CROSSROADS

CROSSROADS
THE LONG WAY HOME

VINCENT L. HOWARD

Charleston, SC
www.PalmettoPublishing.com

Crossroads
Copyright © 2022 by Vincent L. Howard

All rights reserved

No portion of this book may be reproduced, stored in a retrieval system, or transmitted in any form by any means–electronic, mechanical, photocopy, recording, or other–except for brief quotations in printed reviews, without prior permission of the author.

Paperback ISBN: 979-8-88590-727-9
Hardcover ISBN: 979-8-88590-728-6
eBook ISBN: 979-8-88590-729-3

TABLE OF CONTENTS

Foreword vii
Prologue 1
Chapter 1   Which Way Is Up? 13
Chapter 2   Lovely Day 38
Chapter 3   Cloud Nine 64
Chapter 4   Castles Made of Sand 96
Chapter 5   You Got to Pay the Price 124
Chapter 6   Who's Gonna Take the Blame? 153
Chapter 7   Don't Let the Green Grass Fool Ya 180
Chapter 8   Somebody's Gotta Win, Somebody's
            Gotta Lose 208
Chapter 9   Everything's Coming Up Love 235
Afterword 263
It's My Turn: A Message from the Author 265

FOREWORD

Home is a physical place. It represents a strong bodyguard, a mighty defender, blocking any difficulties the world and its occupants throw into your path. Whether the tiniest hut or a magnificent palace, it amazes in its ability to provide comfort whenever it swallows you within its walls.

Home is a mental place. It's any situation where your mind is at ease, clear, and sharp. It's where the fires of stress are doused by the cool hose of mindfulness watering any personal discomforts with your strengths, talents, and values. It's where confidence forever reigns supreme.

Home is a social place. It's being in the presence of those who purposefully utilize the tools of mutual admiration, respect, and love combined with healthy doses of laughter, honesty, trust, wisdom, fun, and sacrifice—all toward the principle of maintaining each other's best version of self.

Home is a spiritual place—a place inside your mind or outside your body that feeds your purpose and provides unrelenting invisible advocacy for your core being when life is at its darkest or when you are facing fears threatening to erase your place in the world.

I dedicate this book to those whose crossroads have taken them to distant places far from where they want to be physically, mentally, socially or spiritually.

And to those whose crossroads have brought them home—welcome back.

PROLOGUE

The sounds of Elton John and Kiki Dee slowly invaded the sleep-induced unconsciousness of the groggy fifteen-year-old. As he tried to squeeze a few more moments of slumber out of the early morning, the words of the song coming from the radio ran through his mind.

It wasn't a bad song...it was the opposite, it was light-hearted and fun—it was a pop tune. He'd heard these pop tunes so much, sometimes he sang along in his head. But it reminded him he needed to get home after school. This was San Diego in the late Seventies, and they only played black music on the radio from 4:00 p.m. until 7:00 p.m. on 92.5 FM. So he needed to make sure he was home and ready to hit the record button on the cassette player at exactly the right moment if one of his favorite songs came on. He loved sleeping and waking to music and there was always new music to record. Eyes still closed, he mentally practiced dance moves to some of his recordings for later, but his thoughts were rapidly replaced by an emotion born of a different thought.

"I hate school."

This thought went through the mind of Benjamin Frazier just about every day, at least until he was on vacation or school was out for the summer. Lunch time was good; school dances were fun too, but for the most part, school was the place where adults went through the motions and out of their way to purposely bore everyone…or at least that's how it seemed. The teachers didn't even TRY to be interesting; plus, they obviously loved bossing students around but they were suddenly absent or out of time whenever anyone needed anything really important. Half of the them seemed scared—the other half probably didn't care about anyone except for the super geniuses.

Benji, as his mama fondly nicknamed him, opened his eyes and stared for a moment at the ceiling, thinking maybe if he lay there completely still long enough, the necessity of going to school would magically disappear. But as he continued to lie in his bed, he shook his head gloomily and grimly remembered times past; you just never knew when it was your day to serve as the target of the inevitable verbal onslaught that goes along with living where he lived. His turn had come recently:

"This cat got a name sound like he a runaway slave."

"Sucka so black, when he fall down in the street, look like a skid mark."

"Nah, Doo Doo ain't just black…he blackety black black BLACK! Doo Doo the "hide & seek" champion of the world…ain't NOBODY finding home boy…lookin' like everybody's shadow…"

And other similar barbs. Sometimes the attacks came out of nowhere and once initiated…were relentless.

But that was just how they played around in Benji's Southeast San Diego neighborhood known as Skyline. Supposedly it was all in fun; when someone said something funny, Benji had to laugh, even if the joke was on him. In truth, Benji normally gave as good as he got though; sometimes he could be pretty clever and even got the better of them all in the ghetto sport called "basing," which was probably their second-favorite pastime—after slap boxing, of course. But this morning, he frowned remembering the sting of some of their insults—even though he laughed it off, as he usually did. But when it went too far, his hidden irritation was very real. Like when even one of the girls randomly screamed in the cafeteria, "Benji so black...he look blue!" and another followed with "No! Benji so black, he PURPLE."

Benji didn't like being attacked by girls because he couldn't attack them back—basing on girls crossed the line for him. So he shrugged it off but honestly thought at the time, "Where'd THAT come from? And what are they all talking about anyway? Ain't we ALL black? I don't get it." It was around then for the first time, Benji noticed he had darker skin than anyone else in his family.

By far.

He'd never really noticed before.

But the litany of dark-skinned jokes wasn't nearly as bad as the name Benji despised more than any other; the name he was ultimately stuck with—the aforementioned "Doo Doo." The hated nickname stemmed from Benji's extremely bad eyesight, which forced him to wear glasses with very thick lenses. Last year, a group of Skyline teens was all over him again:

"Yo glasses so thick, I bet yo ass can see the future!"

"Them glasses so thick, I bet you solve the mystery faster than the chick on Scooby Doo do!"

Scooby Doo…do.

I didn't get it at first.

The insults got a huge laugh from the crowd, though, and the final insult stuck. Initially, it was Scooby Doo Doo…ultimately, the nickname simply got shortened to "Doo Doo"…which also doubled as an offensive reference to his dark skin, "which made it even more funnier to everyone", Benji supposed with a shrug.

The real problem was, when the streets are laughing because they've decided to nickname you something like "Doo Doo," you only have a few choices…and none of them all that great. You can choose to not answer to it or get indignant, which brings attention, shows sensitivity or the perception of having hurt feelings, generates more laughter and lets people know without a doubt it bothers you—but doing it displays a vulnerability. You can respond with something extra clever to make people forget, if you can think fast on your feet—but there was always the chance of someone being even MORE clever which could escalate the situation and result in an even worse name. Or you can stay non-reactive, go on about your business, ignore it or answer like it's no big deal, until the name either dies on its own or becomes so normal, people forget why and how you got the name in the first place. But the problem is—if the name doesn't die, you're stuck with it. Maybe forever.

Or you can fight.

"Doo Doo" was way better than being nicknamed "Velma" though. She was the girl with the thick glasses in the Scooby Doo cartoon who always solved the mystery. A few people tried to make that nickname stick, but it didn't take hold. It was a good thing too. "Doo Doo" was bad enough, but if "Velma" would have stuck…

It's fight time. Every day.

Even people who didn't know why he was called Doo Doo started calling him Doo Doo…and though they shouldn't be allowed to, a few teachers even called him Doo Doo. There should be a rule or a law to make teachers call students by their real names. Or let students call teachers by some crazy, insulting nickname too. It was just a guess, but Benji figured not too many teachers would enjoy being called Mr. Butter Tooth or Ms. Booty Breath to their face. They'd probably think it was a little bit disrespectful.

In any case, Benji hadn't laughed during or after the "Scooby Doo do" incident. Honestly, he seriously considered punching the offender in the face, but since everyone laughed so hard, Benji was forced to just let it go. Because like I said—the problem is, if you get too emotional about things, it gets even worse, and the attacks get even more personal. There's a price to pay when you show any level of weakness in Southeast Dago, so a lot of the time, it's better to just shine it on. That's just the way it was. But that meant Benji would often not wear his glasses, especially in school. Even though it meant not being able to see the board or follow the lesson—and taking beatings from Pops because of repeatedly losing his glasses. Truth is, he just set his glasses down and walked away. He thought it a small price to pay; Benji was like that sometimes. He often thought, "If I do this, I'll probably get a beating later." Then he'd still do it anyway.

Ah well.

It was time for Benji to get dressed. Nobody who lived in Skyline had a lot of money, but if clothes didn't match, were dirty, torn or didn't fit—that was ammunition. Floods were a definite no-no too. You could see those white socks from way down the street no matter how much you tried to pull your pants down to pretend like they were really the right length. Wearing the same thing multiple times in a week would also not escape notice. Even Mama knew—school shopping options were limited, so Benji and his little brother usually wore hand- me-downs. So for the few clothes Mama could buy from the discount store, she was always careful to buy clothes where the colors complemented each other. "Everything matches black and blue," she always said. So Benji could make a lot of different combinations from his three pairs of school pants and four school shirts—when his sisters remembered to wash and iron clothes.

Benji had two older sisters, and it was part of their chores to take turns washing and ironing clothes, but now they were older, so when Mama wasn't around, they were always complaining, "I ain't your maid, boy!" Then they would either not do it, do a lousy job on purpose, or not do it at all and say they did. "I should snitch on them like they always snitchin' on me if they don't do it today," Benji thought with a chuckle. "But nah…way more fun to front them in front of their boyfriends or put some hard government peanut butter spread on the inside of their dresser drawer handles—or on their panties!" Benji thought with a devilish grin. "It doesn't spread too well on bread, but it works pretty good on my sister's underwear." Only problem was they always knew who did it. It's not like Benji could blame some invisible peanut butter fairy for flying around and sprinkling cheap peanut butter on underpants.

By the time he was ready for breakfast, Benji's father, Pops, a garbage man or "sanitation worker" as he was supposedly known, was already at work. Pops couldn't care less about what he was called. He said call him whatever but he added, "I make honest money, and if I stop doing my job, people can swim in their own shit and they gonna call me 'sir' and beg before I'll come back, so don't piss me off." It sounded angry, but it was funny how Pops said things like that and Benji always quietly laughed at his Pops's rants—Pops was hilarious. But he laughed quietly because his father was not a man to laugh at unless you KNEW he was joking…everyone giggled as soon as he left the room though, even Mama. Benji often thought Pops knew they were all laughing at his rants, and just maybe he did it to make them laugh—because laughing was free for poor people. One time, though, when he thought his father left, Benji came out of the kitchen after laughing and his father was sitting in the living room. Benji thought, "Shoot—Pops heard!" but his father just looked at him with a little smile in his eyes, gave Benji a wink, and left for work. So Benji thought his Pops knew the deal…but he wasn't 100 percent sure. Better to not take chances, because Pops worked hard and was very proud. Even during those times in the past when the Frazier family was forced to make Christmas presents for each other from whatever they found in the house and wrap them with newspaper, Benji did not remember a single night of ever going to bed hungry like a few of his friends did sometimes. That was because of Pops…a man of few words, a man whose words counted when he decided it was time to be heard on any issue he felt was important, and definitely not a man who would suffer disrespect from ANYBODY.

As powerful as Benji saw his hard-working father, it was his mother Pauline who really directed the day-to-day comings and goings of the Fraziers. Lina, as she was known to her husband and close family, was passionately dedicated to the welfare of the five Frazier children and was known for her intense devotion to them. She would stand against anyone, including their father, when their welfare was at stake. Blessed with a powerful impact, incredible insight, and a tireless work ethic, she sacrificed her energy almost to the point where she had no time or desire to care for herself. In addition to regularly dispensing wisdom, Benji's mama meted out doses of discipline coupled with huge measures of humor and affection. Benji truly adored her, and their connection was a special one. Like when he was younger and Pops worked two jobs, Benji's mama would wake him at 1:00 a.m. to ride with her to take his father to work or pick him up. Benji liked having alone time together with his mother. He had fond memories of sleepily keeping his mother company as they rode through the dark city streets together. In fact, sometimes he would wake to his mother singing along to James Taylor songs like "Carolina ", the only kind of music on the radio at that time of the morning. Benji didn't really know what the song meant, but after he heard it a few dozen times, he liked singing along anyway—there was a line in the song saying something about love being the best thing or whatever and Benji would always look at Mama with a finger to his lips and say "Shhhh" right before the singer got to the part where he requested his girlfriend to whisper something soft and kind for him. Mama always beamed and turned up the volume a little when she knew that part was coming up because she thought he was so cute back then. It was no real surprise decades later, Benji found he was a huge James Taylor fan. Mama was too; it was like their own special thing together.

Benji took it further and eventually liked Jackson Browne and Gordon Lightfoot too. In secret, of course. Benji's eclectic musical tastes would have surprised his peers, but apparently, listening to folk music and actually liking it was a slippery slope.

Yes, Benji tried to make Mama smile during those special mother-son moments when he had Mama all to himself. He also tried to make her laugh when he found himself in trouble—as was often the case. A very mischievous teen, Benji demanded the majority of her time, even more than his younger brother.

Sid was in the seventh grade, two years behind Benji. Sid got teased too, but Sid was blessed with a personality that always lightened the mood. Sometimes he would start acting out a scene from *Good Times* and play the parts of every actor and actress in the scene and everyone laughed, even though it had nothing to do with what anyone was talking about. Sid was the only one of them who could've gotten kicked out of Cub Scouts for talking too much and still not get in trouble—because that's what had happened.

Marcus was the oldest boy, extremely athletic; a senior, played football and baseball, had lots of girlfriends, and was always lifting weights or doing random push-ups for no reason. Everybody liked him and nobody teased Mr. Touchdown. He thought he knew everything too. He was a good big brother but he always felt the need to give advice; it was like he thought only he knew the super secret code of how to be the perfect Frazier man and he felt compelled to constantly share it. Was pretty cool to go to his games, though.

The brothers were quite close—it hadn't been too long ago the three would pretend they were in a singing group like the Spinners, complete with dance steps and a perfect lip sync to the song *"Mighty Love"*, really believing they were going to be the newest musical sensation. And when they were even younger, they would fashion a makeshift football out of a bunch of rolled-up socks, then challenge Sid to score a touchdown in their living room by trying to get past his older brothers with socks in hand. They called their made-up game "Goal Line Stand." Sid mostly got demolished…a few times he got hurt, but…to the brothers' surprise, he actually scored a few times too. And all of the Frazier brothers celebrated when Sid scored.

Benji's oldest sibling was his sister Angela; she was extremely smart and going to community college; she was also the bossiest girl in the world. She even bossed Marcus—Benji thought maybe his big sister thought she was everyone's mom when Mama wasn't around. Angela still called him "Stinky" because she changed his diaper when he was a baby. But now there were no more diapers to change, so she tried to check if Benji was doing homework and who he was talking on the phone to and what music he listened to.

Benji's other sister was named Nicole, but everyone called her Nikki—she was as annoying as Angela was bossy. She never stopped talking—she would say, "Bridgette saw you playin' ball today, Benji" when she knew Benji wasn't allowed to go to Thompson Park, although he went there to hang out anyway. But leave it to Nikki to make it into a discussion topic. Nikki was a reporter; if you did it or said it in front of her, might as well write a letter to Mama about what you said or did, because Nikki was probably going to tell.

As Benji entered his kitchen, it seemed like any other school day. Pops was gone to work, Mama was singing along to her gospel cassette, Angela had left for her classes, Marcus and Sid were eating cereal, Nikki was complaining her brothers were smacking and slurping too loud when they ate—but Mama knew there was something special about today. She could feel it.

So did I.

Benji couldn't see me though. Or hear me. He never could.

But I've been with him since he was born. He could only feel me in his spirit at times and occasionally in his conscience. You see, I am Benji's guardian…a shadow, but not an angel…definitely not an angel. More like an advisor—I'm his guide. Although Benji usually ignores my advice.

But I know helpful things. For example, Benji doesn't think there is anything special about this day, but I know this isn't true. Because on this day, I know that on five occasions, Benjamin Frazier is going to be at a crossroads. I am not permitted to see where the crossroads will ultimately lead, but I am permitted to sense these five crossroads will present Benjamin with choices. And the decisions he makes or doesn't make have the potential to take him far from home, away from his place of comfort…and alter the course of his entire life.

CHAPTER 1

WHICH WAY IS UP?

Mama wasn't much for the funky sounds of the 1970s, but as Benji entered the room, he was comforted by the sounds of Mama singing along softly with one of her favorite gospel songs, "*I'm Going Away*". Truthfully, he enjoyed many of the gospel songs Mama subjected them to pretty much every day and the gospel choir at church was probably the second best thing about going to church.

The first best thing was those crazy old ladies—they were really funny. Those old ladies would go crazy catching the Holy Spirit and falling on the benches, running up and down the aisle ten thousand times babbling about something or even better, rolling around on the floor and wailing at the top of their voices. Benji had his favorite performer—Miss Nadine was the best. Not only did she give the craziest performance of screaming, crying, kicking, and fighting ushers off like a gangster, but Benji also caught her numerous times saying "mother fucker" after church. It was a sport to the Frazier brothers to bet on which one of the old ladies would be the second one to catch the Holy Spirit—loser let himself get punched in the stomach. There was no need to bet on who would be first to catch the spirit…it was always Miss Nadine.

But the gospel choir at Valencia Baptist was definitely the second best thing about church and that choir was COLD! They didn't just stand up there…no, when the families came into church, there was nobody where the choir stood—somebody would be at the podium saying something or making some announcements, but the Frazier brothers really didn't care because it wasn't interesting to the brothers; probably because it usually was something to do with Jesus.

But then, all of a sudden, the piano and the organ would start the introduction to *"We've Come This Far By Faith,"* and Frazier brothers' attention was immediately transferred to the back of the church where the choir was gathering, lining up and preparing to march in wearing those BAD purple robes. Once the song started, the choir would come walking down the aisle two by two, stepping to the beat of the music, singing loud. First were those girls with the highest voices; then slowly the sound would change to the girls with high voices, but not as high as the first girls'. Then next came some girls, but mostly guys, and the sound changed as the voices got deeper. Lastly—the men. All of them seemed enormous and they all sang with deep, strong voices, walking all slow and hip. By the time they finished their march, the whole church was rocking with all the singing! They always sang the same song. The same verse…over and over and over and over…every single week. "They must really love that jam," Benji thought. "Me too."

Benji liked the song Mama was listening to right now too. It was real slow to start, but by the time the guy got to the chorus, Benji was ready to boogie. He loved this beat—in fact, he was inspired to practice a few dance moves. Benji thought he'd just about perfected a lot of the moves he'd seen on *Soul Train*—the Soul Train Line was something he looked forward to every Saturday, and the hard beat of this gospel song gave him a chance to work on a few moves like the *Soul Train* dancers. He was in his own world as he locked his arms, popped his shoulders, and moved his feet and teenage hips in what he thought was a funky rhythm, and for a minute, he imagined he was under the spinning disco ball, dancing with the most beautiful dancer in the room in the Soul Train Line - Damita Jo was the one, she'd probably ask Benji to be her partner if she was there right now. As he danced with Damita Jo down the line in his mind, Benji got lost in his fantasy and kind of forgot where he was…until he opened his eyes.

Marcus just shook his head and rolled his eyes without looking up from his cereal. Sid was reading the cereal box, but Mama and Nikki were looking at Benji like he'd lost his mind.

"Benji, this is GOD'S music."

Mama's look left nothing else to say.

Benji sheepishly stopped dancing and avoiding Mama's disapproving scowl, started over to the kitchen table where his brothers sat. Benji avoided looking at Mama because he knew she did not play when it came to God but thought, "It's not my fault, Mama! The song was fresh, the chorus kinda sounded like…Con Funk Shun maybe? Still though, smart enough not to have any kind of look on his face, Benji quietly sat and addressed his younger brother.

"Lemme get some cereal, Sid."

"No, I'll pour it."

Sid did not want to give Benji the cereal box for fear he would not get it back. He loved reading the back of the cereal box to see what prizes, games and offers were there.

"You ain't pourin' my cereal. Gimme the box. I'll give it back."

Benji loved reading the back of the cereal box too. Benji had no intention of giving the box back, but he didn't think Sid needed to know it.

"Y'all both stupid. There ain't nothing on the box anyway, and anyway, it's the same thing there as it was yesterday," Nikki chimed in. Benji narrowed his eyes into slits and glared at his sister to mind her own business.

Benji reached over and tried to yank the box out of Sid's hand, and Sid held on, so a cereal box tug-of-war ensued. The brothers started alternately laughing and arguing over who would get the cereal box, with Sid saying in a "louder than necessary" voice, "Stop, Benji! Stop! You play too much!" Benji responded, "I just want some cereal. Gimme the box. You a baby!" The battle raged for a few more seconds, and then all of a sudden, Benji heard the sound of a chair scraping against the floor.

Mama was coming over.

"Give it to me."

Four words ended the battle immediately. Mama took the cereal box, poured Benji's cereal, and returned the box to Sid, who smiled and said, "Thank you, Mama."

"Man, what a chump —that kid is a baby! Mama gives him everything he wants. He makes me sick!" Benji thought angrily as he put sugar and milk on his cereal. He knew they were both a little too old to argue over a cereal box but…he stepped on Sid's foot hard under the table anyway. His brother responded by kicking Benji, who retaliated by kicking him back harder. The brothers glared menacingly at each other, but no words were spoken. They sometimes fought like brothers do, but Marcus, Benji, and Sid never snitched on each other. One time, Benji stole money from Pops's wallet; the brothers all knew Benji stole the money but when Pops lined the boys up and declared "I know one of you knows: *who stole my money*? All y'all coming in my room and if nobody don't tell me—EVERYBODY getting a beatin'!"

Pops already knew he would not get an answer—because he knew the Frazier boys don't snitch. Not ever. No need to ask the girls. Pops realized if the girls knew, they would tell.

Quickly.

Well anyway—the three Frazier boys all took a taste of Pops's belt that day. Wasn't the first time or the last. It never occurred to any of the brothers to raise their hand and say, "I did it, Pops. Don't whip them. It was me." Snitch on themselves? Wasn't gonna happen—the Frazier Boys just don't snitch. Especially on themselves.

"Benji, what are you going to talk about at the youth conference? It's a pretty big deal. Have you started thinking about it yet?"

Benji transfixed Nikki with his most hateful scowl. "You know I don't wanna do that stupid shit! I ain't speakin' at no youth conference! Why you always frontin' me anyway? You ain't Mama!" Benji thought to himself. Benji didn't want to do this and I knew he meant it. Because Benji, like most good people, did not usually think in profane terms. Often, he spoke profanity if he was sure his parents were not within earshot because that was the way of Benji's world. But his thoughts were not often littered with random profanity as they were now.

So I knew Benji truly had no desire to participate. But I did not know why yet.

In Benji's mind, youth conference was an annual three-day event at the church where square teenagers read from the Bible, sang, made speeches, and even preached while the adults applauded and gushed stupidly over the corny kids they convinced to get participate. Benji did not even want to attend.

"I ain't sure," Benji mumbled with a bored shrug.

"How about singing? No, don't sing…you can do a speech though. Or maybe read…you know how to read…"

"Nik!!! Come on! What did I do to you?" Benji thought as he scrambled for a response—because now Mama was looking at him too. "Nikki definitely getting it later for this one," Benji thought angrily.

But what to say now?

Benji decided to just ignore his sister—pretend like he hadn't heard. He wanted to just leave the room. However, leave too fast and it might signal Mama that he was uncomfortable. Then, Mama might start making speeches of her own and asking questions to pin him down. So Benji just played it real cool. He finished his cereal, sat against the counter for a little bit, opened the refrigerator for no reason, said "hmmm," closed it, got himself a water glass, got some water from the sink, leaned against the counter again, sipped some water, took it all in, put the glass in the sink—then when the phone rang, Benji started to slowly make his way out of the room. Benji could hear it was his Aunt Rose on the phone, so thankfully this phone call was probably going to take a while.

Aunt Rose wasn't his real aunt, but her and his mama were real close friends, kind of like play sisters, so that made her an aunt. She was also the attendance lady at their school, so she knew when everyone ditched. She didn't always tell, though. Sometimes she just yelled at the kids to scare them into going to class or threatened to call their parents if they ditched one…more…time—which was way better than telling. Benji was in enough trouble, so he thought Aunt Rose was a pretty cool aunt for not tellin' ALL the time.

Aunt Rose's boyfriend or maybe he was her husband, Benji didn't really know…that was Mr. T.—Benji had no idea why they called him that but everybody in Southeast called him that. But he was funny, like all of Pops's friends, and Mr. T was always bringing frozen meat over for Pops and the family. He called it "wholesale". Benji didn't know what it meant but he figured it probably meant "cheap". Definitely meant Mr. T was hustling though, so he was pretty cool too.

Their kids were jheri curl kids—they were one of the first ones in the neighborhood with the new hairstyle. Benji wanted to try it too but Mama wouldn't let her kids get a jheri curl, it was too expensive. The Fraziers were more of a "hot comb and braids" kind of family, probably because there were so many heads to take care of and both Angela and Nikki could do hair; much easier to maintain if it was braided...cheaper too.

Aunt Rose's kids were OK though—when Aunt Rose and Mr. T would come over to drink and play cards, all the kids would stay in the back rooms and cut up. Their oldest kid, George, was always reading or doing this goofy Russian dance like in the Bugs Bunny cartoon; that kid really made Benji laugh. Vince was in one of Benji's classes but he ran with a different crowd. Jason and Robert were the younger brothers, and, well...Benji didn't know too much about them; they were too young for Benji to pay much attention to, but he and Vince talked about girls in their school and showed off their latest pop-locking moves. Jason and Robert danced sometimes too—then they all battle danced, except George - he always did the Russian dance thing while the rest battled. Marcus would judge when he wasn't busy because he always thought he was the expert at everything. Just the boys would dance, though; Nikki was the only girl and thought all of the boys in both families were stupid. Seemed like maybe Vince really liked Nikki or something; Benji busted him staring at her a couple times—jheri curl kid had poor taste apparently but Nikki wasn't gonna like no young boy no way. Benji didn't care about it very much either way. What he DID care about was how long Aunt Rose could keep Mama talking on the phone right NOW. He figured they would yak for a while, like they usually did. Then he could escape.

"Close one," Benji said to himself as he continued to ease out of the kitchen with a sense of relief.

He should have known better.

"Do you even know what your worth is?"

Mama stopped mid-conversation with a "Hold on, girl… I'll call you right back. Don't worry, we're going to find him." Then she seamlessly delivered a mother's strong words, stopping Benji in his tracks. He turned to look at his mother, expecting to be met by flashing anger in her eyes. Or the look of disappointment and pain he saw at times when he messed up…again. He saw neither. But he was shocked at what he did see.

His mother's eyes were soft, hopeful, and full of love. She was smiling the way she did when he was little.

"Do you even know what your worth is?" she repeated softly.

Benji's mother loved all her children equally and for different reasons, but right now she was totally focused on Benji as she gazed at him with a wide smile and touched his face tenderly. Benji had been special from the beginning of his life. He was born at twenty-seven weeks, ten weeks premature with undeveloped lungs. Lina's third child spent the first eight weeks fighting for life within the neonatal intensive care unit. Because of his underdeveloped lungs and the resulting breathing problems, Benji began life on a ventilator. His mother remembered the crushing guilt of being unable to nurse her son as she had nursed her other children—her guilt was not numbed in the fifteen years of Benji's life. She always kept a silent eye on Benji—as Benji grew, he had gotten into more trouble and received more beatings than all her other four children combined. He entered life struggling to breathe, she knew how bad he felt that he couldn't see well either—she wondered if Benji was perhaps in a constant state of trying to prove something to somebody. Perhaps to himself. But it seemed as if he'd been fighting since the day he was born.

Mama thought all this in an instant as she gazed at her beloved Benji. He was in more and more trouble every day, but she knew he was something special. Sometimes she felt she was the only one who could see it—the only one who believed. Her son was talented and she knew it…and she wanted the world to know it.

And she wanted Benji to know it.

Mama felt this event was Benji's chance. Tears welled in her eyes as she remembered how he struggled to take every single breath, and there were times she silently wondered if he would survive—and if she bore any fault for his condition. But her son was strong now. Perhaps life began with him struggling to make a sound or take a breath, but now was his chance to speak and be heard by everyone. It was his chance to break out and be known for more than how he saw himself - the funny-looking kid with thick glasses. This was his chance to be seen as something positive and powerful and good. And Mama could see the aftermath—the accolades he would receive and the pride he would inspire. This youth conference opportunity was for Benji, but he had to want to do it.

"Mama…what do you mean?" Benji said.

Mama's eyes were somehow soft but powerful at the same time, and her whispered words of encouragement, accompanied by her almost imperceptible nodding, were somehow louder than any scream.

"What I mean, son, is do you know your true talent? Your strength? Your character? Your power? We are much more than what the world sees when it looks at us. But when we look at ourselves as through the eyes of God, it no longer matters where we live, how much money we have, or what we do…no power on earth can change what opportunities God has given us to advance His purpose. And this is your chance, Benjamin…this is YOUR time! I see greatness in your eyes…just like I see in Baba's eyes…"

"Baba" was how she lovingly referred to Pops, and Benji stood in awe of even being compared to the man. Pops was powerfully built, proud, charismatic, and people were always drawn to him. Many was the time Benji came home and there was a circle of men around his father—Mr. T the meat guy, Steve the electricity guy, Herb the cop, Jerry who owned Jerry's Market, the Mailman—and Pops would hold court as the men drank, laughed loudly, and argued.

Another time, Dink Jefferson, a ferocious gang banger, was severely beating his girlfriend in the street. It was Pops who came out of the house and stopped the beating. Benji peeked out the window and saw Dink's girlfriend crawling under a car in an effort to escape Dink's rage. Benji had been terrified when saw his father approaching Dink and ashamed he'd been too afraid to go outside and protect his dad. But the next thing he knew, the neighborhood's most notorious gangster was sitting in HIS house at the kitchen table with sad eyes about to cry..but nodding with head bowed at whatever Pops was telling him.

Benji could never imagine having the toughness, courage or the wisdom of his father. He thought he was only thinking it, but in reality, he said it softly under his breath, "I can't be like Pops...not gonna happen..."

But Mama heard him.

She forced Benji to look at her and her tone changed to one resembling that of the preacher in church.

"You don't have to be your father or Marcus or anyone else, Benji...it is not who you have to be or even who I want you to be. You are Benjamin Frazier Jr.! You have an opportunity here not just to glorify God but also to uplift this community with YOUR talent! I see something in you—I see your talent with a mother's eyes, and you would make me so proud if you would share it. What is talent if it remains hidden, Benjamin?"

Benji beamed with pride inwardly when she said this, but he did not see himself as talented or special in any way; her words sincerely confused him, so he responded quizzically, "Uplift the community? How would I help anybody?"

Benji's mother locked eyes with her hesitant son. Her eyes were on fire, and she seemed to roar as she pointed to Benji and exclaimed, "Your words and your knowledge are key—they matter now! You matter...and it is time for YOU to be heard!"

Mama's voice softened a little as she continued.

"But you don't see it...you hold back...you can't see it yet..."

Mama drew a deep breath, kissed her son on his forehead, and said one final time, "I love you, son—I know you will do what's right and if you do it, you will know the answer to this:

Do you know what your worth is?"

Her words commanded the room—and when she was finished, there was dead silence except for the sound of gospel music playing softly in the background.

Benji couldn't exactly see them—his eyes were now fixed upward toward the ceiling—but he could feel them. They were all staring at him now.

Sid was wide-eyed, expectant and amazed. The youngest Frazier was not used to these types of words from the family matriarch. Mama was a powerful woman—but this was something entirely different. Sid now looked on and silently waited for Benji's response.

Marcus looked up from his breakfast and was looking at Benji—but not with the scorn or dismissiveness he normally reserved for Benji. Marcus was looking at him like a real big brother…or maybe like…a friend? Marcus looked right at him and winked.

Nikki stared with a smugness—though she tried to hide it. She thought there was zero chance Benji would resist such an impassioned plea from Mama. Nikki smiled at her mother…then returned her gaze to Benji to wait for his inevitable acceptance.

Mama was now looking at Benji with an affectionate smile. She walked over to her middle son and hugged him as she did when he was little. Benji put his arms around his mother and hugged her tight. "She smells like Mama," Benji thought.

Benji's mother rocked him a little bit while they stood, and Benji felt the tenderness of a mother who loved and was proud of her child. Benji looked into his mama's eyes, and she looked back smiling. It was a moment—like their moments in the car listening and singing to James Taylor with nobody else around.

Benji felt a surge of love for her, and he knew he could not disappoint his Mama.

That feeling only lasted for a second.

Maybe less than a second.

More like a split second.

Or a flash.

"No," Benji thought. "I'm not doing it. Not a chance. I don't care."

I moved in closer to Benji. I whispered to him, "Why not, Benji? Why does this trouble you so? Do you see the look in your mother's eyes? You are about to tap into a talent you don't realize you have…why are you resisting?"

Benji did not hear me, of course. I was only an echo in his subconscious, a fleeting thought. It would be so much easier if Benji could actually see me and hear me. We could get a LOT done together that way. Unfortunately, that's not how it works.

Benji began to ponder the situation, though. And the fact was, in Benji's mind, he was starting to get somewhere good in his life.

Benji remembered a couple months ago he'd been at his school locker and seen Teri Shaw and Shante Clay walking and laughing out of the corner of his eye. He didn't really take note of it, but as the sound of their laughter got closer and closer, he saw Teri approaching rapidly, laughing even louder, with Shante in hot pursuit. All of a sudden, Teri broke out into a run! And as she passed by Benji, she yelled out, "Shante likes you, Benji!" to which Shante screamed, "No I don't! Stoppp!!!" Then both girls ran off giggling.

This never happened to Benji before—Benji pretended to have lots of girlfriends, like Marcus. He often successfully tricked his homeboys, and even his family, into thinking he had a lot of girlfriends by waving at strange girls from a distance...they normally waved back because in the passing two seconds, the girls didn't realize they didn't really KNOW Benji. It tricked everyone but the fact was Benji didn't really know how to approach girls, much less talk to them. He didn't even know how to ask them to dance at the after-school dances in the cafeteria. So instead he just copied Marcus' style, said hip stuff like Marcus did, and kept his glasses off at all times. Even so, Teri and Shante was a first... Benji smiled at the memory; he still didn't quite know how to make a smooth first move with girls but thought, "If I'm confident, cool, and keep my glasses off, I don't have to make the first move...girls are making the first move on ME!"

He didn't know why. He didn't care why. He was just glad it was happening.

Benji swelled with happiness knowing pretty, light-skinned girls like Shante were talking to him, smiling, and wanting to hang around him. Shante even agreed to braid Benji's hair...meaning three whole hours with his head in her LAP; that was WAY better than one of his sisters doing it. So, he wasn't going to let no stupid youth conference mess that up. Benji loved his mother. He'd never purposely disappointed her. It was more likely one of those spur-of-the-moment, lack-of-judgment situations. But this time was different. Teri and Shante had shown him things were about to get different for Benji.

But there were other reasons too.

Benji's best friends for as long as he could remember were Brian Weaver and Enrique Escamilla.

Brian was a short, brown-skinned teen who was always laughing and thought himself the most knowledgeable of the trio. He seemed to know something about everyone. Benji was pretty sure even if his friend didn't know something for certain, he made it up and put a humorous spin on it. Slightly overweight but already a really talented guitar player and singer, Brian also had the largest appetite of anyone Benji had ever seen—there was nothing he wouldn't eat. In fact, when the friends ate, Benji would not leave food on the table for ANY reason. On more than one occasion, he left food and come back to find it gone and Brian with a sheepish grin to go with a ridiculous explanation like "the wind blew it on the ground, so I just threw it away."

Now, Enrique, whom everyone called Ricky, was a slightly built Mexican, a tad shorter than Benji, with slicked back hair and a definite wild streak but not a malicious one. With Brian, there wasn't anything he wouldn't eat but with Ricky, there wasn't anything he wouldn't DO. He was fearless, and it made him funny in a different way than Brian was funny. Like one time, when Benji ran away from home fearing a whipping from his father for losing his glasses again, Ricky, before he even knew the reason why they were running away, promptly said, "OK, me too!"…even though he had no reason to go. And Ricky was fiercely independent— he seemed utterly unaffected by the peer pressure affecting most young men and women his age. For example, he was the only one in the neighborhood who refused to call Benji "Doo Doo." He would either call him "Benjiiiii" in an exaggerated Mexican accent or simply "G," short for Benji.

The three were inseparable...but things were changing.

Last week, Benji passed by Nick Thomas. They'd been in school together since kindergarten, but Nick was now an ominous hard-core teen— an intimidating, vicious Skyline gangster. The kind who was dangerous to talk to or even look at unless you got an invitation. It was true even for adults—teachers were clearly scared of him and content to just give him passing grades, even if he didn't learn anything, as long as he stayed calm. In the past few years, Benji rarely heard him even speak, but last week, Nick was standing around with other gangsters and spoke...to him.

He'd said, "What's happenin', Ice?"

Ice?

After the greeting, Nick laughed, gestured toward Benji, and said to his homeboys, "Thought dude was square but he cold - little man was scrappin' with Tootie the other day and straight spit in that muh fucka's face! Y'all see that shit?"

Which was true.

Tootie Mo was bullying Benji to the point where Benji could take no more—he walked into class one day and on a bet, without any provocation, for no reason at all, he slapped a sitting Benji hard in his face; so hard, he fell out of his chair. Benji angrily scrambled to physically retaliate but he was restrained by classmates—thankfully, in his mind. He was glad somebody held him back—otherwise he might have to actually fight.

But the memory lingered of Tootie laughing and yelling, "Let him go! Let him go!" In the aftermath, Tootie was removed from the class, but both teens promised to settle it after school.

Benji was frightened. He couldn't believe Tootie hadn't been suspended, what did it take to get suspended in this school anyway? But it wouldn't have mattered. Benji would still have to fight eventually unless he was OK with every gangster in school slapping him without warning whenever they felt like having a laugh or were bored.

Tootie had been left back, had hair on his face, was older than the rest of them, and ran with a local set. Benji was truly terrified to fight, but the unprovoked slap and accompanying laughter from Tootie's bullying pushed him to a point where he really had no other choice. When school ended, Benji noted a larger than normal crowd slowly drifting behind him as he started on his way home, and he imagined each one of them could hear his heart, which seemed like it was ready to leap out of his chest in terror with every beat. Benji wished somehow Tootie wouldn't show, or maybe he would forget they were supposed to fight, but no…there he was, surrounded by his crew, waiting at the vacant lot down the street from the school. Benji hoped maybe an adult would drive by and stop the slaughter. Maybe a teacher would drive by and help him.

Or maybe he was on his own.

As they faced each other, Benji remembered Tootie's dismissive smile, and he thought his panic would overwhelm him. Tootie was bigger than he was and supposedly had gotten some girl pregnant—he was like a man to Benji. And as the fight began, Tootie danced around like Sugar Ray, talking, laughing, and taunting. Benji kept his hands up, afraid to throw a punch. Then Tootie stopped dancing long enough to punch Benji square in the face. Hard.

Twice.

But the punches had a strange effect on Benji. The punches really hurt. They hurt a lot. His eye immediately felt puffy, the salty taste of warm blood filled his mouth, and the same blood now flowed freely from his nose, but none of that was Benji's primary focus. The pain of Tootie's fist and the facial injuries caused did not increase Benji's fear.

They took the fear away. And it made Benji mad.

Benji didn't realize it, but when he fought, he didn't even see Tootie. He was fighting against all the bullies who called him so black, so ugly, so poor, so dumb…and he unconsciously recalled all the times he took their insults with only a returning joke in response. So when Tootie Mo hit him, Benji growled like a wild animal, momentarily distracting his larger foe. Then, summoning everything he had in his nose and throat, he gathered a huge loogie full of blood and phlegm in his mouth and spit it all right in Tootie Mo's face.

Then he picked up dirt from the vacant lot they were fighting in and threw it right in Tootie Mo's eyes.

Then he kicked Tootie Mo right in his balls. Hard.

Then…he proceeded to beat the…well, I'm a guardian…a spiritual advisor…a guide…so I don't use profanity but…Benji proceeded to beat the living "you know what" out of Tazwell, a.k.a. Tootie Mo.

This is the incident Nick was referring to. The gangsters loved it, thought it was funny, and could not stop laughing about it. Benji was overwhelmed by their acceptance, so he just grinned, nodded, and shrugged through it all, but the thought came to him: "Look at who I'm laughing with though like it ain't no thang...these guys are the ones even the teachers fear and they think I'm cool..."

Well...perhaps "cool" was too strong a word.

Still, not only were these gangsters friending Benji, inviting him to parties, hanging around, and treating him like he wasn't a square but it also seemed...or maybe it was only in his mind...most people weren't calling him "Doo Doo" anymore. More and more called him "Ice" like Nick did—with respect.

Benji did not want to let that go.

But there was still ANOTHER reason he did not want to surrender to his mama's wishes.

Benji believed in God. He did and I was glad he did. It was not he didn't believe, it was more like...it wasn't a priority. So he found himself doing things even when he didn't exactly know why he did it. Like the time when Benji was playing two-man baseball with Sid. Benji and his younger brother used to love to pretend they were the famous baseball players they saw on television. The boys would imitate the chaotic wind-up of Luis Tiant, the smooth, left-handed batting stance of Rod Carew, Joe Morgan's shoulder twitch... the boys even copied the powerful forearm batting stance of Steve Garvey, and they would all argue over whose imitation was better. But one day, Benji got angry when Sid struck him out, and he chased Sid with the bat because his little brother refused to "throw it right." When he couldn't catch his brother, he threw the bat at him instead. He'd injured him so bad, Benji carried a bawling Sid back to the house and Mama tool him to the hospital. Mama looked at Benji like she knew Benji had something to do with it, and both she and the doctor asked Sid a million times how his injury happened.

Sid never told though. He said he fell down a hill.

Then there was the time Benji saw the gargantuan jar of quarters his grandpa was always adding to and kept in his work room. Benji loved his grandpa—his grandpa told funny stories and defended him against his mama when Benji messed up. He explained things to Benji…they walked his Grandpa's dogs, Duke and Bo; he was the caddy when his Grandpa golfed; his grandpa took him to the amusement park and the barber shop and he never got tired, and he talked to Benji about life—he was patient with Benji. Nevertheless, all those quarters were too tempting a target. Benji would regularly sneak in when he thought no one was looking and steal some of those quarters and use them to buy sweets. Benji didn't realize his grandpa knew all along… his grandpa told him on his deathbed as he was dying from stomach cancer and asked to see him. His grandpa revealed what he knew, but he smiled, held Benji's hand, looked at him with big sunken eyes, forgiven him, and told him how he knew he was destined to be a great man, but he had to do good. Benji knew his grandpa forgave him, and he promised to do good. Even so, Benji cried in his room alone when his grandpa died a week later.

Benji forgot his promise to do good after a while, though.

He didn't stop stealing either.

Then there was church. Benji thought it was the most boring thing ever, and he NEVER remembered anything anyone ever said or did there, unless one of the old ladies went crazy catching the Holy Spirit or something. On most Sundays, Benji found himself trying to keep from falling asleep rather than understanding anything the preachers said who seemed to say the same crap week after week after week. Some days, Mama would send them to Sunday School early while she was getting ready for the main service. Two hours of Sunday School, then a break…followed by two or three hours of the main service made it easier for Benji to convince his brothers to take the money they were supposed to give in Sunday School and spend it on a bunch of day-old donut holes at the donut shop instead. Whenever Mama asked, "What did you learn about in Sunday School today?", Benji would reply for the group with something simple like "Ummm…Jesus?"

Regardless, Benji believed in God, but he thought the whole thing had a kind of "Maybe I'll worry about it later" feel to it. So how could he stand in front of a bunch of people at youth conference?

They would see right through him.

So no…Benji loved it when his mama looked at him like she was looking at him now, but this was something he could not do. But the question loomed— how could he say no to Mama?

Easy. Too easy, actually.

He'd agree to Mama's ridiculous expectation, but then… the morning of the stupid revival or whatever it was, he'd fake being sick. It was easy—Marcus showed him how to fake it but warned him not to do it too often, otherwise Mama would catch on. The boys had a few tricks. One was to sneak to the bathroom to drink hot water, but this method was sometimes difficult; for one thing, sometimes it was hard to sneak to the bathroom. More than once, Benji tried sneaking to the bathroom only to hear Mama call out, "Benji, is that you? Who's up?" Once he was spotted, the trick was useless. The other problem was if a long time passed from the time Benji drank the hot water until the time his temperature was taken, he wouldn't have a temperature anymore. Marcus said to hold the water in his mouth for as long as possible, but sometimes it didn't work.

The third problem was the water. It was hot. Really hot. And who wanted to have a mouth full of hot water unless you were SURE it was going to work?

Another method was to shake the thermometer really hard while holding on to the tip. When Benji tried it, he instantly thought Marcus was a genius. Benji practiced this in secret so he knew exactly how many shakes it took to raise his temperature just enough so he could stay home from school but not raise it high enough to cause Mama to take him to the doctor. The trick here was Benji had to wait until he heard Mama busy cooking or doing something else she couldn't break away from. If she was busy, she would either send one of his sisters in to take his temperature or come in, take his temperature, then go back out to take care of whatever was on the stove. If Mama wasn't busy, she would always sit with him while the thermometer was in his mouth, so there would be no chance to shake the thermometer. One time, Benji tried to roll over with a pretend stomach ache so he could try to rub the thermometer tip with his tongue really fast hoping it would increase his temperature.

That method fooled the school nurse a couple of times. It fooled his Aunt Ann too, his mama's older sister, whenever she came over back in the old days to watch them when Mama worked. She loved Benji like he was her own child. He wouldn't really have a temperature but Aunt Ann just thought maybe the thermometer was broken.

But it never fooled Mama. Not once.

Benji's favorite method of faking it was to complain he was cold. If it was not overused, it was almost foolproof. Benji really thought he deserved an award for his ability to fake a few shivers, which really sold the deception. It was important to eat a little more the day before, too, because under no circumstances could he say he was hungry or accept food while he was supposedly "sick." So complaining about being cold, dressing warm with blankets, and a few shivers combined with faking not being hungry was just about guaranteed to work; it was also a good idea to act extra energetic the day before. Benji hadn't tried this one in a few years because it was important to mix it up, but since it'd been a while since he'd tried it and because it was so successful, Benji thought this was the perfect opportunity to use it to avoid speaking at the teen church thing. Marcus would know he was faking but he wouldn't snitch— the Frazier brothers don't snitch.

Benji's mama was still gazing at him with an adoring look. Benji smiled back, but not for the reason his mama thought he was smiling. His mama thought she'd gotten through to him.

But Benji was smiling…because he knew.

He knew he was going to deceive his mother.

And he knew it was going to work.

CHAPTER 2

LOVELY DAY

It was a Friday morning, and though Benji loathed school, he felt upbeat as he departed his home into the Southern California morning. For one thing, he felt pretty good about how he planned to deal with Mama and the youth conference mess. Plus, he was pretty sure it was pizza day in school, it was the last day before spring vacation, he was going to see Shante after school to get his hair braided, there was a house party later—and he was allowed to go.

It was going to be a great day.

As Benji exited his home into the Southern California sunshine, he could hear the faint sounds of Heatwave's "*Groove Line*" coming from the distance. The song immediately brought forth images of the after-school dance last year. "*Groove Line*" was always guaranteed to pack the little dance floor created at school when the lunch tables were pushed against the wall. Skyline's teenagers loved to scream the chorus in unison, except they replaced the song's "Groove Line" lyric with "Skyline." It was a fun party, but unfortunately, it was also a day of Benji's humiliation.

Back then, Benji had a huge crush on Lisa, a light-skinned girl he thought was mixed with Italian or something because of her last name, but he thought she was the most beautiful girl in the entire school…probably in the whole neighborhood. Maybe even in all of Southeast.

Same thing he always thought when he had a crush on a girl.

As the dance ended, they started to play the song "*Last Dance*" like they always did and bring the lights up. Benji locked eyes with Lisa (or thought he did), and he really wanted to go ask her to dance—he'd been looking at her and wanting to dance with her all afternoon, and this was his last chance. Just as he thought he had the nerve to do it, she turned her back and started walking way. Then the song ended.

But that wasn't the worst part. Not even close.

Benji followed along behind her, but at a distance—it seemed as if he were hypnotized, but he just wanted to see her walk away, get on the bus and leave school. When she turned around and saw him, he waved at her as he often did. But this time, something different happened—something Benji didn't expect. Lisa waved back, like girls always did, even when they didn't recognize him. But he heard the group of girls she was walking with break out into simultaneous laughter, and one girl looked back and dismissively screamed out, "Lisa don't like you, boy!"

Benji was frozen.

This wasn't like the basing he did with his homeboys which was often cruel but really was no more than insults intended to be funny without much truth attached to them.

This was different. This was real. Benji could tell it was 100 percent true, and even so, it wasn't meant to hurt him— it was just a fact. A fact Lisa couldn't bring herself to tell him but her friend could relish in revealing in front of everybody. In an instant, Benji could see the truth as well—he was a joke to Lisa. Pitiful and pathetic. And he wondered how many other people Lisa told, how many other people knew the dark chocolate kid with nappy hair and thick glasses wouldn't leave her alone.

Then another horrifying thought occurred to him— had his homeboys seen or heard? Because if they did, they would show no mercy.

Benji swallowed hard as he slowly surveyed the immediate area. No one was paying any attention to him at all, but out of the corner of his eye, he saw a familiar face approaching him—it was Ricky.

And he was laughing.

Benji was struck by a feeling of terror for an instant. He had no idea what to say or how to respond. All he knew was—now, everyone was going to know. They were going to know all the waving, all the pretend girlfriends, the whole thing, was complete bullshit. He would not be able to take it; he would want to hide in his house forever, but that would make it even worse. Maybe he could make a joke out of it or something? Or pretend like they had a huge fight and he didn't like her anymore anyway? Or even make up a lie about her to make her look bad? Benji was scrambling for answers.

As Ricky approached, I moved in close and whispered to Benji.

"Calm down—it will be OK. We'll get through this. You'll see."

Nevertheless, Benji prepared for the worst.

As Ricky approached, he was laughing even harder with his eyes squarely on Benji. And the first words out of his mouth rocked Benji to his core:

"Fuckin' Brian, G! That *puto* is always hungry!"

Benji stared at his friend as Ricky went into a story involving Brian that was supposedly amusing at a level just short of Fred Sanford having another heart attack— and it might have been. Benji didn't know. He could see Ricky's mouth moving and heard a humming sound, but it sounded nothing like words Benji could understand. Benji's mind was clouded by a single thought.

That's it? That's what's so funny?

Really?

Benji continued to stare at his noise-making friend who truly thought he was telling a funny story—he stared until Benji finally heard words coming from Ricky he understood.

"C'mon, *vamonos,* G – let's go find that fool…"

Ricky didn't know. Nobody did. Benji kept looking for evidence his private humiliation had been discovered, but the evidence never came. Benji felt a weight off of him that was indescribable. He felt light. He felt happy.

And that was the last time in his life he would ever wave at a girl he didn't know.

"What it is, Doo?"

Johnny Davis's morning greeting interrupted Benji's momentary trip down memory lane. Johnny Davis was Benji's next- door neighbor—he was one of those kids who was on the fringe of gang banging. Maybe he wanted to be one but he wasn't a real gangster. It was more like, he was always in the know, always into something, always up on the latest slang and the latest music, and anyway— he was somebody else Benji could copy when he was trying to front.

Benji looked at his neighbor, shrugged lazily and quickly nodded a silent greeting to his neighbor. He'd watched Marcus return greetings this way a hundred times. Benji thought it just looked so smooth; it was like saying, "I hear you, and you're cool and all, but I'm feeling mad slick and can't be bothered to actually talk to anybody right now."

I was glad. I was not a fan of Johnny Davis; he was a young man destined for trouble. I tried to urge Benji to give his nod and keep walking.

As usual, I was unsuccessful.

"I need a favor, Doo."

Benji looked at Johnny Davis and remembered Marcus also telling him it wasn't good to ask questions…especially to women. Marcus heard him asking Shante when she was going to braid his hair and informed him, "Women ask questions! Men don't ask women questions…they make STATEMENTS." Benji looked at him curiously and considered what Marcus had just said. And he was right. He would have sounded way stronger if instead of asking Shante when she was going to braid his hair, he said, "Hey, Shante, I'm gonna come by so you can braid my hair after school tomorrow." or "I need my hair braided." He hadn't responded to Marcus, but after considering what he said, Benji vowed to make more statements and ask fewer questions.

His older brother's advice came back to him instantly as his eyes focused on Johnny Davis, and he thought, "Johnny Davis knows the rules too. He didn't ask a question; he made a statement."

Interesting. Marcus was right: it did sound stronger. Benji made another mental note.

"What's up?"

"Damn it," Benji thought. That was a question, but there was no other way to respond. Maybe he should have just looked at Johnny until he spit it out. Yes, that's it…much better…Benji made another mental note.

Johnny looked hurriedly around, and his voiced lowered to almost a whisper.

"Check this out, Doo…AP is out of town. I want to dip in his crib real quick and see what's ringin'."

Benji caught his meaning immediately, and he was stunned.

He wanted to rob AP.

What??

AP was Arthur Parker, who lived across the street. Arthur Parker was an OG, an original gangster. He didn't say much anymore, but Benji knew his reputation— he was the type of guy Nick Thomas and Dink Jefferson aspired to be. He'd done anything and everything Benji could even think of; he'd been to jail and back numerous times, but he was rarely seen anymore. Whenever he made an infrequent appearance, it seemed like a hush fell over whatever group encountered him, but he was definitely not spoken to unless you were a gangster paying respects or a fellow OG and truly knew him. The constant look on his face and even the way he breathed inspired either reverence or dread…but it was commonly known while he was capable of an excessive amount of rage and occasionally put in work, he was for the most part out of the game.

And Johnny Davis wanted to rob him.

Why??

Benji was rendered speechless by Johnny's statement and stared with perplexed eyes at Johnny.

Johnny smiled diabolically and continued, "I KNOW his ass caught seven days on some shit…my boy's homeboy work wit him and overheard him trying to get a week off, but my other boy know he got some shit pending because he got it off this girl. And I know it's today cuz I saw him leave, but he didn't leave at the regular time like he workin'—he left late with a bag. I know he ain't going to no work; I KNOW he goin' in for seven cuz my boy say he got his week off! So where he goin'? C'mon man, I been watching; I know he got LOTS of shit in his place, and he ain't gonna know! Looky here, man— we ain't even trying to lift that much that he gonna know it's gone. Plus I know dude ain't tryin to fuck wit the man, nigga don't wanna go back to the pen over some bullshit."

His voice returned to a whisper as he said, "We can climb in the side window, baby…we hustlin' now, Doo, in and out. Come on, man!"

I have to admit I was amazed as Benji looked across the street at AP's house. I didn't think he would need me to make this decision. But I watched him contemplating. And I was afraid for Benji.

To my amazement, Benji was considering it. I remembered Benji stealing his grandfather's money. I also remembered the time Benji found the wallet with forty dollars in it. The person's name and address were clearly marked on the driver's license found in the wallet, and I literally screamed at Benji the right thing to do was to return the wallet to its owner. I really thought he heard me this time. I was disappointed but not surprised when Benji pulled the cash out, tossed the wallet, then spent the next month buying as many honey buns and slices of pizza he could eat.

Benji really loved honey buns and pizza.

He also loved stealing too.

Anyway, that was different. That was bad...but this was dangerous.

Benji heard the sound of Johnny's voice, but as was his habit when deep in thought, he made no effort to respond to his neighbor because his mind was dominated by a single penetrating thought.

Benji did not want to do this.

He could talk the talk too. Maybe not as good as Johnny Davis, but he could talk it. Plus, he was perfectly comfortable with his more delinquent or even violent friends...well, they weren't really friends anymore, more like people he knew. But he never judged any of the cliques that roamed Skyline—he figured smart kids studied, funny kids told jokes, holy kids went to church, athletic kids played sports, that one kid George did the weirdo Russian dance, and gangsters did gangster shit...it was just the way things were.

Benji had no problem with any of those cliques, but as he was being challenged to act by his next-door neighbor, the reality of the situation hit him. And the reality of the situation was Benji was no delinquent. He was no gangster. Not even close. It seemed fun when the real gangsters spoke to him and Nick called him "Ice" - it was like he had a gangster name now. As a matter of fact, that's probably why Johnny made this incredibly stupid suggestion to him.

Well, maybe Benji had a gangster name now and maybe people thought he was something he wasn't because they saw him with Nick, but in truth, he could not even see the fun of doing what Johnny was suggesting. Benji was mischievous, but he couldn't understand why Johnny or anybody else would get any excitement from doing it or talking about it. And right then, Benji wished he were somewhere else. He wished he'd never run into Johnny Davis. He wished he'd just kept walking to school. He wished he didn't know Johnny Davis and Johnny Davis didn't know him.

But here he was. And I knew— Benji had a problem. His problem was he didn't know how to say no. He couldn't even say no to his mother's plea from earlier in the day. He couldn't say no to her…he couldn't say no to boys…he couldn't say no to girls. I knew people would talk him into things and ways of thinking that would really harm him in the future. Unless maybe, just maybe, if I could make him understand, I could keep him from a lifetime of followership that would not end well for him. So since I knew he really did not want to do this, I decided to try. I got close to Benji's ear and whispered:

"Crossroad…"

Then I watched for his reaction.

He looked thoughtful for a moment. And I was hopeful.

As he proceeded down the street in the incident's aftermath, Benji looked back, and he noted Johnny disappeared. As Benji surveyed the scene, he was suddenly filled with contempt for his next-door neighbor. And he made a silent vow to himself—he swore he would never again be influenced by Johnny Davis. His quiet rage was real...he did not intend to avoid Johnny Davis. No need. He did not fear Johnny Davis. He did not want the respect of Johnny Davis. As he surveyed the scene, it was if he saw Johnny Davis clearly for what he was—an irrelevant nobody. Benji realized no one else seemed to fall for his neighbor's ridiculousness. It was almost as if Johnny smelled a neediness coming from Benji, a need to be accepted and belong to something. The realization gave birth to a new feeling of disdain toward himself. But no more. He was done with Johnny Davis's bullshit.

And I knew he meant it.

It was a short walk to Ricky's house—Benji wasn't late; he always left a little early if he was going to Ricky's...but even if he was a little late, Ricky wouldn't care, if he was going to school at all. Benji thought if Ricky wasn't going to school, it wouldn't be because he was sitting outside making plans to rob a gangster. It's more likely he was just too sleepy to get up in time. Benji was no huge fan of school either, so no patience was required, but whenever he went to pick Ricky up, it would take his friend twenty minutes to wake up, put on a sock, talk ten minutes, put on another sock, sit there speaking Spanish, comb his hair for another ten minutes, argue with his sisters, eat, lie back down for a minute, and just generally find everything to do but get ready for school and leave. Still...Benji's mama did not react well to calls from school, so Benji tried not to be late too often. His Pops reacted even worse.

Benji didn't realize how much he loved his neighborhood as he walked toward Ricky's house. It would hit him as an adult, but as a teenager, he didn't truly appreciate the chilly sunshine-filled mornings, the houses lucky enough to have breakfast smells coming from their windows, the preacher at the corner church where they played football preparing to mow the church grass, and school buses taking kids to school. Benji looked up when he heard the rumbling of the big yellow school bus; he truthfully missed riding the bus a little. As he watched the bus slow to a stop, then take on children, he remembered. He remembered how they all sang, "No more teachers, no more books…no more teachers' dirty looks!" on the last day of school when he was little. He remembered, it was probably a couple years ago, he was riding the bus and a song by the Carpenters, *"Top of the World,"* started playing on the bus radio speakers and about halfway through the song, all the girls on the bus, were singing the chorus at the top of their voices. They weren't just singing either…they were raising their arms, holding hands, swaying, laughing—they were truly into it Jackie Norman even slapped Benji in the back of the head, but not hard. He wondered if there was a message in her slap…she always smacked him at the "love" part—Benji wondered if that meant something. In any case, the irony escaped Benji at the time, but whenever he recalled the bus ride as an adult, he smiled at the thought of a busload of black kids from Southeast Dago loudly and proudly singing along to a song by the Carpenters like it was James Brown singing "*The Payback*." He even grinned a little bit even now—he just didn't realize why. Not a problem…he would understand completely when he was older and smile every time he remembered the moment or heard the song.

As Benji turned the corner, his senses were almost caressed by the smell of Mexican breakfast combined with the soft sounds of Rosie and the Originals' "*Angel Baby*" seemingly hanging in the air. Benji knew immediately that meant Ricky's brothers were up and listening to those old "*Happy Days*" songs Benji heard on television sometimes. Benji's guess was they were outside pretending to fix some old bucket that hadn't run in years and would never run again, smoking up a storm, and just generally cutting up. Sure enough, there they were: Francisco, Miguel, and a couple of other Mexican gangbangers Benji didn't know, leaning on the car, smoking, and laughing loudly. They were drinking something Benji was about a million per cent sure wasn't coffee.

As Benji approached, the Mexican quartet switched their focus and eyed him warily as he got closer and closer. Under normal circumstances, Benji would probably have crossed the street—in fact, under normal circumstances, he would not even have been in this neighborhood. Being Marcus Frazier's little brother would not save him here, any more than it rescued him when he got trapped in a phone booth and terrorized by what seemed like fifty Mexican gang members until they got bored.

"It was only three boys," I whispered to Benji with a smile. Benji looked my way as if he could really hear me, though I knew that was impossible.

Benji continued drawing near to his friend's house, and though the older Mexican boys continued to stare at him hard behind hard eyes and gangster brims, it did not escape Benji's notice when Francisco nudged one of the strangers and quietly said with a wink, *"Mira listo, carnal…"*

They were going to mess with him a little. Not a big deal, though; it was a test he'd passed numerous times.

"What the fuck you doing here, *puto*?"

Even though Benji knew it was coming, the steel in Francisco's tone shook him up a little bit even so. Benji stayed calm though.

Benji stopped and faced the group— he nodded like he saw Marcus do, head pointed up. Benji nodded by dipping his head once and got slapped in the head by his older brother for not doing it "right".

Benji knew the brothers already knew why he was there, so there was no need to answer the question. Instead, he came up with a response he thought was instant genius.

"I'm chillin'—gimme some of what you got in that cup though."

Not a question, Benji noted wryly…I made a statement. He was learning.

The Mexicans broke character and roared with laughter at the irreverent remark. Benji wanted to smile, but he knew it would be a mistake; these were not his peers. Instead, he assumed a quizzical look and spread his hands in a way which clearly said to the group, "What's the big deal, fellas? You gonna gimme a drink or not?"

Questions were feminine but questioning looks were definitely OK. In fact, Marcus said talking without saying any words was always considered cool. He said that's what true players did.

As the laughter started to subside, Francisco nodded to the door and said with more than a hint of merriment and a dismissive wave, "He inside. Get the fuck outta here, schoolboy...*pinche negrito*..."

Benji shrugged his shoulders, nodded at the group, and headed for the front door. Ricky's brothers and their partners in intimidation were still laughing as Benji walked away, and since his back was to the group, Benji allowed himself a grin as he heard Miguel call after him, "And you better tell us what you learned in school when you come back, *puto*, or I'm gonna beat your little ass!"

The Mexicans erupted in laughter again. Benji allowed himself a smile, but he didn't look back; the test was over.

Until next time.

Benji could hear the house's activity through the screen door, but before he could rap on the door, he heard his friend's voice drifting in from a back room.

"*Venga*, G...chill out. I be ready in a minute."

Benji thought it was a little funny. His friend was definitely 100 percent Mexican all the time, but at home? Two hundred percent. Ricky's mother was born in Mexico. Her English was broken, but she and her children were proud of being Mexican. Some things were met with scorn in this house and this neighborhood. Benji remembered a conversation he overheard in the house when one of the neighborhood *chicas* had a daughter and named her Julie or something like that. He didn't have to be fluent in Spanish to feel the scorn dripping from everyone present as they discussed the issue.

Benji opened the squeaky screen door, entered, and made his way through the house to hang out in the living room as he'd done a hundred times before. In the hallway he passed by Ricky's older sister Leticia, who was walking while applying the bright red lipstick all high school Mexican girls seemed to love. Benji edged to the wall to give her room to pass, but as she passed, Lety lightly stroked Benji under the chin and then on his cheek with her hand, smiled, and said, "Hi, Benji," without missing a beat before disappearing out the door.

"Well…that was pretty exciting," Benji thought.

Lety was nice…very very pretty too…but she mostly ignored him. Probably because he was just her little brother's friend, a little young *negrito* nobody. But it was right then Benji decided he liked girls touching his face like that.

He liked it a lot.

I knew Lety would never do it again, though. She was just being nice that day. Who knows why, but I sidled up to Benji and whispered, "Lucky day, huh?" Benji smiled… sometimes I really wondered if he could actually hear me.

Benji passed by the open bathroom and saw Ricky greasing his hair and combing it to the back like he always did. The two boys nodded at each other without speaking, but Ricky gestured to the living room. The fact Ricky was even up was kind of surprising—Benji figured maybe he was bored so he'd go to school to hang out. Sometimes they'd jack Ricky's brothers for cigarettes, ditch class and smoke down the hill or right outside the hole in the fence surrounding the school. Sometimes they'd steal some Boones Farm Strawberry and drink it before class to make school more fun or if they could scrape up a couple dollars, they'd try to convince someone older to buy them some Old English Malt Liquor or some Mad Dog 20-20. They had to pay double because they had to buy one for whoever bought it for them but the fun, carefree day it guaranteed in school was worth it. Then again, sometimes Ricky would just hang out and wait while Benji went to class; and sometimes Ricky would go to class too. Whatever he did, though, he did it with a laugh. Ricky didn't ever seem bothered about anything.

Benji heard the sound of water and dishes clanking in the kitchen. Ricky's mother was probably in there, so he went in to greet her and show respect. She was at the sink, rinsing off plates as he entered the kitchen, and when Benji entered and said, "Hola, Señora Escamilla," the overweight but kindly Mexican matriarch did not return the greeting as she turned to look toward the voice— but her eyes crinkled into a welcoming smile. With the water still running, she went to the cupboard for a plate, scooped mounds of still-warm refried beans and eggs from the cast-iron frying pan onto it, and set it down along with a fork and a soft "*Come, Benito,*" before returning to rinsing off dishes and putting her kitchen back in order.

Benji had already eaten at home, but it was rude to refuse her…so he sat and ate. It was really good too. Benji marveled at how Ricky's mom could make simple beans and eggs taste like THAT. Even with no chorizo.

Benji'd just finished wolfing down breakfast when Ricky sauntered in, grabbed a big wooden spoon, piled it as full of beans as the spoon could hold, opened his mouth as wide as possible, and shoved every morsel into his mouth—just in time for Ricky's mother to come and unleash a barrage of rapid-fire Spanish at her son. The only word Benji could make out was "*cochino*," but he was sure he could translate the rest of the verbal bombardment. Probably "Put that damn spoon down, get a plate and a fork, sit your raggedy ass down, and stop eating like an animal, you dirty, stinky, filthy, disgusting little pig!"

Or something like that.

Whatever was said clearly tickled Ricky, who was barely able to keep the food in his mouth while trying to stifle a laugh. He did manage a cheerful "*Lo siento*, mommy" as he swallowed the last of his breakfast under the stern gaze of his mother. Even so…Ricky's mother almost imperceptibly offered her cheek to her son as he approached to give her a goodbye kiss—even though a stone-faced grimace remained displayed on her countenance.

As the boys exited back toward Benji's neighborhood to get Brian, Benji considered the rationale for going out of his way to get Ricky and then heading back in the opposite direction to get Brian before quickly dismissing the notion. None of the three ever really questioned it; it was just the way it was: Benji got Ricky, then the two got Brian. It'd been like that ever since the boys began heading to school together. Though Benji was oblivious to his unconscious rationale, the reason he normally picked Ricky up was he was protecting Brian from having to go to Ricky's neighborhood alone. Brian wasn't scared or anything, but he was just a happy-go-lucky Skyline teen—he liked to laugh, make other people laugh, eat, and sing. Nobody would bother Brian, but still…Benji had been jumped there before. Benji knew he'd do better at talking his way out of trouble, and he was a faster runner too. So though all three friends were unaware of the true rationale, the tradition continued.

Ricky began singing the chorus of a popular Stylistics slow jam in Spanish, an interpretation which brought grins to the group.

"What's up with that 'Rock to Bach,' *ese*?"

He was referring to the school's annual "Bach to Rock" music festival. Mrs. Springer was the school's music teacher; young and pretty, she was the most popular teacher in their school. Her classes included dance, choir, and band. Then once a year, her students put on a nighttime show consisting of her advanced band playing while students sang a variety of songs from classical to current. It was a nighttime event, spread over two evenings; the auditorium was always packed; even gangsters stopped for the night to hang outside the school to listen and chill as live music and singing filled the air in the Southern Californian twilight.

Brian was in Mrs. Springer's advanced band class. Benji thought back to the previous year's concert—he was just going to attend and hang out. He knew Brian was playing, and it was dynamite to see him doing his thing. Benji turned away during an intermission, but his attention was suddenly yanked back toward the stage.

Hey! That's Brian! Singing with a girl! And it's good! Girls are screaming…for Brian!

Brian stayed humble through his mini-celebrity, and as friends sometimes did, even though they were mightily impressed, Benji and Ricky kept it cool, limiting their accolades to "Gimme some skin, blood…you was pretty good."

But Brian was more than "pretty good." Though he could not put it into words, Benji admired his short, slightly heavyset friend...because like Ricky, he always seemed unconcerned with who people thought he was. He was content with being himself, and his self-confidence seemed to give him a power, a sense Benji himself did not yet regularly feel. Benji could not put words to it, but he often felt like he was trying to fit in— as if he never perfectly fit in without trying, except when he was at home. He wasn't a *vato loco* like Ricky, he wasn't an artist like Brian, he wasn't a superb athlete like Marcus, he wasn't charismatic and cute like Sid, he wasn't a handsome ladies' man or funny or smart or a gangster or popular...he didn't know what he was, so he was always frontin'. But Brian seemed to know exactly who he was and was secure in the knowledge.

Brian shrugged his shoulders and was noncommittal; he didn't enjoy the spotlight and rarely, if ever, called attention to himself. He was content to hang with his two best friends, play his music, tell funny stories, and eat. So the boys trudged onward to school, making easy and free- flowing conversation as they crossed the field, made their way up the steep dirt hill, and slipped through the hole in the fence that served as their shortcut to school.

The bell rang as the threesome made it to their lockers and the boys went their separate ways to class, in tacit agreement they would meet for lunch and probably head home together—although for some reason, they sometimes made their way back home in a combination of two or even solo. Probably because each boy sometimes had things to do after school...band practice in Brian's case, just hanging out in Ricky's case, and sometime in Benji's case— detention. Nevertheless, there was a definite unexpressed comfort in heading to school and having lunch together, plus their lockers were all side by side, so they would often see each other throughout the day as well to catch up and cut up.

"Come on, Benji."

Benji grinned at the greeting from Tina Ngono, the girl he shared his locker with. Benji was the only one he knew who shared a locker with a girl, and it made him look like a player, kind of…he knew Shante and her friends didn't like Tina too much, but he didn't care. Tina had a ready smile and light-hearted personality—it made her seem different than the other girls in their school. Like…older. She was also funny and playful and really smart.

They weren't boyfriend and girlfriend, though. Tina was new this year and was wandering the hall looking for a locker on the first day and just stopped behind him as Benji was opening his locker.

"*Samahani kaka habari asubuhi jina lako nani?*"

All three boys turned around at hearing these strange words they'd never heard before and a girl none of them had ever seen standing there, right in front of Benji—-pretty girl but she was just standing there, staring expectedly and innocently at Benji, waiting for Benji to answer what was obviously a question.

Benji looked over at Ricky, standing on his right; his friend shook his head and shrugged his shoulders.

Clearly, she wasn't speaking Spanish.

Benji then looked to his left at Brian.

His hungry friend had no response other than continuing to chomp greedily on the Milky Way which seemed to have magically appeared from his jacket pocket.

Benji returned his gaze to the strange, but pretty girl who'd continued to fix an innocent gaze on him, awaiting an answer.

Then she broke out in a beautiful laugh.

She continued "I'm sorry, I'm just kidding—-that's Swahili, I was born in Cameroon…it means 'Hi, what's your name?' I'm Tina"

Benji tried to deliver a smooth introduction but he fumbled—he was taken aback by the sweetness, simplicity, and sincerity of her statement. After he answered, her next question was likewise straightforward: "Are you sharing your locker with anyone? Do you want to share with me?" And from there— the friendship blossomed. Her real name was Tatiana and she kind of looked like the plastic statue of that African lady's head Benji saw in his grandpa and grandma's house…but prettier. She was easy to be around, and after the first morning, Benji wasn't nervous around her…he could just relax and be himself. She laughed and teased him when Benji was awkward; she even laughed at her own awkwardness and goofiness. She said weird stuff and she didn't care if it was weird, like the time she said "Do you know what you are, Benji? You're an enigma."

After which, Benji had to go ask Angela what "enigma" meant.

He looked up where Cameroon was on his own.

Benji really liked her a lot, but they were truly just friends. Even so, though…there was one time they went on a nighttime field trip to the telescope place. It was a 45-minute ride there and Shante didn't go, so they sat next to each other on the bus. They'd talked excitedly all the way to the place; they'd spent the entire time together. She'd smiled, told Benji about stars and planets, called him *nzuri* which means "cute", and walked around holding on to his arm the entire time. Then on the way home, Tina fell asleep on his shoulder, and they'd held hands in the dark all the way back to the school. Benji had his eyes closed too but he was wide awake. Somebody's radio was playing Natalie Cole's "*Our Love*" too. It was perfect.

Benji hadn't wanted the bus ride to end; he figured Tina didn't want it to end either; he wondered if she hadn't been pretending to be asleep just like he was. Her mom was there to pick her up when the bus dropped them off at school so she ran off fast, but she smiled when she left. Still…the next time he saw her, they were back to being just friends again. Laughing on the phone, playing basketball in her driveway while she watched…friend stuff.

And Benji was reminded once again that he really didn't understand girls.

At all.

Benji grabbed Tina's books, and she released her books into his control as they made light-hearted banter on the way to English class. Tina sat next to him in English—she was a calming influence on Benji in a class she knew he struggled with. Tina knew Benji wouldn't wear his glasses in school and even though they never talked about it, she knew why. But since he couldn't see the board, he lost interest most of the time…all the time, to be honest. So Tina would quietly help him with what Miss Crouch was writing on the board. Benji felt pretty stupid sometimes. He thought back to fifth grade and his struggles with math— he'd been the only one in his class who couldn't do long division. He just couldn't follow along when the teacher was explaining it, and his failure to get it made him angry and hate school even more. Too bad Tina wasn't around back then. Maybe he would have learned long division before he entered junior high.

But Benji had real problems with English and Miss Crouch though. One day when Tina was absent, because he was bored, Benji had decided to unbraid his hair in class— it was starting to itch. Miss Crouch took one look at the monstrous steel comb known as a "cake cutter" and immediately accused Benji of threatening to attack her with it. She started screaming hysterically and told Benji to put it down. Benji was truly confused…he really didn't understand what she was saying or why she was saying it. She couldn't seriously be talking about…his comb?

No way…so he ignored her and kept on taking out his braids. When she ran out of the class screaming, the entire class had been confused; everyone was looking at each other. *No one* knew what her problem was. Then she came back with the gigantic big-bellied shop teacher, Mr. Guerrero. He'd come over to Benji and said softly, "Let's go, son… no one wants any trouble." Benji still had no idea what was wrong or why the teachers were excited all of a sudden, but he left with Mr G. He sat outside the vice principal's office for at least two hours before Mama came. He'd been suspended that day because they believed Mrs Crouch - I guess they though Benji was going to do something to her with his comb, but Mama wasn't even mad. In fact, she went back in, and Benji could hear her yelling at the vice principal…and he wasn't yelling back. Benji thought it was pretty funny.

But when Tina was around…that sort of thing didn't happen.

With English done, Benji proceeded on to Shop class—Ricky was there, but in Shop, his Mexican friend really got into working with his hands. Most of the boys did…nobody sat, and Mr. Guerrero was alright for a teacher, but Benji didn't like the class too much Not being able to see made school really difficult at times. And even making one of those little metal hammers required a precision Benji didn't have; he just couldn't see well enough. The shop teacher didn't fail anybody, he still got a "B" but Benji made nothing in Shop class. And Ricky knew enough about his friend to never offer to help or even mention it. The boys were often entertained by making fun of each other, but Ricky instinctively knew shop class was off limits. Too humiliating.

Then physical education…math…pizza for lunch, just like he thought…social studies…homeroom…and to end the day…the class Benji hated worst of all: General Science.

And the only teacher besides Miss Crouch Benji could not stand: Dr. Deen.

Benji could fake his way through the other classes. He had Tina for English; Shop and PE were easy; he could figure math out later, or his sister Angela would help, and Social Studies was kind of easy too, Tina was there…but General Science was uncompromising and unforgiving. Benji did not understand the topic. The conversations went over his head, and he had zero motivation to even try to understand. And moreover—the way his fellow students presented themselves made Benji feel downright hostile. He despised watching them demonstrate their excitement and speak in such a scientific way.

And then there was Dr. Deen.

Benji hated her.

In addition to loathing the subject she taught, Benji thought she was so obviously biased toward the science geniuses. She gave off a clear disdain for Benji and the rest of the science dummies. If she even bothered to speak to Benji at all, the way her glasses sat on her nose and her expression said it all: "You are unintelligent. You are beneath me. I have no respect for you. I wish you to stop speaking to me and never think of speaking to me again."

Or that's what he heard, anyway.

Benji knew he would fail this class and hated it and her so much he was happy to fail it. Their science fair projects were due today, and Benji would be happy to proudly report he had not done one. He probably wouldn't be happy when Mama found out…he'd be even less happy when Pops found out. But today he didn't care one bit. Deen wouldn't care either. She was too focused on the eggheads.

The good part about today, though—everyone was so busy rushing around, finishing their projects before spring break and sucking up to each other, no one noticed Benji at all. In fact, he even left a couple of times.

When the bell rang, it signaled not just the end of the school day but also the start of spring break. He wasn't focused on science or even on his boys…he wanted to get going to catch Tina before break, them go see Shante and there was that party later. Everything school related was already been forgotten.

"Benjamin, may I see you for a moment, please?"

It was Deen.

This was surprising. And for Benji…annoying.

Deen kept her head down as Benji stood and stared, waiting for the teacher he loathed to speak so he could leave.

The science teacher lifted her head and for a moment, teacher and student locked eyes. After what seemed like an eternity, Dr. Deen seemed to dip her head, and the stern expression on her face silently directed Benji to approach.

"Benjamin, I noticed you did not turn in a science project. I believe this is a mistake. Your project—or stated more accurately, your lack of a project—is troubling in that it is indicative of a lack of thought. Because when one is thinking, one is learning or reinforcing what has previously been mentally digested. It is not the complexity of the project that is most relevant."

Benji stared and wrinkled his brow as though she were speaking a foreign language but remained silent as she continued.

"You will turn in your project when we return from spring vacation. If you do not, I will assume you do not intend to do so. Have a pleasant vacation, Benjamin."

And with that, Benji knew he was dismissed.

"That's it?" he mused with a little laugh. "She wants me to do a project…on spring vacation?

"She could have saved her breath. Too easy. Not doing it. Feel free to fail me."

CHAPTER 3

CLOUD NINE

Benji stopped by his locker before he left school for vacation and was mildly disappointed when he saw Tina wasn't there—she must have left already. "I probably would have seen her if it not for that idiot Deen," he thought with a frown. In truth, there was no reason to go to the locker anyway…as was often the case, Benji didn't take any books to any class. There was not much point in it. Since he couldn't see anyway, he wasn't doing any schoolwork until he got home and could put his glasses on. Not only that, no books made it easier to run if necessary. Sometimes he'd leave his books at Ricky's or Brian's and then scoop them up later before he went home.

But deception was unnecessary today, so he was light hearted as he proceeded to Shante's house on his way home. He thought it was pretty cool to have a pretty girl waving at him for real, passing notes and messages from other people, sitting by him…as a matter of fact, he liked having someone to dance with at the after-school dances too—he wasn't standing on the wall with the others, wishing they were dancing. And at the house parties, he had someone to slow dance with, and he didn't even have to ask...she just appeared, and they'd start dancing. Ricky and Brian would be standing on the sidelines, pretending they couldn't see him on the dance floor so they could pretend they were interested in what the other was saying. Shante looked good... REALLY good...but even though she was kind of interesting, they really didn't have much to say to each other even though she never seemed to stop talking—it wasn't easy convo like it was with Tina. He'd almost kissed her one time though, but it was too awkward, so Benji just kept swaying with her to Danny Pearson's "*What's Your Sign Girl?*" and holding her. When they talked on the phone...it was kind of a chore. The conversation was forced and full of "hold on" and "wait a minute" and Benji was relieved when the phone calls were over. Benji started asking Mama to say he wasn't home sometimes...but Mama wouldn't do it. Neither would Nikki. Benji found himself annoyed when Nikki would answer the phone and call for him loudly with fake sweetness, "Benji! It's your girlfriend!!" In truth, Benji could not quite figure out why Shante liked him...but she was pretty, and even though she dominated their conversations, since Benji didn't really know how to talk smooth to girls anyway, maybe that was kind of OK.

"I bet she likes me because of these," Benji thought to himself with a smirk as he glanced admiringly at his own now flexed bicep and patted it lovingly. "I've been doing push-ups."

But all of a sudden—he didn't feel like going over there right now. The last time he'd been there, he'd sat around while Shante talked with somebody on the phone. Even now, Benji would usually do pretty much whatever Shante wanted him to do. But as his confidence grew…so did his independence. His mental independence anyway. When she was around, he still did pretty much whatever she wanted.

But she wasn't there right now.

And he'd just decided he didn't want to go to her house.

It wasn't often I agreed with decisions Benji made, but this one I agreed with. Shante was not an bad person…but I sensed she and Benji were not the best combination. I didn't like how Benji just seemed to do her bidding. She was good to give Benji experience in relationships and different types of people, but I sensed their usefulness to each other was reaching its end. I didn't know it for a fact. But I sensed it. So I was happy to see Benji take this step.

As Benji was deciding on his next move, he looked up, and there was Topaz Marks coming toward him, smoking a cigarette, with two other guys he didn't know. And although he didn't know the accomplices, Benji sensed he knew what Topaz might want.

Revenge.

Benji may not have been so confident in his dealings with teenage girls, but this was a type of situation he was becoming increasingly familiar and comfortable with.

He scanned quickly for potential allies—there were none. He saw his escape route clearly so he knew where he'd run. It'd be easy as long as they didn't surround him, so he needed to make sure that didn't happen. He'd been jumped before, and those beatings typically didn't last too long, but he saw Topaz had some sort of stick in his hand;

as the boys approached, Benji saw it was not a stick…it was a golf club. He'd never been hit with one of those, but he'd have to make sure to stop at a far enough range where he couldn't get hit with the club or surrounded by the boys but close enough so they would not assess him as being afraid or intimidated by them. This situation was unavoidable, but he'd only run if necessary—if they sensed fear, they would probably come after him again and again…and again…day after day. Until they got him.

He was ready.

As he approached, he noted none of the group headed toward him moved to his side or attempted to come in behind him— after a quick glance behind to ensure no extra members of the group magically materialized behind him, Benji was slightly more at ease. Once he was within hearing range, Topaz began twirling the golf club and addressed him.

"Heard you been scrappin' with my cousins…"

Benji stopped and eyed all the group calmly but warily. It was true. He'd gotten into a fight with Topaz's cousin Sean. They'd all been walking home in a large group, and Sean started in on him on his dark skin, a normal topic and all in fun at first. But as the boys went back and forth, Benji's verbal retaliation enraged Sean; he chose to escalate the war of words to something physical. Benji remembered Ricky, laughing so hard, egging them on, yelling and in the middle of everything. Brian was quieter, kind of just standing there, but Benji knew he wanted it over. But because they were surrounded by excited teenagers, the fight was inevitable… and despite the heat of the moment, it wasn't long before Benji almost felt sorry for his clearly overmatched opponent.

Every time Benji knocked him down, the assembled crowd hollered, and Sean got up and charged again. It became almost comical. Then Benji saw Sean's brother Lee ready to jump in; Benji didn't know if Lee wanted to break it up or get in the fight. Brian and Ricky wouldn't have allowed Lee to jump in but Benji dropped him with a single punch too just in case because Lee was standing too close to him… and Lee started crying. Both brothers got up and ran off… and Benji thought he saw tears in Sean's eyes too.

I felt sorry for the brothers, but Benji was unconcerned. He was no bully—he hated bullies, in fact, but he was sick of being bullied himself. It was happening less and less, but still, anyone who came at him got whatever they got.

However, now…here was Topaz. Older, and with two friends. Benji was absolutely aware of the price he might now have to pay. He made note: he would tell his brothers later…Ricky too…even Brian.

Benji shrugged his shoulders and said nothing in response to Topaz's statement. What happened next was surprising.

Topaz chuckled.

"It's cool, it's cool…my cousin trippin', so you took that mother fucker to the next phase, huh?"

Topaz's friends laughed heartily as Topaz added, "Actually…I guess you planted both of them niggas…"

Benji was smart enough not to fully join in on the laughter; he allowed himself the smallest of grins and repeated his shrug. Anything more demonstrative might have been viewed as disrespectful.

Topaz lazily stuck out his hand, Benji dapped it, and the three went on their way. Benji proceeded on; he didn't turn around, but he listened for the telltale sound of shuffling feet alerting him the boys were launching a sneak attack from behind. No such attack was imminent, but they did stop as Topaz called out, "Check it out, though, young blood… come on by the ABC on Market…we got a gang of young brothers over there sparring and learning and shit. Archie Moore run it."

"Bet."

It was the only word Benji spoke during the entire encounter.

Benji knew about the ABC…it was the "Any Boy Can" center, run by boxing legend Archie Moore, a fighter who fought Rocky Marciano, Muhammad Ali and commanded respect from everyone in Southeast Dago— even the hardcores. Benji knew they learned boxing there, but also responsibility and tutoring and a bunch of school stuff. They'd even been doing the Pledge of Allegiance one time when Benji wandered by and looked in the window. "Nah," Benji thought almost immediately…plus he'd heard Mr. Moore was kind of a hard man with all the discipline and what not. Benji already had Pops at home; who needed all the extra stuff?

But then Benji had a thought.

He loved fighting, and he truly admired fighters. The Olympics was big a few years back, and all of Sugar Ray Leonard's fights were on television now. Benji and his Pops watched Larry Holmes and Ken Norton fight on ABC's *Wide World of Sports*, and it seemed like the whole neighborhood was watching and screaming when Muhammad Ali beat Leon Spinks in the rematch. Benji loved it— even more than watching the San Diego Chargers. But the other thing Benji considered was since he started fighting in the neighborhood, people respected him more. Look at Nick... Topaz too. Nobody was teasing any more. They weren't calling him Doo. Even the gigantic shop teacher spoke to him calmly and respectfully when taking him out of English class. He walked with a lot more confidence now; he was unconcerned with bullies, and maybe...just maybe...that's why Shante liked him so much. As a matter of fact, he was certain that was why. All because of fighting.

I watched Benji with some amusement. I knew he was considering it; I knew the excitement was building within him, and I knew something else. I sensed it. I didn't know exactly what was going to happen...but I knew where we were.

I got close to Benji's ear and whispered:

"Crossroad..."

Then I watched for his reaction.

Benji wanted to get home so he could prepare his cassette player to record songs off the radio. He felt a surge of independence as he passed Shante's street without stopping by her house like she wanted him to do. He was thinking more and more about his lockermate Tina. They were good friends, but...sometimes he wondered why weren't they a couple? He knew she felt the connection between them at the field trip, but afterward? It was like it never happened, at least in Tina's mind. Benji couldn't figure it out, but one thing he knew: the more you chase girls, the more they run. Like...his girlfriend Shante. If he called her when she said to call her, sometimes she would answer, "Call me back later," and hang up the phone so abruptly, Benji would wonder if he'd done anything wrong. But when Benji ignored her, refused her demand to change lockers or acted like he didn't see her (he really didn't wave back at times because his glasses weren't on), those were the times she was much nicer and even affectionate. So his friend Tina would have to stay his friend until she decided they would be more. He couldn't chase her. It wouldn't work; she would just run anyway.

"Hi, Stinky."

Benji smiled at the greeting of his older sister Angela as he walked in the door of his home. Benji often felt annoyed when Angela tried to mother him, but secretly I knew he also found comfort in it too. The oldest Frazier sibling was strong in her own way— she was quiet and smart, and Benji knew Angela and Mama often sat in the kitchen to discuss what Mama needed for the younger Frazier children, and Mama knew Angela would make sure it happened. Angela wasn't like Nikki, who wasn't fast but was a little boy crazy… Angela had a boyfriend, but she just didn't care as much about hair or make-up or parties. It seemed like she only cared about school, her part-time job, and family. And the truth was, she never seemed mad, never bothered; even though she had her own boyfriend, she always took time to listen to Marcus, braid Nikki's hair, babysit, cook, study, or do whatever was needed. And for Benji, she seemed to just know when to give him space to think or to learn and when she needed to be available to talk. Like one time Marcus came home really late from being with some girl. He was mad or upset or something and somehow…even though he didn't say anything, Angela just knew. She came in the room and they started whispering; Benji pretended he was asleep and strained mightily to hear, but he couldn't quite make out what they were saying. They left and talked some more, but all Benji knew was in a couple days, Marcus was back to being Marcus. Benji wasn't quite sure how she did it, but he knew it was because of Angela.

Benji settled in his room to relax and listen to the radio. Sharing a room with two brothers, it wasn't often he could count on having the room to himself, but Sid was out playing somewhere and Marcus wasn't home yet, so Benji took the time to just lie on the bed listening to the radio. It was still early; he figured he would just relax for a while. He was supposed to meet Shante later, so he hoped Pops would sneak him some change. He decided not to ask…easier to sneak two bucks out of his mom's purse than to hear the inevitable lecture followed by a "no".

Bobby Womack was on the radio now, singing a song that made this Harry Hippy guy sound like the hippest guy in the world, walking around day just singin' and cuttin' up; Mary Hippy was his down chick; this song was a little old but Benji liked it so he settled in to listen and thought to himself as soon as the song ended, maybe he'd get up and start recording. He reminded himself to add Bobby Womack to the list of people whose songs he wanted to record.

Then the phone rang.

"Benji!" he heard his sister calling for him.

He asked his sister, "Who is it?" He wouldn't have bothered asking Nikki; she would just say something stupid. And he definitely wouldn't have asked Mama; she might have started a lecture or conversation about not staying on the phone too long or something embarrassing right then and there in front of whoever it was - probably Shante. But it was Angela hollering for him and the look on her smiling face told him everything he needed to know.

It was Shante.

"What you doin'?"

"Check this out," he began.

He ran through the story of how Deen jumped on him after school, how he had no idea what to do, didn't care, and had no intention of doing a project.

But he'd forgotten…when Shante said "What you doin'?" she did not truly want to know what he was doing. It was just something to say before she launched into whatever came to her mind. Because she seemed wholly uninterested, and there was a noticeably uncomfortable pause before she spent the next forty-five minutes talking about what she was going to wear later, how so-and-so got on her nerves, the television show she liked, new music she heard, what time he needed to go at her house so they could walk to the party, why hadn't he come over earlier and of course…how much she hated Tina.

Benji always smiled when she got to that part. Shante always called Tina "your little girlfriend" in a voice literally dripping with scorn and disgust. Benji used to defend her, saying, "She not my girlfriend," but Shante would hit back with "Oh, so you gonna defend her?? Why she in your locker then?" and then angrily hang up in his face…before calling back again…and again…and again. Now Benji just let her rant, but for some reason, he still enjoyed her obvious discomfort. It was kind of funny.

He didn't realize Angela stopped to listen outside the door from the moment she heard "Check this out."

Angela did not think Shante was good enough for her little brother, but she kept her opinion to herself. She knew many "little fast girls" just like her—too loud, too fast, too basic, with nothing going for themselves except popularity and looks. In fact, some of the girls Angela herself went to high school with now found themselves out of high school, still desperately but unsuccessfully trying to hold on to what they once were. Angela thought Shante was on her way to being one of those girls; she also knew it was useless telling Benji; for one thing, he was obviously girl crazy and for another, he was always trying to keep up with Marcus. But what she just overheard was her chance to drive Benji towards something positive.

"I can help you."

Benji looked up from his pad of paper, where he was writing the words of the song he recorded earlier.

"What?"

"With your project. I can help you."

Benji realized his sister had overheard him talking. He didn't care. Angela and Nikki were always doing stuff like that; sometimes they quietly picked up the phone to listen to his conversations. Well…maybe they probably didn't go that far; Nikki probably did but not Angela. But Benji and Sid definitely listened in on their calls though. Listened to Marcus's calls too sometimes. Angela's calls were usually pretty boring, like about school stuff, but Nikki? Pretty interesting convo…Benji learned quite a bit about girls from listening in to some of her calls.

"I'm not worried." he said dismissively to his older sister. Angela helped him with his homework a lot, but he was just so uninterested in General Science, there was nothing about it that could possibly get him anything other than an F... so there was no point in trying. Besides, he'd told Deen to fail him. He didn't say it out loud but he challenged her in his head to fail him and he meant it. He'd take the punishment for it later.

"Really? You sure? I have an interesting idea for a project though...it's fun too. It's about all your little girlfriends," Angela continued with a laugh as she started to leave.

Benji remain uninterested.

Wait a minute.

The realization hit him like a ton of bricks. He stared after his sister, slightly confused and a thought came to mind.

"Did she say...girls?"

I saw Benji conflicted now. He watched his sister leave, but I saw the wheels turning, and I knew he was curious. On one hand, there was nothing about science that could hold Benji's interest for longer than two seconds. On the other hand —Angela clearly said "girls," and despite himself, Benji found himself interested in what she meant. Was it a trick?

I sensed something. It wasn't a trick. I got close to Benji's ear and whispered:

"Crossroad..."

Then I watched for his reaction.

Benji settled in. He'd intended to record music off the radio but instead decided to just listen to what he'd already recorded—he was strangely tired after what seemed like a very long day. There was comfort in the music he recorded— sometimes he recorded the music, sometimes he listened to words of the songs…sometimes he wrote the words in his notebook so he'd have something to say when he talked to girls, as long was the song wasn't too popular. For now, though, he was content to listen to his handiwork in total solitude as the Southern California Friday afternoon slowly turned into the Southern California Friday evening.

Every song he'd taped meant something, and Benji sunk into his bed to relax as his recordings played. He recorded fast music too so that he could practice dancing, but this was his slow jams cassette. Benji secretly recorded this one song *Baby Come Back* which was playing now…Benji hadn't originally intended to record Player's pop tune, but the beginning was pretty slick and he'd listened to the lyrics - just as he was doing now. He knew his brothers would laugh at him if they heard it, so he always scrambled to turn down the volume or hit the fast-forward button if anyone surprised him while he was listening. But right now, though he could hear the voices of his brothers and sisters coming from the living room and kitchen, he felt comfortably alone.

As he listed to those Player guys plead for some girl to please come back, thoughts of Shante flooded the young teen's memory. The truth was—Shante Clay was the best girlfriend he'd ever had. He liked her too. She was a little loud, and like Benji, she wasn't too interested in school, which was no big deal - but there was just something about her. She was confident, outgoing, and funny…she always seemed surrounded by a bunch of people, both girls and boys. She was pretty and fashionable and loved to dance — in fact, she was everything Benji was not. But the thing was…not only was she pretty, she was loyal too. She was often randomly affectionate to Benji no matter how many people were around. She'd even walk away from her crowd to sit with him or jump on his back or scream across the cafeteria, "There's my baby!" He couldn't figure out why, but…it felt pretty good…so as the song played on, Benji found himself regretting not going over to her house and for the life of him couldn't remember why he hadn't gone. Because Shante could choose someone else way better than him, and then what?

The song changed now…and though it was Donny Hathaway singing about getting closer to Roberta Flack, in his mind, it was Benji thinking about his locker mate Tina Ngono. Their night at the telescope place and the bus ride there and back was the best night of his life, and he knew she felt it too…and then as quick as it came, it was gone. And it never came back. It was as if it never happened, and Benji almost got angry sometimes trying to figure out why. And another thing Benji noticed…Shante talked about Tina often, and her jealousy was obvious, but Tina never talked about Shante…like she didn't care whether Shante was his girlfriend or not. Why? And why'd she tap him on the shoulder and asked to be his locker mate anyway? And why did they laugh so much and talk about things like being an enigma and stuff? And why did she let Benji carry her books like a boyfriend? It was so confusing. Did she even have a boyfriend? She was the one who was an enigma…

The afternoon turned to dusk, and Benji felt more and more relaxed as Bobby Debarge and Switch threatened to rock Benji to sleep. Not even thoughts of Tina could push away the thoughts of the dark-haired girl he saw around from time to time; she always captured Benji's attention, and he did not know why—because he'd never spoken to her. He almost talked to her one time, though. Once, at the school trip to Magic Mountain, he'd seen her with a girl he thought was her sister...and she waved! Benji was so rattled he didn't even wave back, he didn't realize who she was waving at because he wasn't wearing his glasses...and the moment passed. Later that evening, Benji won a gigantic stuffed giraffe by shooting baskets—and when the guy gave him the monstrous toy animal, Benji walked around for an hour, intending to give it to the dark-haired girl from his neighborhood...but he couldn't find her and ended up giving it to Shante, who squealed in delight. Benji wished he was as smooth as Bobby Debarge from Switch. His last thought before his eyes closed was "I'll whisper something in her ear...yeah...Bobby Debarge always knows what to say..."

I looked at Benji and smiled.

"Do you ever think about anything but girls?" I said to his sleeping form.

He smiled drowsily with his eyes still closed.

Just as he threatened to fall into a deep sleep, Benji woke with a start. His cassette reached the end of the tape, so silence now teamed with darkness to fill the room as Benji forced himself awake. It was dinner time, and it appeared as though Pops brought his family a rare Friday night treat... the tantalizing smell of McDonald's french fries beckoned Benji to rejoin his family.

Benji's nose had not led him astray, and his mouth watered at the thought of the treats held within the crinkled white bags, but it was not his father who delivered the family's Friday- night feast. It turned out his cousin Jimmy, who joined the military last year, was home visiting and bought dinner when he came over. Benji's focus was on the McDonald's bags. He was hunting for Quarter Pounders; he loved the box containing the quarter- pound burgers because the melted cheese always spilled on the box, and he could scoop the cheese with a french fry…or his finger. The Big Macs were OK, but the cheese didn't fall on the box, sometimes the cheese never melted at all…plus Big Macs had all that stupid lettuce and red mayonnaise on them that had to be scraped off. Mama would pull out a quarter-pound burger to save for Pops and sometimes for his sisters too; then the boys would battle for the remaining burgers. Last one to the table might get stuck with a regular old cheeseburger. Or worse…a hamburger.

Benji dived into a bag and struck gold…the yellow Styrofoam container which held the cherished Quarter Pounder with cheese. But as he settled down to eat, another thought came to Benji's consciousness before he could take a single bite.

His cousin Jimmy.

He was different from before.

Jimmy had always been kind of a…well…kind of a… nothing. Even though he was older, he wasn't big, strong, and popular like Marcus; he wasn't super smart like Angela; he wasn't cute like Nikki…and Benji couldn't believe the word "cute" had even come to his mind when it came to Nikki— she wasn't cute; in fact she was nothing but annoying. But Jimmy wasn't even annoying…he was just a nobody cousin who just kind of hung around and blended in to whatever crowd he happened to find himself in—in fact, he was kind of like an older version of Benji. He wasn't a bad person, he wasn't mean or anything, he just…he didn't score any touchdowns; he wasn't interesting; he didn't do anything particularly well. Benji remembered Mama feeling sorry for his cousin because Jimmy's date for the prom came home after an hour because she had another date on the same night as the prom. Jimmy was kind of like oatmeal with no butter and no sugar—that's what Marcus said back then, and everyone laughed…because it was true.

But this was a different Jimmy.

He was telling military stories, Marcus was laughing and Sid was mesmerized; Nikki was looking at him like he was some kind of enchanted prince, and Benji thought he knew why. Jimmy was talking with power and confidence now… he even moved around the room like he was in charge or something. Pops came in, and when Jimmy stood to greet him, Pops shook his hand like a man and put his hand on his shoulder like Jimmy was…like…a hero or something? But what really struck Benji was how his cousin looked. He was stylish, dressed all in matching purple pants and a purple shirt with a fresh wide collar, and he just looked…strong. He was muscular now in a different way than Marcus was; Benji could kind of see muscles under Jimmy's silk purple shirt, and though he tried not to stare, Benji found himself enthralled with his military cousin just like his sister and everyone else seemed to be.

"Benji, come here."

His father's command cut through his altered focus and beckoned Benji to join him where he was deep in discussion with Jimmy and Marcus.

"Yes sir?"

Benji's father gestured toward Benji as he turned to Jimmy and said, "Tell my son what you were just telling me, Jimmy."

Jimmy stuck out hand and said, "Hey, lil' cuz."

"His voice is even deeper," Benji thought to himself. "He sounds like a man…is this even my cousin?"

"Listen," Jimmy continued. "We got a program out at the base where we bring in teenagers to work for the summer to get working experience. Might be a good opportunity for you to make some extra money and see how the military works. I can try to make it happen if you're interested."

Benji's father looked at him expectantly.

The fact his father hadn't said that Benji was going to do it meant Benji knew he had a choice in the matter.

Benji thought to himself, "Doesn't sound all that good… I don't know about all that working and stuff. I want to chill in the summer time, and I'm not trying to be out there getting yelled at and marching around and getting my hair cut and everything."

Then he thought again.

"Jimmy looks real smooth, though. Do I get a uniform? I could use some money, but do I have to work every day? Would Pops let me keep the money? I can do some things with money, but…what about Shante? And…what about the boxing thing?"

I could see Benji was very conflicted but I sensed something. I knew where we were so I moved a little closer and got close to Benji's ear and whispered:

"Crossroad…"

Then I watched for his reaction.

Benji knew he had a lot of thinking to do, but now he needed to get ready for the party. Mama didn't always let him go…sometimes he snuck out, even knowing the beating might be waiting when he returned home. Sometimes he lied and said he was going to Brian's house…never said he was going to Ricky's because the answer would still be no, Mama thought that part of Southeast was too dangerous at night. But this time, Mama said it was OK as long as he came home on time. It was a different level of comfort not having to sneak and lie.

Of course—Benji still said he was walking to the party with Brian. A minor lie, but it was much closer to the truth than where he normally ended.

There was no need to dress up for a regular house party. Benji made that mistake once before after saying he was staying over at Brian's house…not only had he been teased for months for wearing "church clothes" to a house party, but once he got home, Mama grilled him about where he'd really went. Because when Benji tried to sneak the clothes back into his closet, it was obvious they'd been worn somewhere. Benji tried to stick to the lie no matter what, just like Marcus said he should…Marcus said when you lie, stick to it forever, no matter what—but Mama wasn't buying it. When the matter got turned over to Pops, the refusal to tell the truth earned Benji a beating. Pops seemed to know what the truth was…

Marcus and Sid wouldn't have told—the Frazier boys don't snitch. But the Frazier girls? Benji figured Nikki found out where he went and probably snitched. He could tell Nikki was a little bit sad in the aftermath of his beating. Probably a guilty conscience.

Some kids could get away with dressing up for a house party, but Benji was not one of them. His normal house party style was to wear school clothes or maybe something just a little bit better than he'd wear on a normal day—like what he'd wear on picture day, maybe. Shante would out dress him, but that was OK—she always did and besides, she was a girl. Nick and the other gangsters never dressed up for house parties, so even regular clothes were OK for guys.

Having decided his denim bell bottoms and matching shirt would work (after asking Nikki what would look good— it was one of the few times she didn't get on his nerves), Benji jumped in the bathtub and then went to work on his hair, picking out his hair until it no longer seemed lopsided to him. He examined himself in the bathroom mirror and was pleased with what he saw…he only wished he had a chain or something to wear around his neck like the guys on *Soul Train*, but all in all, he thought he looked ready.

Benji felt good as he prepared to depart his house to head over to Shante's; school was out, and he wasn't sneaking or hiding, so he wasn't nervous, even though he was supposed to be home before midnight— he'd have to see about that one. It was going to be a great night, and he was looking forward to seeing his girlfriend. He'd really missed her that afternoon, and what he didn't realize until that very moment was that they were rarely alone…in fact, they'd never been alone. Her friends were always around; they were even at the house when he went over there to get his hair braided. And if not her friends, her little brother or sister was running around. The only time they were alone was on the phone. So walking to the party tonight was going to be a first for the young couple.

"You look so handsome."

His mother was cleaning the dinner mess and beaming at her middle son. She had that sparkle in her eyes Benji loved to see…it was like he was her baby again. Benji was surprised Mama would let him walk to their party, but it was if she finally recognized Benji was growing up.

"Angela! Your brother is ready to leave. Can you drop him off?"

He should have known better.

And there was no sense in debating it. Mama was so protective; he should have expected something like this. Or even better— he should have just snuck over to the party like he usually did.

"Come on, Stinky."

Benji's father looked up from the show he was watching to give Benji a little smile and wink as the two departed the house. Pops understood…Benji knew he did. But no one was standing up to Mama on something like this… not even Baba. Pops's wink said, "Don't worry…this won't last forever."

Benji wasn't so sure.

"And be outside at twelve so your daddy don't have to wait for you" Mama added.

Great.

Benji was silent as his oldest sister climbed into the car and began to make her way through the darkened Southeast streets.

"Where are we going?"

Benji peered at his sister. He didn't want to go to the party and then head backwards to walk with Shante. He didn't even want to be dropped off in front of the house where everyone could see, but he thought he could convince Angela to drop him off down the street from the party or on the next block. She'd understand.

But then Benji got an even better idea.

"Can you drop me off at Shante's?"

It was a question, not a statement. But that was OK in Benji's mind; Angela wasn't a girl…she was his sister.

Angela looked at Benji in exasperation. She was the oldest; Mama and Daddy depended on her. She said no to her siblings often when she was left in charge; it wasn't easy being the oldest. And besides…her brother was too good for that little fast girl anyway.

But even through the dark, she could see the almost pleading look in her brother's eyes. She was not much for parties herself, but she understood.

"Benji and Nikki are not so different," she thought with a smile. "She's a female version of him; he's the male version of her. Both of them are love crazy"

"Does Daddy know where to pick you up?"

Benji nodded.

Angela silently adjusted her navigation to drop Benji off at his girlfriend's house; Benji stopped staring at her, but she felt his warmth and gratitude through the darkness.

When they arrived, Benji hopped out and looked back as he headed for Shante's door. The Fraziers were not an "I love you" kind of family…especially the brothers and sisters. Maybe Mama was sometimes, but the rest? The family did love each other, but it just wasn't something they went around saying to each other all the time.

Or some of the time.

Or ever.

But as Benji and his sister shared a moment in the dark… no words were needed. Angela knew. And Benji knew. And they each knew the other knew. The actual words were unnecessary.

Benji approached the door as his sister drove off, but no one answered when Benji rang her doorbell. He was about to ring it again when Shante's older brother appeared at the window, pulled back the curtain, and made a loud announcement through the closed window.

"Shante ain't here. She left already."

And with that statement made, he closed the curtain. And Benji was left standing there.

At first, he wondered if Shante was really there and just not ready. Or maybe she'd changed her mind and decided she didn't want to go to the party. Or maybe she was mad at Benji for not coming over earlier. But he'd just talked to her, and they'd made a plan to walk to the party together, so for a moment, Benji was stunned.

And then it became clear. Shante left…probably with her friends. Because as usual, Shante was going to do whatever Shante was going to do…which was whatever she wanted to do, whether they'd made plans or not. And Benji wasn't mad though.

This time—he was just done.

He'd had it with this girl. This was it: tonight he would quit her. Yes, he would quit her, and tomorrow he was going over to Tina's house and not play basketball…he'd talk to her about their time at the telescope place. He was going to call her an enigma, and he wouldn't ask Tina any questions either…he'd make lots of statements, like Marcus said.

Or even better…he'd find that dark-haired girl and tell her his name. She wasn't going to get any questions either… all statements. Then he'd suggest going somewhere, and she would be thrilled and they'd make a plan. Oh and he was going to tell her about the toy giraffe and find out what her name was too.

Maybe he wouldn't tell her about the giraffe.

But Shante? He was done with this chick, he had options now…or so he thought. For a split second, he considered not going to the party, but he felt so good, he decided he wanted to go. And he hoped he saw Shante there. In fact, he practiced how he would ignore her like she was no big deal all the way to the party.

Benji heard the party before he got there. The Bar-Kays' *"Let's Have Some Fun"* played faintly in the distance and got louder and louder as he approached. There were a bunch of kids outside, and as Benji walked in, he heard a male voice yelling.

"There that nigga is! Punk muh fucka bet not come over this way! Punk ass mutha fucka…scared ass nigga, I'll beat that ass.…"

It was Tootie Mo.

He'd never gotten over their fight and was always trying to instigate another conflict. But it was here where Benji's poor sight was a huge benefit to him.

To everyone who witnessed the incident and to Tootie Mo himself, it appeared as though Benji stopped, glared at Tootie Mo with absolute malice, decided he wasn't worth beating up again, and proceeded inside, completely unaffected by his gangster tantrum.

I knew the truth.

In actuality, Benji heard the voice and turned to look at the voice. Since he didn't have his glasses on, he thought it might be Tootie Mo, but since the music was loud, he wasn't sure. He also had no idea if the voice was addressing him specifically, so since he couldn't see the culprit to accurately read the situation, he looked for a minute and then went on about his business.

Things were not always what they looked like. It was odd how that worked sometimes.

As the rest of the night unfolded, it didn't go quite like Benji imagined it would go.

The music was good…Cameo, the Sylvers, Brick, Rose Royce, Bootsy…Benji knew just about everyone there and was comfortable. He'd go inside and hang out, move out to the garage where the strobe light was flashing and someone had some different music playing, then outside where the gangsters mostly hung out…then he'd reverse the process and repeat it. Over and over.

But something was missing.

He wasn't sure if he'd seen Shante or not. Without his glasses, he could have walked right by her and not recognized her in the dark. Which he did several times. But it wasn't that.

The thought just occurred to Benji that the party was fun…kind of…but he had even more fun just hanging out with Brian playing electric football or eating beans at Ricky's house while laughing about whatever. He had a good time with Sid…the brothers sometimes just created games to play with discarded dice from several board games and old playing cards, then spent the evening arguing over who won. He had more fun playing basketball at Tina's house, and he wondered what they were all doing.

But the rules were you had to act like you were having fun at a party…and Benji was acting like he was having fun.

Kind of.

It was just a weird feeling. Benji couldn't put it into words…so I did it for him.

"It's like…wherever you are…whatever you're doing… you don't feel like you quite belong. There's always something missing…something lacking. Right, Benji?"

Benji stood almost frozen as the words I whispered to his subconscious thoughts struggled to make their way and find an interpretation his conscious teenage mind could comprehend.

"Come on, boy, and dance with me. You know you like this."

Shante beckoned as the jungle cry of *"Aqua Boogie"* introduced the beginning of Parliament's hit song and broke Benji from his stupor. As she grabbed his hand and guided him to the area serving as the dance floor, Benji didn't know if by "you want this" she meant he wanted her…or wanted to dance to one of his favorite songs.

He wanted neither.

When he'd said he was through, he'd meant it, and for a brief moment, he considered just walking away—seemed kind of a feminine thing to do though. Even so—he imagined the look on her face, and she'd probably make a scene… but he didn't care anymore. The only thing that kept him from leaving was the fact that the makeshift dance floor had rapidly filled up, and exiting was no easy thing right then. So he danced.

Benji heard the music enough to stay in rhythm, but it was an uninspired dance performance. Even for an average dancer like Benji. He was just waiting for the song to end so he could head outside with the gangsters. He knew they'd be up to something funny or crazy. Anything to get out of there until his Pops came to get him. Benji fully intended to head outside when the song ended.

But something else happened.

The musical tinkle of bells at the start of the slow dance song that followed seemed almost magical. And for the first time that night…maybe for the first time ever…Shante was really looking at Benji. Really looking…and as she was drawn closer and closer to Benji, she reached out for him… not to grab his hand though.

But to hold it.

This was a different Shante than Benji had ever seen. Thoughts of her selfishness, her constant chatter, her leaving for the party without him disappeared as her being seemed to just fade into the warmth of Benji's teenage body.

And Benji held her.

Cliff Perkins's effortless falsetto serenaded the two. "*Body and Soul*" enchanted the teenagers and Benji held on a little tighter as Cliff sang the words Benji wanted his girlfriend to hear.

The teens held each other tighter and swayed to their own slow rhythm, almost oblivious to the melodic beat… but not the words. For his part, the song captured Benji's feelings exactly. Shante had been disrespectful; it was just like when Tootie Mo slapped him out of his chair. If he didn't do something, the slaps were going to keep on coming.

Shante just gave different kinds of slaps.

It seemed strange - he still really liked her in a way but even so, he couldn't stay with her, even with as sweet as she was being right now. Although…he'd never felt her caring more than he felt at this moment. She was responding like she needed Benji. Like she wanted him and it could be no other way.

Body and Soul.

Just like the song said.

Benji and Shante continued to dance together in the dark with Shante holding Benji tight, Benji holding Shante tight, and the music holding them both…tight and warm in the dark. Shante broke contact long enough to look up at her boyfriend, and when he looked into her eyes, he was met with something he never expected to ever see.

"I'm sorry."

It was her eyes saying it…but it was as if she'd said the words out loud, and she might as well have…her eyes didn't lie.

Eyes can't lie. Not ever. It's impossible.

And as the young girl's eyes threatened to overflow with tears, she buried her face into Benji's chest to be comforted by his warmth and the beating of his heart. And now Benji was again torn. Thoughts of Tina evaporated, and in the moment, the dark-haired girl also ceased to exist—there was no Ricky, no Brian, no Sid, no Marcus, no nobody…there was only Shante and a something that was happening that threatened to overwhelm them both.

Shante reached up and began tenderly caressing Benji's neck and face, and before either could plan for it or be nervous…they were kissing. It wasn't sloppy…it wasn't rushed… it was the deep, sweet, pure, fresh kiss of youth, of innocence and of teenage passion. It was a kiss that announced to everyone there were only two people in the room…only two mattered. Everyone else had disappeared.

The song was only three minutes long, but it seemed like it lasted three hours.

They stared closely at each other as the song ended. And then, without a word, hand in hand, each knew… they wanted to leave. Benji thought Shante would have to make an announcement to her friends before they left, but the teens just walked out wordlessly into the night air and then started off together in the direction of Shante's home.

Still holding hands.

And they talked. Really talked. And laughed. They talked about their day, they talked about school, they laughed about the party and agreed it was dumb. There were no apologies, no mention of Tina; nobody dominated—it was just a light-hearted, free-flowing, easy, back and forth talk between two teenagers who liked each other a lot.

And neither wanted to let go of the other's hand.

And neither wanted the walk to end…but both had to end eventually.

They kissed again on the sidewalk on front of her house…quick this time, so no one would peek out her window and catch them.

"Don't forget to do your project, boy!" Shante playfully called out as she broke away to go in her door.

Benji was all smiles; he still didn't care about the project but…she'd remembered. So that meant…she'd been listening all along.

As he ambled toward his own home, something pulled him to look back at the spot where he and Shante kissed before she went inside. And when he looked back, he was met by a face in the window.

It was Shante. Smiling. And waving. And even though his eyesight was poor, he felt he could clearly see the look in his girlfriend's eyes and what it meant.

It had been a fantastic night…funny how the right three minutes can make for the perfect night. He walked home slowly so he could relive it, and the memory made him smile.

But doubts lingered. The night was special…even better than the night at the telescope place. Way better. But Benji remembered some things—things about Shante, but what he really remembered was Tina. They'd had their evening too, but the next day, it was like it never happened. Was this night going to be forgotten too? Shante was already his girlfriend, but…girls were tricky. He didn't forget that he didn't understand them at all.

And I remembered too.

I wasn't so concerned with Tina, but I was definitely concerned with Shante. Benji wasn't focused on it, but I remembered the forced phone calls. I did not forget the selfishness of leaving without Benji earlier that evening and ignoring him for most of their time at the party. Shante was not a bad person, but I definitely sensed something. So I moved a little closer and got close to Benji's ear and whispered:

"*Crossroad…*"

Then I watched for his reaction.

Benji got home a full hour before curfew. Everyone was asleep, but Pops was watching the cowboy movies he loved. His father loved cowboy movies, they reminded him of his own childhood. The look on his father's face now said he was happy he would not have to go out to pick up his son. When Benji walked in, his father told him, "Wait here." He went into the kitchen to pour himself some VO Canadian Whiskey, his favorite drink. He added some water and a few ice cubes and sat back down to watch more of the movies. Finally, at the commercial, he eyed Benji and said, "I haven't seen you much today…how was school? How was the party? How's everything?"

Benji figured he had about two minutes before the commercials ended.

"Well…" he began.

CHAPTER 4

CASTLES MADE OF SAND

Benji did not regret his decision to accept Topaz's invitation to make his way to the ABC Center because he rapidly learned he loved everything about boxing. He loved the training…the increased confidence…the skills he learned…the camaraderie with the other fighters…the sounds of the gym He loved hearing the trainers yelling, the sound of jumping rope, someone thumping the heavy bag, the grunts of fellow fighters when sparring—even the smell of the gym was attractive to him. But more than anything else, he loved the mental aspect of fighting: the intensity, focus, and resulting sense of purpose. He'd dived deep into it from the beginning; it'd consumed his entire life over the past six years. And now here he was, a highly trained fighter, a promising boxer with a strong amateur resume ready to make his living and find his glory through legalized combat.

His eyesight was not a liability in his chosen profession; rather it dictated his fighting style—he wanted and needed to get in close to his opponent. It was a style that required he train to be stronger than his opponents and it also made for more exciting fights. In boxing and in life, he was trained to accurately assess the situation, determine what his strengths were, analyze the weaknesses of the enemy in front of him, determine the validity of any assumptions, and then almost immediately determine the proper course of action—even if the action was to retreat temporarily. He knew he was mentally powerful, physically lethal and clear minded with a resolute refusal to let any situation overwhelm him. It was a process—the instantaneous process of a fighter. It was a skill that served him well over the course of his young lifetime and in the boxing ring.

So why did his heart threaten to pound through his chest right now?

It was because…she was coming.

To his place. Alone.

Their first meeting was at random, but she looked really familiar—he'd seen her at his first professional fight. She happened to be attending this fight with her sister, who was a fight fan and enthusiastically cheering on the fights—her?

"Not so much," he remembered with a grin.

She seemed bored by the spectacle.

He saw her almost immediately as he exited the locker room and made his way toward the ring. When he was an amateur, his prefight routine involved intense concentration on what he was about to engage in, and it was even more important as a professional. A fighter had to be focused—his chosen endeavor was a dangerous and violent confrontation between two powerful men unconditionally committed to causing the other pain and separating the other person from consciousness if given the opportunity. Every single time Benji entered the ring, he remembered losing was not the worst pain he could possibly endure—a moment's lapse could result in severe injury, permanent damage to the body and mind…or death. So his attention remained on the matter at hand—every time. No mistakes allowed.

But he saw her. And his concentration was broken.

At first glance and probably due to his focus on combat, he did not see her clearly, but even through the darkness of the arena and his poor eyesight, she instantly caught his attention and broke his focus—he definitely remembered her. She was the dark-haired girl he'd always seen around the neighborhood, but now, her extraordinary beauty was even more apparent. Her dark hair was pulled back to accent her features, and she wore large designer sunglasses even though she was inside—like a movie star. She took them off and her coal black eyes seemed to look right into the fighter's soul and warm it as she innocently watched Benji walk to battle. Though she wore very little make-up, her soft burgundy lipstick seemed to light the entire dimly lit arena.

Benji noted how she turned to say something to her sister and both women laughed as he walked past. Maybe it was his imagination…but he thought he saw her glance his way with a smile that seemed shy, flirtatious, and glamorous, all at the same time.

She was the most beautiful woman he'd ever seen.

"They're talking about me," Benji thought.

They weren't.

But in Benji's mind, he summoned a new motivation anyway. A different type of power welled up inside him, and he was filled with a new passion…and he made a silent vow.

"I'm not losing. Not with her watching."

He was scheduled to fight Melvin Foster, who was undefeated in seven fights. When the fight was offered to Benji, he'd been nervous— it was his first professional fight and Foster had been at it for a while. But his team's confidence strengthened him; his opponent was more experienced, but Benji was ready to begin making a name for himself. His team convinced him he was the better man…and Benji was ready.

Melvin Foster was powerfully built, intimidating, and a dangerous local fighter; in addition to being undefeated, he had knocked out all seven men he fought. His back was turned when Benji stepped through the ropes, but he turned around and fixed Benji with the cold stare of a master assassin and an appearance that projected the personification of pure malice. He was a dangerous man, and every single person in the arena knew it…including Benji.

Benji's trainer knew it too. "You have to fight this man, B.G.," he said softly, without looking at him. "You have to get his respect."

Benji nodded but did not look at the diminutive trainer. Nor was he afraid of the animal standing across from him in the ring—he was a deadly, well-trained, professional fighter himself now. He could no longer hear or see the crowd. And his expression did not change as his mind was focused on a single, penetrating thought.

"I'm not losing. Not with her watching."

As the bell rang, Benji dominated his muscular opponent. Benji's technique was flawless, and he seemed to hit Foster at will. Despite his opponent's obvious power, Benji's hands were faster, his feet were faster, and his reflexes were honed to avoid his foe's dangerous punches. Benji did not celebrate. He remained focused because he knew this was a dangerous man that could render him senseless with a single punch.

Then…he almost did.

When Melvin Foster hit him, Benji froze. He didn't fall, but his legs seemed paralyzed and he no longer had any idea where he was, though he could hear the crowd's full-throated screaming for his demise. He could not feel his arms and had no idea if he was protecting his head as he had been trained to do…and Benji was afraid. Not afraid of Foster. Not even afraid of getting hurt. He was afraid of losing.

Because she was watching.

But Benji was powerless to stop it. His strength, his boxing intellect and his boxing talent all somehow betrayed him at the same time. He could not physically defend himself from the coming assault; thunderous punches we're on the way from a powerful man any second now, a combined force that would batter him, knock him out, steal his victory, ruin the vow he'd made, and demolish his dream. He waited for Foster to finish him.

But the punch never came.

After what seemed like an eternity but was really only a few seconds, Benji felt his legs again. He felt his arms… they were still raised and poised, ready to defend and ready to strike. His vision was the last thing to return, and amazingly…the fighter in front of him was not advancing to finish him off. He was circling around Benji and eyeing him warily as if he was unsure how damaged Benji was.

So Benji punched him hard in the face.

And the rout was on.

Benji systematically stalked and destroyed his nemesis through punch after merciless punch. With his opponent in full retreat, Benji stepped to his right and feinted with his right hand to attempt to lure his rival to move to Benji's left. When Foster obliged, Benji fired two rapid left-hand bombs…one each to Foster's body and head. His opponent's eyes rolled, and he fell into the ropes with his arms lowered, all inferences of malice gone.

From the corner of his eye, Benji thought he saw a white towel being thrown in the opposite corner. It was the universal signal of surrender.

"No," Benji thought. "That could be a T-shirt or a reflection of the arena lights. No mistakes allowed.

So now…I'm going to kill this mother fucker."

But as he moved in, the referee stepped between the combatants and waved off the fight, signaling the brutal battle was concluded. Benji roared and ran to the ropes to accept the raucous accolades from the now adoring crowd. He scanned the audience for her. He knew she was cheering wildly; everyone was. He wanted to find her, point at her, pose with his masculinity on full display, pound his chest, lock eyes with her, and let her know this victory was for her. He wanted to signal to her to wait for him.

But she and her sister were gone.

Gone.

He didn't know if she'd even seen their victory.

Benji had to check on his opponent first, then left the ring quickly. He wanted to shower fast and come back…

maybe she was still in the building. He hurried to the dressing room with the crowd still wildly cheering his victory.

He didn't care. He had to find her.

He walked into the locker room to applause from his fellow fighters—he managed a smile and acknowledged the accolades from powerful men he respected, like-minded warriors whose veneration was hard earned and, once given, not easily relinquished. They recognized one of their own had just stared down hardship to defeat painful adversity, and they knew it in the way only those who placed themselves in the same dangerous circumstance could possibly know. As a weary Benji sat, he continued to acknowledge the subtle nods he received from those who likewise conquered, as well as the wide-eyed admiration from those who had not yet joined their fellowship.

His vanquished opponent entered to a more muted reaction, though even the defeated warriors were congratulated for a good fight. Drained, he walked slowly to where Benji had settled and sat down next to him. Both warriors' faces were expressionless as the two, who only moments before were bent on the other's destruction, now sat quietly and turned their battered faces to look at each other.

Then Melvin Foster stuck out his hand.

"Great fight, G."

Benji accepted his hand, and the fighters stood and embraced, placing their other hands on each other's shoulders and resting their foreheads lightly against each other's foreheads in the manner of the Congolese warriors.

As Foster ambled away, Benji sat, closed his eyes, and leaned back against his locker, soaking in the magnitude of his victory this night, clearly physically, mentally, and emotionally spent.

From his victory.

Their victory.

His eyes sprang open, and the thought occurred to him. The main event was still five fights away…it was not likely to start for a few hours or more.

"She might still be there."

I whispered to Benji. This time…he listened to me.

Benji leapt up, showered, and dressed in record time.

Benji left the locker room and scanned the place where he thought the dark-haired girl had been standing, but it was no use—she was gone.

But Sid was there.

Mama and Angela wouldn't watch him fight. Pops and Marcus watched every chance they got when he was fighting in the amateurs, Nikki only rarely. Nikki said it was because fighting was stupid, but Benji knew by now—his sisters were afraid he'd get hurt. So it was OK.

But Sid was always there. Every time.

"Hey, champ, you looked good out there—let's get something to eat, though, unless you want to watch the fights…"

Sid was right. Getting something to eat was a pretty good idea—the fight game was very disciplined, he'd learned you needed a mental break sometimes. A break meant no fights, no watching what he ate, no getting up early to train, no intense focus during sparring. He'd won his first professional fight so he'd earned a break, but laziness was contagious, so he'd allow himself one evening of food…maybe some drink too. Take a full day off tomorrow…then back at it.

"Let's go, champ."

Benji stared absentmindedly at his brother as they began to pull out of the arena parking lot and leave; he felt surprisingly numb in the aftermath of his first professional victory—a huge triumph and the result of many years learning his craft since the days of the ABC. And that's when he knew—he needed to forget the dark-haired girl. Put her out of his mind in all respects…because if he didn't, if he was wondering about her, trying to find her in the audience, trying to guess whether or not she would come to a future fight or was attending one, he could be badly hurt. He would be badly hurt. His focus must be singular…he had to train with full intensity because that's what his future opponents were doing. When fighting, only two people mattered—Benji and his opponent. The rest of the world disappeared. So Benji made his second vow of the night: the dark-haired girl didn't exist. In fact—she'd never existed. What dark-haired girl? It was time to eat now, to celebrate the first of what Benji knew would be many victories. The first step on the road to a champion's destiny.

And then she was there.

On their way out of the parking lot, there she was… standing by the entrance to the arena, just talking to her sister. As Sid stepped on the gas to head out the exit, Benji leaned over and elbowed his brother; with a grin that his brother could sense in the car's darkness, he said, "Hold on, Sid…slow down…"

"What?"

"Just slow down, black."

Sid looked where Benji was looking…and he knew. Two girls. He grinned too. Benji was glad Sid knew instinctively to not slow to a crawl…that might scare the girls, like they were doing a drive-by or something creepy. "Just do the parking lot speed limit, man," Benji thought.

"Shorty is mine," Sid said with a laugh. "She likes me."

Benji responded, "Oh no, baby brother…Shorty is out of your league. You got the tall one; dark-haired shorty is mine."

The brothers engaged in light-hearted banter as they sauntered past their targets in the gold '75 Toronado Pops let them drive. As they started to pass, Benji rolled down his window—he was tempted to yell something out the window but thought that might scare them. So as they passed, Benji said nothing. He just leaned out the window…smiled…and waved.

And she waved back.

Benji felt his heartbeat as he hurriedly told Sid with a huge smile, "Drive around and roll by again…"

Sid protested, "Why? You ain't even said nothin'! You scared. C'mon, Sir Smooth…let's go eat. I'm hungry…"

But Benji turned the radio down and said, "Later for that. Swing her way one more again…"

Sid shook his head but drove around the arena until they were again approaching the women. As before, Benji hung out the window, flashed a friendly smile, and though he was unsure if she could see from that distance, he winked.

And she waved, and this time…she laughed too.

"Go back again, Sid."

Sid just shook his head and said under his breath, "All right man...damn...you all slow...they probably gone now anyway."

As Sid sped around the arena, Benji thought his brother might be right. They could either be gone or think he was weird. It was time to make a move.

"OK, bet...pass this time...then park."

Benji noted from a distance the women saw their Toronado approaching again, and they were pointing at the oncoming vehicle and laughing together. So as Sid pulled in and parked, Benji jumped out of the vehicle, walked to the smiling duo, and addressing the object of his affection directly, he stuck his hand out like Billy Dee Williams in "*Lady Sings the Blues*" and smiled.

"Hey, baby girl. Listen, we really tired of driving. Would you hold this for me while I go for a walk?"

For what seemed like an eternity, both women stared at him as though Benji had lost his mind.

Then...both women started laughing, and the dark-haired girl looked at her sister and exclaimed, "OK, THAT'S cute!"

Then the dark-haired girl looked slyly at Benji and said with a big smile, "Do another one."

Without missing a beat and with his charm at maximum levels, once again channeling his inner Billy Dee, Benji came at her with another line.

"Baby, you fine as wine and just my kind, but on a scale of one to ten, I gotta rate you a nine..."

Then he leaned in and lovingly took her hand in his as he almost whispered: "Because I'm the one you're missing."

All four broke out in uproarious laughter. As the laughter began to subside, Benji chuckled and said, "I'm just playin', girl— I'm Benji Frazier."

And all their conversations had been just that easy ever since.

Since then, they spent increasingly more time together; even after only one chance meeting, they embraced a closeness that grew daily— they shared; they laughed; they told secrets; they developed favorite places like the soul food spot on Imperial Avenue or the pancake place on Euclid. The feeling they inspired in each other was amazing…he met her every day after she got off work or when his training was complete; he felt like she knew him better than any woman he'd ever known, of which there were many.

But he didn't know quite what to expect today. He'd been visiting her at work for a few moments one day, and the outpouring of affection between them was natural. Right before he departed, she looked at him and said almost shyly, "I have my day free tomorrow if you want to get together."

He laughed and said almost jokingly and with his trademark wink, "Come to my place?" He expected them both to laugh and plan to meet for lunch, then see the city, holding hands the entire time. Her smiling response floored him.

"I can do that. What time?"

From then until now— he was stunned. She'd looked at him with her deep, soulful eyes and said in her beautiful soft voice, "It's OK— I trust you. And we're just going to talk, right?"

His return smile was just as sincere as he looked into her eyes, but all he could manage was "Yes."

But thoughts flooded his mind. Even so.

No woman had ever attracted him more but he refused to plan to seduce her or try too. It was not his way.

Well…it usually was his way.

Fighters always got the prettiest girls—always. Every single time. Fighters got paid not just for how good they were but also for who wanted to see them fight, so fighters who didn't play the villain were extra personable outside the ring. They were charismatic and comfortable to talk to. Fighters were like singers in that respect…didn't matter how well singers can sing, what mattered was who and how many wanted to listen.

Fighters were also very confident…they were respected by other men, and since fighters had nothing to prove outside the ring, they walked like giants among men. Also, woman could watch her man playing football, basketball, or baseball…sometimes her man was involved in the action, sometimes not. And she probably screamed when her man scored a touchdown, hit a home run, or dunked a basketball, but when a woman saw her man in the ring, there was an emotional connection, a deep primal focus and feeling that rose and fell with every punch landed or missed. The emotional connection grew with each passing round, each passing fight. When the fighter won, there was a feeling of intimate togetherness because his woman was with her fighter emotionally the entire time. Even when the fighter lost, the connection was there, maybe even stronger because it activated a caretaking mentality a defeated fighter needed to rebound and fight again.

The result was a creation of a mutual understanding of the lows and the highs that generated a powerful and attractive bond. Oh yes, fighters always got the most beautiful women— and due to the emotional connection with their fighters, these women were intensely loyal. Combined with the confidence dripping from men constantly training their minds and bodies, and Benji had no problem getting women— all kinds of women.

But this was different.

With her, the moments were special so he fought against his urge to seduce or to have expectations of her being with him for several hours— of being totally alone with her in his place. Every moment with her was better than the last— despite a burning desire for her, he steeled his mind and convinced himself his only real expectation was he would not be disappointed. Because he had zero expectations. No matter what.

Still, he scanned his apartment and chuckled. Music drifted from his medium-sized boom box; the window shade was slightly open, not quite closed but not all the way open, so as not to flood the room with light. He sprayed his chest with cologne and brushed his teeth...again.

"OK, OK," he thought to himself. "No expectation...I'm just creating atmosphere...no expectation...I'm just creating a moment. No expectation." He smiled.

Then there was a soft knock on the door. It was soft, but it startled him.

It was her. She was there. Right on the other side of the door. She was a little early.

He closed his eyes and breathed deeply. He didn't want his voice to shake. He got up and walked to the door and took a final deep breath. "No expectations," he thought.

He opened the door…and there she was.

She was wearing jeans that accentuated her shape and fit her perfectly to go with a flowered yellow blouse opened right under her neckline. He looked down and saw she was wearing sandals and her toes sported a pink polish complemented by her tiny feminine hands, which displayed the frosted fingernail polish she favored. He gently took her hand and raised it to his face and tenderly kissed her index finger, repeated the kiss for her pinky, then held her petite hands in his boxing-scarred hands and gazed lovingly at the object of his desire. She was still a more beautiful woman than any he'd ever seen in his life. Her deep, dark eyes were so smoky they seemed almost coal black and looked at him with a hint of a smile at the corners. She'd gone with a cherry red-colored lipstick today. She was smiling at him as she greeted him with a light meeting of their lips and said hi in her adorable, almost shy manner.

It was Angela Bofill on the boombox setting the room's mood and atmosphere. He was listening to his mood music before her arrival, but he'd intended to switch it to more upbeat songs before she got there…but she arrived early. He did not want her to arrive to romantic music because it was too obvious an attempt to set a romantic mood. He was worried now she would think making love to her was the only reason he'd asked her to come. He wanted to be alone with her, but with this mistake, he knew her—she would smile and laugh, but then suggest the couple go walking together or go get something to eat.

He figured he'd already blown it.

She walked in, seemingly comfortable, put her purse down, and looked around with a wry expression. She looked back at him, and was it his imagination, or was she smiling a little bit wider?

Smokey Robinson now. Damn music was still playing.

He walked toward her with the honest intention of taking her hand and guiding her to the couch where they could sit close and talk. He wanted to explain. In truth, he was that kind of guy. But not with her. No way. He wanted to explain it. He hoped she would believe it. Because it was the truth.

But when he took hold of her hand—something happened. Without saying a word or making a sound, they came together —he didn't know if it was the look in her eyes or her smile or her scent or the softness of her skin, but something changed his action in an instant. The two looked into each other's eyes, and slowly their lips were drawn together like magnets into a slow, deep, sensual kiss. He could feel the total fullness and softness of her lips; he could taste the inside sweetness of her mouth. Her eyes were closed as they reveled in the most passionate kiss they'd ever shared. Her eyes opened slowly as they broke off the kiss with their faces in close contact with each other. They looked at each other raptly for what seemed like an eternity.

Then they began kissing again.

They married eighteen months later.

By the time they married, Benji was well into his boxing career. He wanted to fight even more because a new fighter's earnings were meager. There were gym fees whether he had fights scheduled or not; sometimes he was paid as little as four hundred dollars but he still had to pay for travel and his hotel. Additionally, the promoter took a percentage of his earnings, his trainer took a percentage of his earnings, the government took a percentage of his earnings…and sometimes, promoters would offer certain fights only if he agreed to give them an even bigger cut. Because Benji was aware a fighter's talent didn't necessarily earn him leverage with promoters— a fighter also sought popularity with the fans, so after his fights, Benji needed to spend time in the audience, talking with the fans, being personable, asking them if they'd enjoyed the fights, all in hopes of growing his popularity. Those were difficult times…Benji found himself working during the day anywhere he could find work to support his growing family while continuing to train in the evenings before sometimes heading to a part-time graveyard shift at the Yellow Cab company or 7-11. Benji also occasionally found part-time work sparring with more accomplished fighters, which often paid more than his own fights. It was tough work, but he needed the money and the experience.

His wife's support never wavered. She found a way to help with the family finances through working as a department store cashier and also found the time to enthusiastically attend every fight. Sid returned from a stint of playing baseball in college, and though immersed in his own growing career, he found time to work Benji's corner for his fights for free. That really helped in those early days.

Benji raised his fight record to eight victories without a single defeat, though. The children started coming soon after…a son first…a few years later another son…added another son a few years later…and finally, a daughter. The children added joy but also additional financial stress on them all, but Benji adjusted by sleeping less and working more. He just added getting up in the morning to be "daddy" for even an hour before collapsing to seize a few hours of sleep before he had to get up once again to sell cars, flip hamburgers, mop floors, or hone his body and mind into a more destructive force. It was exhausting, but Benji was driven. He had to succeed…because he'd risked everything for the opportunity to fight.

He'd won fourteen straight fights and managed the precarious balance of caring for his family, earning extra money, training to a better fighter, and raising his fighter profile, but was twenty-five years old when he suffered his first defeat in the ring. He ran into a fighter that was a little more energetic, a little too fresh, a little too fast, a little too strong. It was a fight where Benji felt drained. He just could not seem to summon the right amount of energy and focus, and when the bell rang, sounding the end of the fight, Benji did not feel beaten up. He thought it was been a close fight—but he knew in his heart he'd been defeated.

His wife and brother were very encouraging—their belief in him strengthened his spirit, and Benji himself felt like he'd just had a bad night. And the crowd responded enthusiastically to the fight, he'd managed to entertain the fans, even in defeat. So all in all, Benji thought this defeat would make him a better fighter and raise his fighter profile. He was excited to resume training.

But then he lost again.

And again.

His third defeat in a row. And this time he'd been badly beaten, leaving the contest with both eyes swollen, a jaw that would not fully open for a few weeks, and a low-level headache that stretched on over a month.

He unconsciously felt that at the level he was now fighting at, he needed to double his training, get even more work sparring, and have an even greater fighter profile so that people were talking about him and wanting to see him fight...not easy for a fighter who'd lost three fights in a row. Nevertheless, in the months and years to come, Benji's children woke up more and more often to "Daddy is training" or "Daddy is working"...only to hear the same phrases repeated as they laid their heads to rest for the night.

Benji began training in the mornings and evenings. Often forgoing work in favor of training put added financial strain on the family. It meant his wife had to work more while still ensuring the four children were cared for. She remained outwardly encouraging; her husband was working as many hours as she, but still...she began to wonder. Now the experienced wife of a professional fighter, she knew Benji's mental focus must stay as strong as his body, so she refused to let her increasing doubts negatively impact Benji. A slip in focus could get him hurt.

But she recognized at some point she might need to step in.

I felt the same way.

Benji's increased focus paid dividends. He went on an eight-fight winning streak. He kept scanning the ratings to see if maybe he cracked any state or national rankings, but even with his record of 22 – 3, no one was writing articles about him. No commission was ranking him yet. He was just a popular local fighter…but that was about to change.

Enter Uriah Grant. "The Boss Man."

Grant's record was 17 – 8, but he'd fought and defeated an aging Hall of Fame fighter; he'd lost a bid for the state heavyweight championship, gone to Florida and won its state championship. But he was coming off a loss in trying to obtain the United States Boxing Association championship. And now, he was trying to make another run at a championship…and he was looking for a fight.

Benji's record was better. Grant's record looked bad to the uninformed, but he was the most accomplished fighter Benji had ever fought.

And Benji got the fight.

Benji trained like never before for his first- ever ten round fight…in fact, he stopped working so he could train almost around the clock, but because he no longer worked outside of boxing, he had more time for his wife and children. This fight would pay him more money than he'd ever made fighting—Benji thought he might even get to enter the ring to music, make an entrance walk like the major stars on television. He didn't get it but he vowed…after he beat Grant, he dreamed of making music-themed entrance walks for big money fights in the future. Benji talked excitedly with Sid about fighting for the U S title…the North American title… even a world championship on television. He dreamed with his wife about being more than just a popular neighborhood fighter, about the hard work and sacrifices and how it was all about to pay off. He played with his children, he laughed, he felt great about this opportunity, and on the night of the fight, he never felt more mentally and physically ready. There was no music to lead him to the ring as he dreamed of, and because he was out of his neighborhood, the crowd reaction was muted, but he heard music in his head. He was ready to grab his glory. He only wanted a chance and now… that chance was here.

And Benji lost.

He tried mightily and had never looked better in the ring. But the Jamaican was never troubled and as before, there was no controversy in Benji's mind…he knew he'd been defeated. The Jamaican was just a different level of fighter.

And he was crushed this time. He'd given his all to it; he had no more to give. He couldn't train any harder; he couldn't do anything different. How could he give this much…and still lose?

He was despondent for weeks after this defeat. And now I moved in to tell him, "You are young…take this money…invest it in your family…invest in yourself. You have nothing to be ashamed of, this fight game is brutal, but you have taken from it all you could…we can do something different now."

But Benji didn't listen to me. Instead, once he handled his disappointment, he continued his new intense training regimen and won four fights in a row to run his record to 26 – 4. We all knew the opponents he defeated were men he would have defeated even early in his career. They were lesser fighters, but they were good for Benji's confidence, a confidence he would need…because we were all shocked when Benji was offered and accepted a rematch with Grant. He trained even harder for the rematch in the knowledge it was the most important fight of his life.

And he lost again.

But it was only when he was battered by his next opponent, a fighter with a record of 8 – 18, that the drug use started.

Fighters in Benji's gym had begun to take Dianabol, an anabolic steroid, to build strength. He didn't work out as regularly, but Benji was an experienced fighter. He knew how to fight. He could resume working out only in evenings and increase his training activity when he knew he had a fight scheduled because the drug gave him strength. The fighters knew how to beat drug tests if they were even tested at all so now Benji had more time for his family since he didn't have to train as much.

Then Benji found Stanozolol, another steroid and Benji felt twice as powerful with half the effort. He won fifteen fights in a row—his fight record was 41 – 6 now…but still, he longed for a fight where he would get to walk to the ring to the cheers of an adoring crowd. He dreamed of what music he might pick. But for now, he was content being an elder statesman in his gym with such a strong record, was seemingly earning one last chance at boxing stardom beyond their gym, neighborhood, and city.

But the chance was forever denied him.

The boxing world caught up with the requirement to test for steroids effectively. Benji's now- sporadic training habits combined with his age, and two decades of fighting had diminished his skills. The fights became more difficult.

The losses started to accumulate. Benji was thirty-nine years old when he looked up and found his fight record now included fourteen defeats.

I saw the effects…the costs. Benji's sense of smell was damaged now. He had difficulty swallowing, and oftentimes, people started asking him to repeat himself because he was slurring his words and his eyes began to further betray him.

I knew it was time…it was past time. His wife now offered no pretense of supporting Benji to continue fighting. After his most recent defeat, she sat at his feet with her head in his lap while he sat forlornly in the dark of their small living room, drinking water glasses full of alcohol, groggy, badly beaten and confused. When he lost now, it hurt…not mentally…it hurt physically. It hurt in a way it had never hurt before. It hurt in a way that gave birth to a new emotion in Benji, a feeling not common to a fighter: fear. And as his headaches were nearly constant now, his wife spoke gently to her husband, holding his hands and comforting him in the aftermath of a battering defeat. She told him it was OK…that she loved him…that she was proud of him…that he was their champion and would be forever…but they all needed to move on now. And Benji was forced to fight back tears as before he fell asleep in a drunken stupor, his wife climbed into his lap, and he reluctantly agreed with her the time had come to stop fighting. They slept in that position—and when Benji woke, he remained convinced he did not want to get beaten up anymore. He was convinced he'd fought his last professional fight.

It lasted almost a year.

He told Sid first. He was depressed and confused and has lost his purpose since he'd stopped fighting. He couldn't seem to focus on anything for long—he was drinking more, out of shape, and increasingly angry. And moreover, he missed being a part of the team of men at his old gym; he missed being a part of a group not defined by any individual's feeling but by a rock- solid commitment to the collective effort necessary to building fighting men. Naturally introverted anyway, he was quieter than he'd ever been, but then, like a miracle, his old promoter reached out with an offer to fight. The promoter was offering to give Benji a reason to get back in shape…to train…to team with the people whom he'd spent the entirety of his adult life with.

Fighters fight. He knew now. He'd just needed a rest. He'd been at it too long. But he was ready now to take advantage of one last opportunity his old promoter was offering him.

Sid was against this. A father with five children himself now, he was no longer the joking little brother or Benji's free cornerman. He was mature and wise and unwilling to validate his brother's desire to fight again. He told Benji bluntly " sometimes your love for something doesn't match your talent for it. It's over, Benji." And he told his brother he couldn't be a part of it…and told him for the first time, he would not attend Benji's fight. He didn't even want to hear about any of it: not the preparation, not the fight, not the result. Benji could not help but feel a sense of betrayal.

Sid's reaction was tame compared to that of Benji's long-suffering wife.

She exploded. Their fight was more vicious than any they'd ever had. She mentioned the financial sacrifices their children made over the years…the sacrifices she personally made. She reminded her husband of the unconditional support they'd all given. Sid informed her about Benji's past drug use, and although she raged at her brother-in-law when told, she was now beyond incensed at her husband. She alternated between pleading and anger when discussing his high blood pressure, slurred speech, faulty memory, diminished motor skills, and confusion, all of which made it difficult for Benji to now hold a regular job but even more importantly, damaged her husband's health…perhaps irreparably.

She begged her husband to not proceed with this fight and was dead serious when she proclaimed, "I love you. If you love me…if you love us…think of us first this time. Don't do this."

Benji thought back to the meeting he'd had with his old promoter. The promoter needed a fighter on short notice. The money was only fair, but the promoter said he would personally supervise Benji's training—which was code for ensuring Benji was discreetly distributed steroids and he would also take care of handling any subsequent drug tests. The promoter made the usual promises: win this fight, and we'll line you up for an undercard fight, maybe even a televised fight on ESPN…there would be big money for a fight like that. Win that ESPN fight and a ranking might follow… or a regular high-paying sparring job with a highly ranked fighter. Or possibly a job as a trainer's apprentice could resuly, where he could end up training fighters and earning a percentage of their income. The promoter told him stories of older fighters who found their glory in their late thirties or even forties…all Benji had to do was take this fight, and there was a chance for all the old dreams to still come true.

Benji stared impassively.

The promoter continued, "I understand the money ain't the best, Champ…but I have fighters who will do the fight for less. So I need to know right now."

Benji was not new to the fight game. If the promoter had fighters willing to fight on short notice for less money, he would have offered the fight to them, and Benji would not be here.

Still…Benji paused before he continued.

"The money is fine."

But clearly there was more; something unsaid hung in the air like a cloud. The promoter sensed it, so he leaned back and waited.

"I want a ring walk. With music. And a spotlight as I enter."

The promoter narrowed his eyes.

"That's it?"

Benji nodded.

"Done."

Decades later…

A significantly older Benji rocked gently in his chair. He understood much of what was said to him, but he didn't talk much anymore because it was humiliating to be forced to mumble unintelligible words that sounded clear in his own head. It was difficult for him to get around…painful…and there was an increased danger of falling, a sad irony that the balance that'd carried him to so many victories had been compromised so badly; plus, he was now legally blind…his eyesight was beyond correction.

So mostly he sat, hummed quietly, and rocked in his chair. He loved to just watch and take in the blurred beauty of the world around him—these were the things he'd taken for granted in his youth and early adulthood, so he loved just staring out the window. Even with his diminished eyesight, he saw and heard some things much more clearly now… birds singing…the brightness of the sun…children laughing. And he felt as if he could stare in awe at the huge mountain landscape all day without saying a word—and he often sat outside and did so.

He sometimes remembered he'd once been a professional fighter, but he struggled to remember any of his fights most of the time; nevertheless, through all his confusion, he constantly remembered one thing…

His ring walk…his entrance music…and the spotlight on him as he entered.

It was the closest he'd ever been to being a champion.

I never left Benji. I bent in close and whispered, "Benji… was it worth it?"

I hated asking. I dreaded it, but it was what I'd been sent to do for Benji's entire lifetime, so I had to ask. But I knew the answer would be the same as always.

Benji looked in my direction but did not speak at first. Or think. He simply looked in my direction.

A single tear fell down his wrinkled face, and then he sadly asked a question to no one in particular…

"Did I win?"

No one answered.

So he went back to humming the song that always seemed to be stuck in his head now.

He just couldn't ever quite remember where he'd heard that song before.

CHAPTER 5

YOU GOT TO PAY THE PRICE

Benji hadn't been able to sleep all night. Today was the big day.

It all started with Jimmy and the summer jobs at the naval station he'd set up for his cousin. Benji was enthralled by the experience: everyone running around in different uniforms, walking on the biggest ships he'd ever seen and just wandering around and taking it all in. He didn't have to do any real work that summer. Every now and then, the guy in the brown uniform or the guy with the glasses would give him a bunch of computer punch cards to feed into some machine, but for the most part, he just listened to the sailors talk and then walked around when he wasn't putting those cards into a machine.

He got a job on the navy base every summer of his high school years. He kept it somewhat secret…military people weren't popular in his neighborhood, and he knew the gangsters jumped sailors whenever they saw them at parties. The only one he told was Tina— she'd started at a new high school when they were sophomores, but even though they weren't lockermates anymore, they talked often. Tina was the one who'd gone with him when he wanted to visit the military recruiters right before they were both supposed to graduate.

Benji was adamant about wanting to join the Navy—he wanted to sail on one of those huge ships or even better… live on a submarine, that seemed like it would be fun. He knew exactly what it was like too, because they let him go on one when he was working one summer. Benji imagined it might be like being on that *Star Trek* spaceship; that was a good show, they had lots of adventures too. Benji intended to ask the recruiter if living on the submarine was kind of like that. Tina didn't think it was like that at all…which annoyed Benji. After all, he was the one who'd worked at the Navy base; he figured that made him a little smarter than Tina about submarines.

The Navy guy wasn't there when they went to visit the recruiters, though and the door was locked. But the Marine guys were there.

Benji saw a few Marines when he was working, but he hadn't seen any up close. This Marine guy who pulled him into the recruiter's office seemed like the guy on the poster— he talked strong, and all four of the Marines in the office stood and shook his hand— they all looked pretty sharp in their uniforms too, all muscular with about a thousand tattoos each. They took turns telling interesting and funny stories, and they drew Benji into their jokes; he felt like he was already a Marine. Then they showed Benji a movie about what basic training was like, and Benji knew what he wanted to do. The Navy was out...the Marines were in. They said it would take eight months to start, but Benji could meet with other recruits to hang out every week until he left. He just had to come back and sign some papers.

Benji was ready to go. But a few weeks later, he saw a tall brother in a blue uniform at the mall who called him over. He was an Air Force guy and very interesting too, but Benji told him he was going to join the Marines. Mr. Air Force laughed when Benji said that he'd seen Benji's scores and asked if he was sure the Marines was what he wanted to do. He said the Marines were tricky and they were making it sound good, but he gave a lot of reasons why the Air Force was better. He put his hand on Benji's shoulder, and looking Benji right in his eyes, he said, "You're too smart to fall for that, aint you, young brother?"

No. He wasn't. He really wanted to join the Marines very badly, but what he really wanted was to just go somewhere...anywhere. Tina was preparing to leave for college, and with Tina going soon, Benji found himself wanting to do something too. Tina kept asking what he was going to do and if he was OK. She was always nice about it but...it was almost like she was feeling sorry for him, like he had nothing going on. He didn't want to go to college but in his mind, maybe the military was even better...or at least as good. And he could tell...Tina thought only people who couldn't get into college went into the military. Maybe she was right but when he came back home in his uniform, he'd impress EVERYBODY...just like Jimmy did. So when the Air Force guy said he could leave in four months instead of the eight months the Marines said it'd take, Benji was sold. He was ready to go..he enlisted in the Air Force as a Security Specialist. A military policeman. Benji liked the fact they carried machine guns and got to wear berets. He was going to wear that beret when he came home to visit too.

Benji's mama was tight lipped about his decision to join the military, but Pops seemed positively delighted; they stayed up many a night discussing the dos and don'ts. Benji loved and admired his father, but his Pops was not a talkative person. He was only dimly aware that his father served during the war in Korea or Vietnam or some place; now, father and son could come together and discuss the military for hours…and often did. Benji always knew he had his mother's unconditional love and affection, but over the next four months, he felt his father's pride in his decision. And making his father proud just felt good.

But now…it was time to go. It was still dark, but his recruiter was coming early, so Benji had to be ready. When Benji got up and went into the kitchen, he was surprised to see Mama already there, making a breakfast big enough for the entire family but was only for him. Mama stayed busy and talkative, like if she talked continuously enough, her middle son wouldn't leave. Right before his recruiter came, Pops came out of the room, got his coffee, winked at his son, and exclaimed "You gonna be the top kick soon!", proudly using the old Army term for "first sergeant". Pops didn't linger though…with a grand smile and a squeeze of his son's shoulder, he went back to bed. Only Mama was awake when the recruiter knocked on the door.

The recruiter went back to his van to wait after he knocked on the door. Mother and son shared a long look. Benji thought she might cry, but she didn't; Mama wasn't a crier. Instead, Benji's mama just hugged her son very, very tight.

And then...Benji got in the van with the recruiter and other recruits, and they all drove off to his destiny.

Only when the van was out of sight did Mama allow her tears to flow.

For Benji, what followed was a day that seemed like it would never end.

After getting firm instructions to remain together, Benji and four other San Diego recruits spent three hours in the airport before boarding their flight for San Antonio, the site for Air Force basic training. Upon arrival, the group of recruits followed the directional signs displayed for new recruits. Benji then found himself congregating with about one hundred other recruits from all over the country...and they waited together another three hours while they were allowed to use the meal vouchers the recruiters gave them to buy food in the airport.

Around 9:00 p.m., a bunch of guys in uniform and Smokey the Bear hats came to line them all up and put them on buses, and Benji thought, "I thought this was going to be hard. I'm a little hungry...but this isn't hard at all."

I smiled.

Because once they got on the base...the atmosphere changed dramatically.

The men in those Smokey Bear hats got on the buses and screamed for everyone to shut up, and the buses drove around…and around…and around…and around. It was pitch black outside. There were no lights outside, no buildings— it was like they were driving around in space.

It must have been midnight when the buses stopped. The Smokey the Bear guys, men Benji would come to know as his drill sergeants, got everyone off the bus, lined them up again , and welcomed them all to the Air Force by teaching everyone how to stand at attention and how to address the drill sergeants by saying, "Drill Sergeant, Recruit Frazier reports as ordered." Then the drill sergeant would give them permission to speak…if they chose.

The drill sergeants informed them all they were to follow every direction quickly and without questioning. When asked if they understood, the group yelled in unison, "Yes sir!" so the drill sergeants proceeded to test whether they truly understood the instructions.

"Pick 'em up!" one drill sergeant ordered.

And the group stood there and stared.

"Pick 'em up!" the drill sergeants yelled again, even louder and with more aggression.

Unsure, a few of the group started marching in place.

"Pick 'em up, pick 'em up, pick 'em up!" the drill sergeants yelled with obvious and increasing rage.

And slowly…the recruits understood the drill sergeants were telling them to pick up their luggage, and one by one, they did so and prepared to go wherever they were going… hopefully to bed. Benji was exhausted.

"Now put 'em down!"

Thinking they'd done something wrong, the recruits put their luggage down.

"Pick 'em up!"

And once again—the recruits picked up their luggage.

"Put 'em down!"

Over and over, the recruits stood there at attention, in the early hours of the morning, exhausted, attacked by Texas mosquitoes, picking up and putting down their luggage on command until after a little more than an hour, they were picking up and putting down their luggage quickly and together, all fifty recruits responding to orders immediately, without question, and in absolute sync with each and every member of the team.

It was the first lesson of Benji's military career…and the end of the first day.

That initial lesson of rapid obedience and teamwork served Benji well through the six weeks of basic training and the eight weeks of technical training that followed to qualify Benji as a security specialist. Benji's world up to then consisted of depending on his family and being comfortable in his neighborhood, but the world in general, and the Air Force specifically, was broader than Benji's narrow viewpoint. There were fights, both physical and mental, as people of different races and backgrounds came together for the first time. There were various ways of seeing the world, different types of interaction and humor, different habits and cultures and languages—but they all needed each other. The tasks the drill sergeants gave them to complete were impossible to complete alone; some seemed overwhelming or impossible…and they refused to tell the trainees how they were supposed to complete the seemingly impossible tasks of increasing complexity placed before them. The only way to succeed was to come together, and when the trainees figured out they would have to break into teams on their own and count on each other or they would all fail, they completed their transformation from trainees into Airmen.

Still, when Benji reported to his first permanent duty station in Nebraska, the feeling wasn't quite like he pictured it would be when he was doing his summer employment in high school. For one thing, Nebraska was nothing like his California home; he felt like he'd landed in a foreign country. He hadn't anticipated being homesick. He missed his Mama, he missed Pops, he was always wondering what his brothers were doing, he missed Angela mothering and smothering him, and…surprisingly, he missed Nikki. He missed Ricky and Brian and Tina—he missed being in high school; he was not comfortable in this strange place. Arriving at his first permanent base was also different from being in basic training or technical training school. There, the drill sergeants were always around— guiding them, teaching them, yelling, but always there.

But when Benji arrived at his first permanent base… there was no one. Just him.

And me, of course.

He wandered around the base carrying his duffel bag, going into each barracks to inquire if that was where he was supposed to be. When he found the chow hall, he stayed there until it closed, just because it was the only place he found that seemed even remotely familiar. When the chow hall closed, he was forced to resume wandering until he finally found the last barracks at the top of the hill.

"Is this the security forces barracks?"

His voice was too high pitched. And he'd already forgotten Marcus's command to not ask questions but to make statements. It was feminine to ask questions...he should have said, "I'm looking for the security forces barracks."

Maybe that explained why the men assembled playing pool all erupted in laughter when he concluded his question.

Damn it.

One pointed lazily to a door marked "Charge of Quarters," and a thoroughly humiliated Benji went to the open door and received his room assignment.

When he opened the door, one of his new roommates, annoyed at being awakened, roughly ordered him to "shut the fuck up, newbie, and don't turn on the fucking light." Benji was immediately angered. That sounded like an invitation to fight, and Benji was ready to accept the invitation... but here? The team came first...so Benji fumbled around in the dark, and resigned to not being able to put away his belongings in the darkness, he climbed into the only open bunk fully clothed. Sleep did not come easy in this place and wouldn't come easy for some time to come.

Benji was having serious regrets about his decision to join the military.

But it got easier over time.

Benji's supposedly glamorous job as a Security Specialist was pretty much walking around an airplane for twelve hours to make sure nobody crossed the red line painted around the plane...which of course no one ever did. But he made friends in the barracks, and as much as he would have liked to call home and speak to his family, it was too expensive...so his fellow Airmen in the barracks served in the role of family. His roommates were Louis Boyd from Pennsylvania and Kevin Hoover from New York…and then there were others in the barracks that formed his group. Jimmy Gaines was the informal leader; then there were Willie Evans, Donnie Brown, and Conrad London. The seven did everything pretty much together…where you found one, the others were usually not going to be far behind. They all worked together, sometimes on different shifts, but they always caught up with each other. They trained on air base ground defense, so in addition to walking around planes, they went into the field to train on security forces defense tactics for weeks at a time.

When they weren't working or training, they were lifting weights, playing basketball, or playing on one of the squadron's intramural sports teams. They'd all get dressed and go to the Airmen's Club on weekends even if they had to work in the morning. Sometimes they would leave from the club, get in uniform, and go get midnight chow together, because you had to be in uniform to eat at the chow hall. But it was worth it, those midnight chow cheese omelets and french toast at the chow hall were better than any Benji ever had. There was just something about stumbling over to the chow hall, drunk, loud, funny, in uniform in the middle of night to eat eggs together. And the seven young Airmen took care of each other…when Benji had his wisdom teeth pulled and was forced to stay in the hospital, it was his roommates who picked him up, and even though the doctors told him to be careful because of the stitches in his mouth, they took him for BBQ beef sandwiches when he was released from the hospital anyway. And when the stitches broke and he vomited blood and BBQ beef chunks, they laughed and made Benji laugh in the aftermath too.

Benji was unaware of something, though. As his comfort grew with his military team, he thought less and less of his family back home. He loved them, of course, but homesickness would not go over well with his military duties. He continued to embrace his military identity and its associated teams.

The process repeated itself as Benji was promoted to Sergeant, reenlisted, and moved on to his second and third duty stations. Benji was growing as an Airman— he was expanding his duties beyond simply guarding assets. He was also learning to enforce the law on base as a full-fledged military policeman, and as a sergeant, he was now responsible for the welfare of other airmen…the welfare of the team. The feeling of homesickness never really left him, though— it was at its worst when he would call home for Mama's birthday, Father's Day, or a holiday. He could hear the revelry going on in the background as assembled family members rapidly alternated getting on the phone and returning to the Frazier family joy. These were the tough times, and the tougher it got, the more Benji had to lean on his team as a family substitute.

Which was confirmed necessary when Operation Desert Shield began in 1990.

This was different. Benji was an eight-year veteran, and his job up to that point was to protect whatever base he was stationed at and to enforce the law on that base. But when his squadron went on alert and ultimately landed in Saudi Arabia to live in tents, it seemed like…war. It seemed like what they all thought it might be when they joined. It seemed like what they'd all prepared for...but uncertainty was thick in the air. They were confident, but they were nervous over the prospect of the unknown at the same time—that Saddam guy said there would be ten thousand dead men in a single battle. Now, there was not only homesickness for his family back in California; there was also homesickness for the people back at his base—Saudi Arabia was a long way from both. The Red Cross helped by passing out phone cards for everyone to use, but it was still no easy thing to stand in line ninety minutes to make a call with a fifteen- minute time limit. The focus on team unity took on significantly added importance during these times. It was a curious dynamic—it wasn't that everyone loved each other... or even liked each other. But the ideals born in basic training grew to adulthood under the threat of actual combat. It was a strength stemming from the collective belief that it was their turn now...many didn't even know the details of why they were where they were; they only knew to succeed, to even have a chance at being America's next generation of heroes or to even survive, they had to come together, count on each other, and believe in each other. Slowly but surely, little by little...Benji's civilian identity kept getting stripped away, and in its place, Sergeant Frazier was emerging as an inspirational, visionary military leader of men and women.

As Benji's career began its second decade, he became a mentor to many while having a grizzled veteran named Master Sergeant Jesse Gibson as his own mentor. The experienced senior noncommissioned officer took a liking to Benji and took him under his wing. He gave Benji an invaluable resource to bounce decisions off of, debate courses of action, learn the ways of senior enlisted leaders, and perform the delicate balance between living a military life and having fun. Master Sergeant Gibson brought Benji home, where his wife, Vicki, prepared them home-cooked meals and the men drank, argued of the merits of their preferred styles of music, and chided each other over whose generation was militarily superior. Benji ended up being at the Gibson residence almost constantly; despite their closeness, he was shocked to come across a memo written by his mentor recommending he be selected as a squadron first sergeant and serve as leader to several hundred Airmen in a squadron. Shortly after being promoted to master sergeant, Benji was selected to serve as a squadron first sergeant— just as his mentor advocated for him to be.

Despite being selected for the prestigious position, Benji was relatively young…just thirty-two years old. There were many older and more experienced senior noncommissioned officers than he. His mentor told him how to best handle those Airmen, and he should know…Master Sergeant Gibson was well over a decade older than Benji himself. He didn't let that fact diminish his pride in his protégé, even though Benji grew frustrated with Airmen coming to his office for help, only to leave with a with a quiet comment to the administrative staff they would come back when the " real first sergeant" had returned.

"First Sergeant!"

Benji was being summoned by his commanding office, Major Lay. As first sergeant, Benji was responsible to the commander for all Airmen's health, welfare, morale, discipline, and training needs. He was the primary advisor to the commander on everything related to his Airmen. Though he was young, a master sergeant had to be talented, experienced, with a high level of leadership ability to be selected as a first sergeant. Accordingly, his commander consulted with him regularly.

"We got an issue, First Sergeant—need your take. One of the guys done put his neck on the chopping block. Drunk on duty. Then the dumb ass cussed out one of my lieutenants. Went home—drank some more. Got into it with a neighbor; Colonel was driving by and stopped— and the stupid mother fucker got into it with the Colonel! Don't know what's going on with these old heads. Six months from retirement, but times are changing, First Sergeant…this ain't the fuckin' bush. We ain't in Vietnam. Anyhoo…took all the statements— witnesses too. Dumb mother fucker lawyered up, but take a look at this shit, and give me a recommendation by tomorrow for what we do about this."

Benji accepted the stack. "This is an easy case," he thought to himself. His mentor was huge on discipline but even bigger on weakness. Though Benji was young for a first sergeant, and the commander decided on punishments at times like these, the first sergeant was the one to administer them. So the squadron was getting ready to find out the new young first sergeant was not a man to b e played with. He mentally played out the future scene when he would put the guy at attention, keep him at attention, chew him out mercilessly, and then dismiss him without letting him speak. Not only would he gain respect from his squadron, but he was also determined to not let his mentor ever regret recommending him to be a first sergeant.

His heart dropped when he looked more deeply at the stack of papers.

Master Sergeant Jesse Gibson was the accused.

And Benji was now conflicted as never before.

Benji read every word on every page on the case the commander gave him, including statements from all the witnesses. They were clear and consistent and described in detail conduct clearly not becoming of a senior noncommissioned officer but also assault of a superior officer while under the influence of alcohol, disrespect to a senior officer, and a litany of additional charges. Though he tried to twist it in every way possible, Benji could only come to a single conclusion.

His mentor was guilty.

But now what?

He had an urge to call his mentor to ask him what he should do—his mentor was more than just a mentor by now...more like his big brother. But there was the obvious reason he couldn't do that. But more than that, if he called, his mentor would undoubtedly appreciate it, but he'd heard his mentor rail...Jesse would also secretly consider him weak. And if his commander or his squadron found out he'd done so, they would likewise think the same.

So calling was out. He was on his own.

But what to advise the commander tomorrow?

Jesse Gibson was one of the most senior Airmen in the entire squadron...what happened to him in this case would be widely known. Benji was a young, lightly regarded first sergeant. If he went light on Jesse, the entire squadron would know he was light…scared…weak…and could be taken advantage of. Discipline issues might increase, and he'd be powerless to do anything about it.

But on the other hand…Jesse Gibson was not only his friend— he'd also given the Air Force his entire adult life. Though his crimes were significant, why should he suffer humiliation after so many years of helping so many? Why did Benji care what the squadron thought? As Jesse told him, "You're a black man first…they're not going to forget. Don't you forget either." Who cared what they thought?

The next morning came way too soon.

Benji gave his advice to the commander and justified it. The commander was impressed with Benji's well-thought out rationale, accepted his recommendation, and directed Benji to notify Master Sergeant Gibson.

Later that morning, Jesse entered Benji's office to hear the decision on his case. He'd expected Benji to come visit him the night before so he could explain; in fact, he was so certain Benji would come he'd asked Vicki to cook. Benji was young, but Jesse knew they could discuss a way for both of them to come out looking OK. They'd work it out together. But when Benji didn't come over or call, Jesse briefly considered calling himself but decided against it. It would show weakness…even fear…and that was not something Jesse Gibson was ever prepared to show, especially to Benji. he was the one who brought Benji to the next level. But Benji was a neighborhood kid…loyal…he knew how to do the right thing.

And now…here he was in his protégé's office, accompanied by his supervisor, the lieutenant. He smiled and sat. When Benji didn't direct him to come to attention, Jesse knew he'd be OK and was relieved.

If it had only been the two of them, it may had been different; but the Lieutenant was there too. She was very young…inexperienced…so Benji knew that even though it was supposedly private, this meeting would be retold in the squadron. He hoped his voice wasn't shaking as he began; because if it did, the squadron would know.

"Master Sergeant Gibson— a senior noncommissioned officer is entrusted with a huge amount of authority…even power. His actions are not questioned because he has earned the right to not be questioned. Senior noncommissioned officers are selected for their expertise in developing leaders at every level…if our Airmen are the backbone of what we do, if our NCOs are our mission's heartbeat, then our senior noncoms are the very soul of the U S Air Force."

Benji paused before he continued.

"On your feet."

It was an order, given to a man Benji respected and admired…a man who until recently had been his senior… yet and still, it was clearly an order, given with dead eyes and a steel tone.

When Jesse looked on incredulously in shock, Benji repeated the order while adding in the unmistakable hiss of malice.

"I said…on…your…feet!"

Jesse rose stone faced with a look of absolute rage on his countenance and stood at the position of attention without taking his intense, almost menacing gaze off his protégé turned first sergeant.

Feeling the lieutenant's nervousness, Benji was compelled to match Jesse's burning intensity and looking him squarely in his eyes, Benji continued.

"You have been found guilty of multiple counts of drunkenness, dereliction of duty, assault, showing disrespect to a superior commissioned officer, and conduct unbecoming of a senior noncommissioned officer. In light of this finding, I find you have violated the core tenets of your current rank, and as such...

"you have forfeited the right to continue to wear it.

"Effective immediately, you are reduced in rank to the permanent grade of technical sergeant."

Now Benji stood ramrod straight.

"You are dismissed, Technical Sergeant Gibson."

Jesse stared incredulously. As the reality of what his friend and protégé said sunk in, his face slowly transformed from a face of confusion to a twisted mask of pure rage.

I thought he might leap over the desk and choke Benji.

With a final fiery glare, Jesse turned around and without waiting for the lieutenant, he stormed from the office, slamming the door shut with force as he left.

The lieutenant remained and just stared dumbfounded at Benji, unsure of what to do in the aftermath of what she had just witnessed.

"Keep on eye on him, L.T.; I'm here if you need me, ma'am"

And with a nod, Benji dismissed the young lieutenant. She seemed to be glad the episode was over.

Benji nearly collapsed into his chair when the session ended. He'd practiced what he would say and hoped he would have the conversation without his voice quivering or his hands noticeably shaking.

Now that it was over, and in light of what I'd just seen, I had a question for Benji.

"How do you feel about what just happened?"

Reducing Jesse in rank was the most serious and long-lasting punishment Benji could administer. Even confinement would have been more merciful…because it had an ending. But Jesse's retirement pay would now be reduced by about $10,000 a year, which meant the true financial penalty meted out was likely in the hundreds of thousands of dollars.

All because Jesse got drunk at the wrong time.

Benji was consumed by feelings of disloyalty to his friend…to his mentor.

He could have recommended a written reprimand be placed in Jesse's military file. He could have recommended a fine, a one-time forfeiture of Jesse's paycheck. He could have recommended probation, or he could have recommended nothing at all…let Jesse be chewed out hard and warned to never exhibit such conduct again. That would have been a harder sell, but he knew just the rationale that would have swayed the commander.

But why, then?

Why did it have to be the maximum punishment?

In truth, Benji wasn't sure it had to be.

"But if I wasn't tough on my first case, how were they ever going to respect me?" Benji thought. "Now at least they'll know…if that's how the first sergeant will treat his friend…how would he treat us?"

But was that the right rationale? For a friend?

Benji doubted himself. He thought, "Maybe I should have given a fine, given out some extra duty, done some more training…that might have been better."

Benji hated doing what he did, and though he hoped to explain to his friend later, that chance would never come.

Because neither Jesse nor Vicki ever spoke to him again.

Why did it have to be the maximum punishment?

Benji carried that internal debate for the rest of his military career.

But the next time an Airman came to see the first sergeant…he didn't leave when he saw Benji was there. He knew the first sergeant was in.

Still, though…

Regardless, Benji's career took off as a leader of men and women. He seemed to have an instinctive knack for employing the right skill at the right time.

When one of his Airmen needed help separating from an abusive civilian husband, it was Benji who faced down the aggressive husband and ensured his Airman was removed from the home without incident. When an Airman's infant child died suddenly but the parents requested no chaplain participation because they were atheists, Benji officiated. When an Airman was accused of murder in the civilian community, Benji stood with him during the weeks-long trial until his ultimate acquittal due to self-defense. When an Airman was drunk and suicidal in his home on Christmas Day, Benji was the first one on the scene and calmed the Airman until medics arrived to care for the distraught Airman. When an airman went to prison, Benji did morale checks, and when he led his unit into combat and the barracks were bombed by terrorists, Benji took command at the scene, cared for the wounded, and brought his squadron home safely. Then - when terrorists flew planes into the World Trade Center, the base went into Condition Delta indicating they were under attack and his airmen thought it was possibly a drill or an exercise. They had exercised and practiced the scenario but many had never been through a real Condition Delta. So, it was Benji who calmed his Airmen's fears and ultimately gathered them into the base theater to rally their warrior spirits with his "lock and load" speech that turned Airman confusion…into Airman readiness to fight.

Benji was all things to his troops…champion, advocate, teacher, counselor, coach, bodyguard, mentor, social worker, motivational speaker, and disciplinarian. His skill resulted in continued promotions— to senior master sergeant…then chief master sergeant…then ultimately command chief master sergeant, the senior enlisted Airman on the entire base, in charge of the base's eight thousand troops.

He was now free to take care of the thousands of Airmen on the base in the best way he saw fit, answering only to the base commander. In short…from a military perspective, he had arrived.

But I reminded him it had been some time since he reached out to connect with his family back home.

It was a good reminder; Benji acknowledged it was something he needed to do and would do, but command chief master sergeant duties and responsibilities were extensive and as time advanced, he forgot my advice to reconnect with his family back in California.

He WAS taking his command chief master Sergeant responsibilities seriously though. Perhaps he took some responsibilities more seriously than others.

Benji wasn't good at—nor was he interested in—providing strategic vision as his duties required. His duties required him to conference with other senior leaders to provide input to initiatives like the Combat Air Force Strategic Plan and the Joint Vision Strategy and to represent the base with civilian dignitaries from the local community during a seemingly endless number of social events.

He could speak to these responsibilities well enough to get by, but in truth— he was uninterested in that part of the job. To him, it seemed like those activities involved repeatedly having the same conversation. However, he relished every opportunity to utilize his true talents.

His skill as a communicator was of huge benefit. Benji was equally comfortable having a one-on-one conversations with Airmen of every rank on whatever topics interested them, regaling small groups with stories that informed or entertained, or addressing large crowds of several hundred people.

He molded each of the many teams that exist on a military base using whatever tool was necessary; he encouraged junior Airmen collectively and individually. He randomly met with the community along with the base commander, as both leaders would go to the Starbucks located on base every Friday morning and talk to whoever came by. He visited his teams of airmen deployed to combat zones…he empowered the base's first sergeants to make changes to base policy without unnecessary bureaucracy.

The ultimate result was an engaged team—eight thousand men and women who somehow all considered each other family, all committed to the team over their individual needs, and all addicted to the joy of serving together, ready at the drop of a hat to come together to jointly produce a combat capability that earned the base recognition as the number one military base in the entire Air Force. Collectively, the United States Air Force was the most dominant aerospace force the world had ever seen—and Benji's base was its best. The mightiest of the mighty.

"We're like The Enterprise in *Star Trek*", Benji thought with a laugh.

It was his crowning achievement.

But now his military retirement was on the horizon.

Thirty years is the maximum years of service allowed, and then an Airman must retire. Benji's career was successful beyond his wildest dreams. He wasn't just good on paper… he was good in reality…and he knew it. With no more military worlds left to conquer and his legacy of personal and team accomplishment secure, he felt ready to end his career on top.

And now finally, before retiring, he decided he could take a visit home. It would his first Christmas vacation with his family in over fifteen years. He wanted to go home sooner than this, but duty was incredibly busy, and sometimes he'd been overseas, so it'd just seemed impossible. But now he could start winding down. He wanted his family at the ceremony his staff was putting together to honor his service.

He decided to go home and make the announcement on Christmas Day.

He'd arrived a few days before Christmas. Pops's physical condition surprised him...though Mama still seemed vibrant for a woman in her late seventies, he didn't realize how frail his father, now in his eighties, had become. All his siblings were home for Christmas this year, and it was great touching base with all of them, their spouses, and their children. He'd lost contact with Ricky over the years, but he'd found Brian on social media— Brian no longer lived in San Diego; he'd relocated back east; but as soon as Benji informed his family, he planned to invite Brian to his retirement ceremony too.

After Christmas dinner and with everyone there, Benji decided it was time to make his retirement announcement, but for some reason— he didn't do it. Something felt a little bit off...for one thing, only Pops asked about his service. No one else brought it up. And though it was his family, they all seemed to know each other...while Benji seemed like he was trying to get to know them again after being away so long. He didn't feel like a stranger—but it was odd to try to fit in with his own people. They all shared stories over the past years that involved each other, and they all knew people Benji didn't know...because Benji had been gone. Their stories involved family members; Benji's military stories involved only him.

So ultimately, the holidays came and went...and Benji never did make his announcement. But when he returned to his base, his staff sent a personal invitation to all family members and then followed it up with a personal phone call to each one.

Benji should have made these invitations personally, but he didn't. He thought he was too busy.

I told Benji this. Repeatedly. I thought I was getting through to him; he seemed to really reflect on what I was trying to get him to understand, but he never did make contact with anyone but Mama.

And he never did contact Brian.

I wish Benji and I could have just had a regular conversation. It would have been much easier, but unfortunately… that's not the way it works.

When the day of the retirement came, Benji found himself uncharacteristically nervous. Most of his family had arrived, but Pops's health made traveling impossible. Angela wasn't coming, but Nikki was smiling and holding on to his arm. Marcus introduced himself to Benji's staff as "Chocolate Thunder", seemingly unconcerned with the embarrassed silence that followed. Sid was also making jokes about how there was no way he could have done "thirty years of hut one, hut two" in the Army and warned Benji in front of everyone that he "was about to leave the easy life and come into the real world." Benji thought his brothers would be proud, so their reactions confused him.

Benji was concerned with the ceremony venue—his staff convinced him to hold the ceremony in the base theater, but the theater held seven hundred people. Even if one hundred people showed up, the theater would look empty. It would be humiliating. Mama was as proud as ever and kept telling the story of Benji's big breakfast the day he left for basic training thirty years previous. Nikki was making constant social media posts about everything that was happening, she seemed to be in awe. But it almost seemed his brothers might even enjoy the humiliation represented by an empty theater; it'd be something else to make a joke about.

He shouldn't have worried. His driver arrived in the VIP van to drive his family to the ceremony, and as they approached the theater, Benji could see the parking lot was packed... fuller than he'd ever seen it.

Inside the theater, it was standing room only. It seemed as if the entire base came out to honor its retiring command chief master sergeant. Benji was relieved and felt a sense of pride in his base...his Airmen. But as the ushers prepared the family to go to their seats by pairing them up with escorts, Marcus began to create a scene by refusing his escort, saying he would walk to his seat by himself and he didn't need any of this "military nonsense."

And Sid was laughing at the scene.

Mama and Nikki glared their disapproval, and Benji fumed. He had no idea why his brothers were acting this way...like they didn't want to be there. But as his two brothers finally submitted to being escorted, Benji noticed how the two winked at each other.

And giggled.

Benji wasn't the only one to notice. The escorts also noticed and shared quizzical sideways glances.

I comforted Benji, saying, "Forget it. Walk tall. It's your day today. Most won't see you ever again after today. You're the base's command chief master sergeant for one more hour. Give your Airmen something to remember."

And Benji proceeded to do just that.

He focused on the volunteer who was proud to sing the national anthem at his ceremony. He focused on the base commander's words honoring him for over thirty years of service. He focused on the flag ceremony conducted by his first sergeants as Tom Waits's haunting "*Lay Me Down*" played in the background. He focused on the thunderous and sincere applause following his final address to his troops. And finally…he focused on the over seven hundred who came to ramrod straight attention as as the ceremony concluded, he went to his wife's seat. She took his arm, and the two began to exit the theater, but not before the entire theater erupted one last time in raucous, spontaneous cheering and applause.

Benji and his wife stopped at the door to turn and acknowledge the well-earned adoration from the men and women he'd led for so long. And with a final wave, Benji and his wife exited into a waiting staff car and were driven away for the last time.

And then it was over.

The thing that had defined Benji and the only life he knew as an adult…was over.

Forever.

And the struggles began.

Benji struggled to grasp his new non-military identity. He'd spent his teenage years trying to fit in…thirty years finding the team he fit with…and now the search for where he fit began again.

He didn't quite fit in with the military anymore. Of course, at the ceremony, they'd said, "You'll always be a part of our military community," but the reality was the active duty service members had to come first. As a military retiree, he couldn't even get his teeth cleaned. He missed the military…but the military moved on without him. It had to.

He didn't quite fit in with the family he'd grown up with anymore. They all had connections to each other that he'd missed out on…he didn't even know many of his nieces and nephews; and they didn't know him. They shared no stories or experiences because they had none to share. To them, their Uncle Benji was a myth who'd always been somewhere else.

He had his wife and children, though, and now he had more time to spend with them. But as he pulled out a football one evening and was playing catch with his fifteen-year-old son, his son remarked, "Dad…this is the first time we've ever played catch!"

"No it's not!" Benji laughingly responded.

But then a thought came to Benji…a disturbing thought. His son was right.

This award-winning, combat-decorated, high-achieving senior military leader, a man who'd led and positively impacted thousands, both in combat and during routine peacetime operations…was playing catch with his son for the very first time.

When he was fifteen years old. The same age he'd been when his cousin introduced him to the idea of military service.

Benji was in a daze as his son dropped the ball, laughed, and said lazily, "It's OK, Dad…it's getting dark, though. I'm gonna go in."

And with that, his son went inside, leaving the football wobbling where he dropped it; Benji watched the football wobble until it came to rest.

As he stared at the football now resting in the gutter, Benji faced his new reality.

His family had also moved on. While he had been busy leading Airmen, his wife had built a life of her own within their house, his son had seemingly grown into a young man without his influence, and Benji recalled seeing his daughter posting on social media about a man who was "like a father to her."

But his daughter had a father…just not a very good one apparently.

Benji found himself wondering "who needs me now?"

Suddenly, Benji felt like a lonely old man, left standing in the dark, in the middle of a barren street, just watching a football now laying perfectly still in the gutter.

I got close to Benji, and trying to make him smile, I whispered, "Let's go home, Command Chief."

The look on his face spoke volumes.

He had no idea where that was.

CHAPTER 6

WHO'S GONNA TAKE THE BLAME?

"Crown on the rocks...make it a double."

Benji grabbed a Newport out of the pack on the bar, lit it, and took a deep, satisfying drag before sipping the brown liquor that'd been placed before him.

He was alone at the bar. It was not like any birthday he'd ever had, and definitely not what he imagined for his fortieth. He was working on his third double of the evening... an experienced drinker, he knew he needed to slow down so he'd be able to drive home later.

The place she was.

The place he didn't want to go.

The Black Frog was nearly empty at this time of the early evening. Benji truthfully felt much older than his now forty years as the DJ honored Benji's birthday request to play music from his teen years. Benji was fairly uninterested in the popular singers of the day— they were all OK, but Benji still strongly preferred the music of his youth. In his mind, they sang about things that mattered. Especially the women. "Women used to sing to a man—about needing a man. Like Dorothy Moore…Patti LaBelle…Teena Marie… them women that made a man feel like one." Benji thought. "Most women today only sang about being empowered or strong or independent or some other such crap."

As the music played, Benji's rapidly reddening eyes glazed over as he lit another cigarette, ordered another drink, and let his mind wander backward to a fateful evening in his younger days.

The party.

The kiss.

Benji had been about ready to do something he didn't quite know how to do, and that was break up with Shante, but their kiss turned everything upside down. He felt a connection with Tina he wanted to explore and there was something about that dark-haired girl too. But the problem was…they didn't like him like that. Shante did. Or at least that's what he thought back then. Girls had always been confusing…women too.

The kiss clarified everything.

And when Shante called him the next day after their kiss to say she was going to the mall, said she would be missing him, then came back later that day with a shirt she said he'd look cute in, he was finished contemplating. As far as he was concerned, this was the one. Because that's the kind of things girlfriends are supposed to say and do.

The teens settled into a pattern. They ate lunch together, they went to movies, they were on the phone even more than before, and Benji went over to her house and they sat outside and talked— to his surprise, Shante even came over to his house a few times, and it was funny how shy she was at first. They were comfortable, but sometimes…Benji felt a little like he was playing a part in a play— the role of being Shante's boyfriend. The result was that slowly, over time, Benji stopped doing the things he'd done before. He walked to school less and less with Ricky and Brian until eventually, he stopped walking with them altogether— they were still best friends, but he went to school with Shante. His relationship with Tina changed as well; Shante changed her strategy of demanding Benji separate from Tina. Benji was powerless against her new found sweetness, and when she almost seductively suggested Benji should share a locker with her, Benji was incapable of refusing her. Truth be told— he didn't want to refuse her. There was no big blow up with Tina— after Benji changed lockers, they just spoke less and less until the former friends would pass each other in the hallway with just a wave. Benji didn't notice the next year when Tina went to a different high school— someone told him about it, but it was no big deal.

The couple stayed together as they entered high school. Shante just always seemed a step ahead of Benji maturity-wise though; she was always a little more popular, a little more in the know, and a little more knowledgeable about things important to teenagers, and at times, Benji felt like he was just along for the ride. He liked his girlfriend, but he was starting to gain a little status on his own. He made the football team, and though he was no football star, Shante and all the girls loved to wear the home jerseys of their boyfriends when they played away games and the away jerseys when they played home games. Benji was growing physically, becoming more confident, partly due to Shante's influence but mostly due to his increasing maturity. He was starting to become more and more comfortable with his own personality and talents; he was turning into a young man, a young man who needed Shante less and less for the reasons they'd come together. Still— Benji was surprised to see Cookie Martin staring at him one day and out of nowhere just coming up to him, holding a conversation and telling him how funny he was…and that it was too bad he had a girlfriend.

He didn't tell Shante, of course.

The prom saw Benji razor sharp in his baby- blue tux, replete with ruffles, and there was no doubt who his date would be— Shante…the same girlfriend he'd been with since the ninth grade. Benji was excited, but not just about the prom. He was now nearing eighteen years old, and though his grades were average, his excitement stemmed from being accepted to an out-of-state university, and he knew soon he'd leave home for the first time. Shante was uncharacteristically moody and upset though— though Benji was maturing, Shante's feelings for him seemed to remain unchanged. She'd even taken to calling him her "Boo Boo Bunny,"…it was a name he despised and thought was stupid— but he didn't say anything. Shante was a little upset at the prospect of him leaving, but Benji knew it was his opportunity to go a different direction. He thought he might even love her, but four years together as teens seemed like a lifetime. Going off to college seemed like an exciting new adventure.

And there were more girls looking at him like Cookie did. This was a change from Benji's early teen years, however subtle. Girls were beginning to take notice for an unlikely reason: his poor eyesight. Similar to when he had been challenged for fights but remained cool because he didn't realized he was being challenged, his interactions with girls starred following a similar pattern. He was often unaware of the subtle clues sometimes sent by teenage girls. Since he was unaware of the clues, he could not acknowledge or respond to them, an act that seemed to indicate a young man's calmness and confidence.

I knew the truth.

It was really just poor eyesight all the time, but the effect was the same.

Things were not always what they looked like. It was odd how that worked sometimes.

Benji sensed the shift though, and he thought he was ready to explore the possibility of filling different roles other than the role he'd played as Shante's boyfriend.

Angela lived at home, while Nikki went to City College and lived at home too. Marcus received an athletic scholarship to play baseball up north, so Benji's parents were extremely proud to have a fourth child in college. He often heard them discussing how to pay for it, but Benji was unconcerned…he knew his parents would find a way to pay for…whatever it was they needed to pay for. Sure enough, envelopes started coming regarding something called a Pell Grant. Angela sat with him to explain what he should do when he got to the campus, how to get his room, how to register for classes but Benji scarcely listened. He was just excited to be going to college out of state. He was the first one too. Not even Marcus went to college out of state.

He was lost from the first minute he arrived.

He didn't know how to get anywhere, he forgot how to register for classes, he got lost trying to find his dorm, and once he registered, he was lost trying to find where the classes were...he basically wandered around all day for the first week, following different crowds until slowly but surely, he got to where he was supposed to be, although it was substantially later than everyone else. He did find the parties, though. All he had to do was follow the music. And with the parties, he found alcohol— more beer, wine and liquor than he'd ever drank before and nobody to tell him not to drink it. Many nights, for the first time, Benji found himself vomiting outside, in the grass, in strange bathrooms, passed out on the ground at times, unable to move. One time, Benji dimly remembered one of the senior football players, a hulking young man, later drafted by the New York Jets, carried him home on his shoulder like a sack of laundry and dumped him in his room.

And he missed Shante desperately. Especially when he was drinking.

He was lost and alone, and the college campus was huge. If Benji felt like he sometimes didn't fit in at home, the place where he'd grown up and enjoyed the regular presence of his longtime girlfriend, now he truly knew the pain of not fitting in—the loneliness, the homesickness, and the depression. And the worse he felt, the more he drank...which made him feel worse...which made him drink more. It was a never- ending cycle. Benji arrived at college looking forward to a life outside of being Shante's boyfriend, but now her letters from home were the only positive thing he had to look forward to. Now he craved her…he wanted her…he needed her.

When he went home for Christmas break, he spent almost every second with Shante. To his delight, she was still all his…the absence apparently made both of their hearts grow fonder. After high school, Shante advanced to a supervisor position at Kentucky Fried Chicken, but she had applied for a job with the Department of Motor Vehicles. Benji was flabbergasted when she told him of her plan to enlist in the Navy; this was a slightly different Shante than the one he left a few months before. She seemed to have eschewed her "popular girl" image and instead, embraced young adulthood; her plan to enlist in the Navy bothered him; he couldn't quite figure out why. He half expected her to add something about getting stationed somewhere and getting married, but she didn't say that or anything like that. He'd never heard her talk like this…she had her own plan, was excited for her own future and though the now young adults were still seemingly tighter than ever, Benji took note of her failure to mention him or them after her planned enlistment in the Navy. Though Benji was unaware of doing so, he started talking Shante away from joining the Navy and almost imperceptibly began showering her with more attention and affection.

But I saw something else.

Benji was unconsciously upset with Shante's plans—way more than he even knew. Because in his mind, somehow, she was one step ahead of him once again.

Benji did not want to return to college after the Christmas break, but when he did, his feelings about both Shante and school flip-flopped. This time, he was fully aware of how much he needed Shante, and he genuinely missed her...at first. Strangely enough, when he returned to school this time, he was ready for it. He knew where to go and what to do. His comfort with the process was increasing, and although he was still drinking too much, he didn't find himself lost or vomiting in the dorm parking lot anymore.

And he was making friends.

Sam Outlaw from New York was his roommate and was outrageously funny. Freddie Stedman was from Detroit and the best basketball player Benji had ever seen in person, even though he was trying to make the college's varsity team as a nonscholarship walk-on.

And then there were the girls.

One was a senior who thought Benji played on the football team—because that's what he told her when they met at a party. Benji had forgotten her name, he didn't want to see her anymore anyway. But Delphia...she was interesting, a beautiful, curvy, brown-skinned girl from Atlanta with the longest, straightest hair he'd ever seen. Stina was a small- town girl from some little city in Arizona—Vail or something like that. She was very studious, a point guard on the womens basketball team and very pretty; his roommate was shocked when she knocked on the door and asked for him. Little Amy was from Pennsylvania - small, petite, perfectly proportioned; she loved laughing, was extra cute and the type to offer a back rub if you said you were tired. Benji knew because he'd said that one day and had fallen asleep in her room during a back rub and only awakened by her gentle whisper: "It's almost curfew…you have to go now, OK?"

When Benji went home for the summer, he felt like a new man…a college man. Shante was still his girlfriend though; he considered her his hometown girlfriend— his real girlfriend. The other girls at college? He just liked their company, that's all…he figured it was just something to do; he rationalized that he couldn't just sit in his room. For her part, Shante got the job at the Department of Motor Vehicles and started at City College herself. But after her initial fervor to enlist in the Navy, she slowed her thinking on that. Though he never came out and said it, her boyfriend clearly did not want her to join the Navy—that meant something. She recognized that she and Benji were growing together; she loved the man he was growing into…she loved him. Shante herself had gone out a few times, but mostly with girls only. Men flirted…she'd ate with a couple of them, but she never considered being with anyone but Benji. She didn't give up on her idea to enlist in the Navy entirely, but she envisioned a future now…Benji was nothing like the ninth grade boy she'd sweetly danced with all those years ago. He'd changed.

She didn't know how right she was.

As Benji went back and forth to college, his grades were almost an afterthought. What was clear was his affinity for women—there were more and more, not enough that he ever thought of himself as a "ladies' man" but enough so that Benji regularly thought, "This would have never happened to me in high school." The actual truth was— Benji still thought of himself as a charcoal-black, nappy-headed, Coke bottle glasses wearing, skinny kid from Southeast Dago.

So when he got attention from attractive women, he didn't turn it down...it always surprised him a little. Shante was just Shante; of course she liked him. She always had; who knows why...but the others? That was something different.

Over time, Benji started developing his own rules for dealing with women. "I'm like Marcus now," Benji would think with a grin. "Now, I'm who should be giving advice."

"Treat the beautiful queens like average girls; treat average girls like beautiful queens. Either way, they're not used to that kind of treatment, and it makes you interesting," Benji repeated to himself one evening as he prepared for a fraternity party.

"Know when to walk away."

Benji surmised if he walked away too soon, he would lose their interest because they might determine he wasn't interested. But if he stayed too long, he would seem too easy, too desperate, not exciting and definitely not a challenge. So the timing on the "walk away" was crucial. And when you left, you had deposit something mentally or emotionally memorable first.

But not a smile.

Smiling seemed disingenuous to Benji; smiles were great toward mothers and sisters and aunts. But for women? Grinning or no expression at all was better...and you could combine it with a little "eye conversation." Benji mastered the art of talking with his eyes, a talent especially important because he thought he couldn't speak that well to women. So less words were better; he preferred to let his eyes and his grins do the talking for him.

But when he went home, he always wanted Shante. By now, all the reasons for being Shante's boyfriend or staying with her seemed to evaporate. Even so, he wanted her available when he came home…he did not want her with anyone else and he did not want her joining the Navy— but every now and then, she'd bring it up. It stopped for a while, but lately, she started up with it again.

Until 1984.

The year Benji and Shante welcomed their daughter into the world.

Benji and Shante were always very careful but less and less so as they traveled the path of their now six-year relationship. Neither professed any real nervousness or regret when they found out she was pregnant. Where as once she was the life of the party, popular and always in the middle of things, she'd matured into a thoughtful and determined young adult. She viewed impending motherhood with joy, and she had no doubt Benji would take these important steps with her. Deep in her soul, she suspected there was a possibility Benji let himself be less careful with her because he wanted to ensure she would not leave him by joining the Navy. She had not intended to leave him, even if she enlisted, though she recognized what the possibilities would have been. Now everything changed— the Navy did not allow recruits to enlist if they had children unless they surrendered their parental rights. Signing over her child was a plan of action that never crossed Shante's mind; it was an impossibility. The change in plans did not anger her…babies were blessings, and if this was the path she was on, she was glad she was on it with Benji, who, though changing, was still the genteel, loyal and caring soul of her teen years.

Or so she thought.

For his part, Benji was in fact pleased, though extremely nervous about telling his parents — especially Mama. Benji was proud...he felt like he was more of a man now, but his thoughts on the matter were curious. One of his prevailing notions was "I got her now...she'll never leave me," and from the moment she told him the news, he immediately stopped worrying she would leave him. And though Benji had matured and grown since their first kiss at the party back in the ninth grade, some of his thoughts on fatherhood were decidedly immature, notably his belief he could return to school and all would be as it was before. As Pops intimated with a smile and a strong hand on his shoulder, "Everything has changed now, but you'll be fine—just be a good father to my grandchild; that's the important thing now. It's the only thing." Benji agreed but still made plans to continue his life at school. Deep in his soul, he suspected there was a possibility that Shante let herself be less careful because she saw he was on the path of success and she didn't want another woman on that path instead of her. It did not anger him— Shante was a steady, and he planned to spoil her and his new baby whenever he was home from school.

But the realities of fatherhood soon hit. When Benji left school to return home in June, he did not fully realize or understand that he would never again return.

Three months later, his daughter Jade was born.

And as much as he loved being a father, he could not admit to himself he missed being at college, particularly the social aspect. And neither Benji nor Shante recognized the real resentment, small at first but growing ever larger over time...in Benji.

Because fatherhood was hard. Really hard.

Even before he left school, Benji felt Shante had become more demanding about things she felt her their unborn child needed. The list seemed endless, and now Shante seemed to assume Benji was going to somehow provide all these things. He didn't understand yet that his parents would help some...Shante's mom would help some...but Shante, her mom, and his parents all seemed to put the primary responsibility on him to provide, and it felt overwhelming. The light-hearted days of college were like a dream...had it really happened? And Mama seemed to have an expectation...she was never angry, but she always seemed to start sentences with "When y'all get married..." or "If you were married, then..." Benji heard the message loud and clear: marriage should probably come next; marriage would somehow make everything better.

So they married in 1986. And Benji proceeded to work harder than he'd ever worked in his life. Janitor and cook at the school on Forty-Seventh...McDonald's...gardener at Balboa Park...and others. He tried the very best he could, but he was fighting a losing battle— Shante became more and more demanding with things Jade needed, and Benji was stung by one of her common refrains: "You have to step up and be a man now, Benji," a comment which never failed to anger him. What did she think he was doing? He left everything to take care of her and provide for both her and the baby. The weight of the responsibility was an anchor to Benji and threatened to avalanche him every day, it seemed.

And their second daughter, Jayla, was born later that year.

And Benji continued to miss being at college. Not just the social life, but now twenty-four, he was recognizing he didn't want to work in the post office or try for the Police Academy like Shante suggested. Toward the end of his college days, he realized what he really wanted to do was be a lawyer. And when he thought back, the pleasant and exciting reality of the past had changed to "She trapped me with these babies, and now I can't do anything." And his resentment grew as the number and level of the couple's arguments increased.

During one of those arguments, Benji let it slip out he always wanted to be a lawyer. He claimed that Shante didn't realize that he'd given that up for her, but Shante recognized her young husband's hard work; she was appreciative, but she was working just as hard— perhaps even harder because the job of being a mother to two young children was never ending. Still, upon finding out Benji was angry about not being able to finish college, she was surprised, primarily because she'd never known Benji to be such an angry person…it was a side of him she was not used to seeing. In search of peace at home, she felt Benji finishing college was good for them all. First Benji would finish…then she would finish. Then they could both provide for their children much better in the future. So Shante advanced the idea that she would return to her work at the DMV and her mother agreed to watch the children during the day. Benji could take classes in the evenings and finish his degree; then later, Shante would take classes to complete a degree as well.

Benji was overjoyed. He signed up and began taking classes. He also discovered soft contact lenses. So college wasn't the only thing Benji resumed.

His womanizing also resumed.

Benji hadn't been listening to me for some time now, but I was constantly in his mind and his psyche. You see, I love Benji, and no one on earth knows how good a man he can be better than I do. But Benji was not acting like himself…he was almost unrecognizable. I asked him often, "Why, Benji? Your relationship is sound— your father was not this way! Why, Benji? Do you remember who you are?" But for Benji, apparently the grip of outside women was too strong. By now, I knew it wasn't even that "poor Benji was traumatized by being teased"—no, I was not going to let him off the hook that easy. By now it was clear…he was making bad choices, he knew he was making bad choices, but he just didn't want to say "no." But with a family depending on him, I needed him to learn how to say no to certain people and certain situations…and learn it quickly.

Before it was too late.

By 1988, Benji had earned a bachelor's degree, and the couple welcomed their third daughter, Janiya, into the world. But this pregnancy was much more difficult than the first two. Shante was in significantly more discomfort, and her weight gain was significantly higher than normal, accumulating mightily on her hips and thighs. For some reason she could not fathom, she found it difficult to get out of bed in the aftermath of this delivery; she was constantly sad and would burst out in tears for no reason. She ate continually, as if she were powerless to control it, and the ultimate result was a weight gain that seemed permanent. The normally confident Shante felt worthless and hopeless and could not shake the sense of guilt because of her seeming inability to care for any of her daughters. The doctor prescribed medicines and told Benji to remain patient; he said Shante would probably be OK after a couple of months, but her condition stretched on with no end in sight.

As Shante's condition slowly started to improve, despite my urgings for Benji to forgo it, Benji decided he needed to begin law school. I was constantly in Benji's ear, telling him Shante needed him to go with her to the doctor, she needed more support than ever before, she needed him to do more than just ask, "What can I do?" I told him he was a husband and the father of three beautiful girls and it was time for him to just do what he knew was necessary without being asked. I knew Benji had only one chance to do this the right way.

And Benji was loving, caring, and attentive...for a month.

Then he started law school.

And he'd taken up with a fun-loving, light-hearted, attractive young woman named Robin.

Shante completed the rest of the slow process of postpartum recovery alone. The only remnant of her condition were the excess pounds she was still unable to shed.

But she recovered a lot smarter than she'd been before.

There were things she should have known before, things she refused to see, things she refused to believe...but now she knew. For the sake of their three children, she still hoped beyond hope...but she knew. Thereafter, she demonstrated that tricky relationship that often exists between hope and faith. Her hope that her relationship would right itself enabled her to eventually resume work while fulfilling her duties as wife and mother just in case her relationship righted itself. But her faith in the man sleeping beside her had eroded to the point that she silently began making plans of her own...just in case her hope didn't pan out.

It was her hope that resulted in the birth of their fourth child in 1993.

It happened just as Benji was graduating from law school— a son she allowed her husband to name Benjamin III, primarily because she'd come to adore her father-in-law so much. Nevertheless, for the first time, Shante experienced a level of regret regarding the birth of one of her children. It was an unintended pregnancy, the result of a moment of weakness, and she fought against the unnatural urges and feelings she experienced in the aftermath of what she vowed would be her last pregnancy. She loved extra hard on her son, and eventually, as it had after her third pregnancy, her mind cleared. Confusion and despair were replaced by focus and purpose: Jade was nine now, Jayla had turned seven, Janiya was five, and she had her beautiful baby Benny to care for. She called him Little Benji in front of her husband...but Benny at all other times when he wasn't there...which was often. Benny's birth delayed her plan, but it did not end it. Shante was tough in a way Benji had never really been... she thought him gentle, sweet, caring, and loyal for the past fifteen years, and that was why she loved him. And he had been once...but since it was clear he was no longer any of these things, Shante knew she would have to act, and like any lioness on the hunt, she lay low and patiently waited for the right time to act.

My concern was for Benji, of course. I was assigned as his guide, whether he was right or wrong. All human beings are flawed, so I loved Benji no less. But I was sad and couldn't help feeling I had somehow failed him because I failed to convince him to return to the Benji we all knew before it was too late.

Now it seemed it was already too late. I sat back now and waited for the inevitable.

He would need me in the future.

I hadn't given up, but I was resigned to Benji's future. I wasn't the only one to see what was unfolding. Benji's father had also taken note.

"Robin called my house for you."

After law school graduation, Benji rapidly found high-paying work as a general counsel attorney. He needed every dollar to care for Shante, his four children…and Robin along with her infant son Brandon, a secret no one was aware of, not even his brothers. Though he saw Robin infrequently now, she had turned into a bitter and vengeful woman. Shante seemed pretty content doing whatever it was she did, but for Benji, when he wasn't taking his girls to Girl Scouts, going to school plays and track meets, or taking care of his clients' legal needs, it was now the beautiful Sonja who took up the majority of his free time. He was annoyed to learn Robin had called his parents' house; he wasn't aware she even had the number. But here was Pops, visiting him in his office, informing him she'd called. Benji's heartbeat sped up a bit as he rose from his seat to close the door and find out what his father knew without revealing his secret.

"Oh, that must be Mrs. Little, Pops…she's a client that…"

"Stop."

His father cut him off and peered at him.

"This wasn't no client. This was a lady looking for you."

"Pops, I…"

Benji's father cut him off again with a wave and a stare before continuing, "I don't know what's going on, but you wasn't raised like this, Benjamin— this just some foolishness. All this education and money and your name on the door and your big office don't impress me none and it don't make you no man. You got a wife and four children, and being a man mean you gotta put them first. Where did you learn being a man got anything to do with embracing the softness of a woman? I slung people's garbage and made my money off of other people's rottenness and trash for forty years, and I still walked like a man because your mama and my children came first. Not me…not my comfort… my family. A man sacrifices for his own, and if you gotta bathe in filth, be dog tired, or go without, that's what a man do for his babies! You can teach them with your mouth, but a man like me teach by example!"

The way Pops looked down and shook his head made Benji wonder if perhaps his father was ashamed of him. His father took a deep breath and swallowed before continuing.

"I thought I taught you this."

Benji was quiet through his chastisement but relieved at the same time: his father didn't know about Brandon. His father was from the old school and he would have lost his mind if he knew there was another Frazier child that wasn't of him and Shante, a daughter-in-law who doted over him as much as Angela and Nikki did; and he loved her as his own daughter.

"Your mama don't know about this, and she don't need to. It'd break her heart. You fix it."

Pops's final command before he got up and left needed no further explanation. Benji knew he needed to fix it so Robin would stop calling his parents' home. He needed to fix it so whatever was happening at home that made Robin relevant got turned into a happening that ended her relevancy. He needed to fix his marriage with Shante.

He needed to fix…himself.

But it wasn't easy. For one thing, there was Brandon, the baby no one knew about. That was problematic enough but the other thing was—Benji just didn't truly need Shante anymore. When they were teens, she attached herself to an insecure teen and gave him confidence. When he went to college, she was there when he was homesick, lost, and lonely; she gave him a reason to keep going. When they were young marrieds, she went to work and took care of their children so Benji could finish college and law school. But now? Her teenage beauty had changed to the slightly overweight body of a mother of four. She worked, but Benji made plenty of money now. Insecurity and a lack of self-confidence were no longer issues he needed her to assuage, and she always seemed busy doing whatever it was she did. He just didn't seem to need her for anything…not anymore.

Until one day…he did.

Benji had been suspended from practicing law. Though he was extremely well paid, it was a financial strain to take care of his family, Robin and Brandon, and romance Sonja too. He developed a practice of borrowing from client trust funds and then repaying the "loan" before it was discovered. It was an unethical practice— he knew it was unethical but he needed the extra money. And he thought since most of the clients were either too old or too young to vigorously check— and he was the manager of the trust— as long as the balances were correct and he always repaid the trust, no one would ever know.

But under a routine audit, it didn't take a genius to figure out something was amiss when a trust that required only one payout a year had a dozen transactions of differing amounts tied to the account.

And he hadn't had time to pay back three of the trust accounts at the time of the audit.

His firm was sued, Benji was fired, and the bar association suspended him from practicing law pending a hearing. He was crushed by losing his job and status, but he was really concerned about the money and how they would replace it to care for his family. Shante always came through in situations like this though; she'd figure it out. First, Benji had to come up with a plausible explanation for being fired, though— he obviously couldn't tell her the truth. But once he had his story straight, he'd tell her whatever lie he came up with and they'd make a plan together. He didn't know what to do about Robin and Brandon, but he decided to figure it out later.

When Benji went home to tell Shante, the house was strangely quiet, but he didn't recognize it at first. He came home earlier than he normally did, extremely talkative, laying out his fabricated story of what happened, how it wasn't his fault, how unfair it all was and how he knew they were going to be OK anyway, they didn't need anybody anyway and wanting to know what she thought they should do.

And then...the unconscious invaded his conscious mind...and a realization hit him.

"Where the kids?"

Shante had not moved from her position sitting on the couch and did not answer his question. It was only then he became aware of the unnatural quiet, a silence violated only by Millie Jackson's soulful voice singing in the background.

And almost as if on cue, outside...the rain began to fall.

There was no food cooking in the kitchen. The window shades were drawn, and the house was unnaturally dark. Benji was keenly aware of the rain coming down harder against the windows as his focus shifted to the bags packed... and sitting in the hallway.

She knew.

And outside - it thundered.

The situation left him speechless as she got up without a word and walked out of the door and into her sister's car that just appeared in his driveway.

As it had been for what seemed like their entire lives... Shante was one step ahead of him.

They divorced in 1999. The judge took no pity on Benji's employment status and in fact seemed angry as he mandated he pay Shante nearly $3,000 a month in alimony and child support. Benji remained motionless through it all. When the proceedings were complete, he unintentionally came face to face with Shante.

He did not intend it, but now that it was here, there was something he wanted to say…something he needed to say. But as he looked into the eyes of his now ex-wife, he recalled the times in college and when he first started his legal career, when he took so much pride in being able to talk to women with his eyes alone and how effective it was.

But even more so, he remembered an evening over twenty years ago, when in the middle of a slow dance, Shante had looked at him through the darkness of a house party with eyes that spoke without saying a word.

Her eyes said "I'm sorry" that night.

It was the same message Benji's eyes were sending now.

And I knew he meant it.

And so did Shante. Her eyes responded in turn, also without saying a word.

Her eyes responded…

"I know."

And as she embraced her ex-husband and kissed him softly on his cheek, for a brief moment in time…Teri and Shante were running the halls of their junior high school, with Teri screaming to everyone within earshot that Shante Clay liked Benji Frazier…and in that moment, the now ex-spouses were fifteen all over again.

Then the moment passed. Shante turned and exited the courthouse.

She did not look back.

Over the next few years, Robin sued Benji for child support. Sonja left. And Benji was alone in his struggles. He considered moving to Wisconsin, where there was no bar requirement and only a law degree was required to practice, but Wisconsin seemed too foreign to Benji, and moving there would have required a relentless determination that seemed to have left Benji. He found work as a paralegal and augmented his salary by working at 7-11, driving a cab, performing work as a security guard, and with his father's words ringing in his ears, doing anything he needed to do to pay his child support obligations.

He did not see his children much, though. The stress of his situation, poor habits, waning discipline, and an increasingly severe drinking habit resulted in a weight gain of his own. As his weight climbed over 280 pounds on his six-foot frame, he stopped weighing himself…when he went over three hundred pounds, he did not want to know. He was not suicidal yet—but his depression was deepening, he'd just stopped caring about what was going to happen; it reflected in his demeanor and his appearance. He did not want his children or Shante to see him like this. He'd rather just pay his child support and have them remember him like he was. He'd seen Shante, though—he'd seen her by chance as he aimlessly wandered a shopping mall one day…and she looked fantastic. She'd lost fifty or sixty pounds and looked like the Shante of their younger days. He'd heard she was working as a real estate agent and doing very well for herself.

He'd wondered though…when did she find the time to get that level of training and set up her new life?

Still…it was another reason to just pay his child support from a distance and remain a ghost. Every now and then he'd call and lie about how good he was doing. But as he ran out of lies and reasons he couldn't see his children, the calls just stopped. His father was right…he should sacrifice for his family. And the best thing he could do for all of them was pay what he owed and let them all remember the strong, handsome, confident, accomplished man they once knew…and loved.

As he drank alone on his fortieth birthday, Benji could not lie to himself…and he couldn't lie to me. We both knew he was a dangerously obese alcoholic, flat broke, and alone. Not completely alone, though— he'd met an older woman named Alyssa, a slovenly, annoying, negative woman with too many children that she didn't take good enough care of. Though he could barely contain his disdain for her, at least she gave him a place to live.

And she was pregnant. Or so she said. Maybe he was going to be a father again. Maybe not. Who knew? His baby? Someone else's?

None of it mattered anymore.

Benji started on a fifth double as the bartender warned him he would not serve him another— which was OK; he had a bottle of cheap whiskey stashed under the seat in his car. In any case, Benji barely heard the bartender through the alcohol-engendered haze he now found himself in. This was a comforting place for Benji now—everything was fuzzy, but he was engulfed by the warm comfort of his own alcohol-infused world, a world where he was always happy, a world where he could forget his numerous failures, a world where he wasn't a disgraced, morbidly obese, disgusting, pathetic alcoholic—a world where he still reigned supreme as its king.

I could not see this twenty-five years ago. I suspected continuing a relationship with Shante might not be the right road, but all I knew during their dance and first kiss was that Benji was at a crossroads. I suspected Shante would be a negative influence on Benji.

What I didn't realize was it was Benji who would have the negative influence on Shante. Not the other way around.

I knew there was a path to redemption for Benji. His failures were numerous, but he was a good man underneath it all. I tugged at his his conscience and whispered, "Let's go home, Benji…let's go home. We'll sober up and plan our way ahead."

Benji nodded as if he could hear me and fumbled for his car keys.

"No, no, no," I warned him. "Call your father…Angela… or one of your brothers. You've had too much to drink. It's not safe to drive. I know you know this. Call someone."

Benji knew he shouldn't drive. But he ignored me.

But I was right. The flashing red lights almost magically illuminated behind his swerving car as he proceeded from the Black Frog.

"*Body and Soul*" blared from the car speakers as he drunkenly pulled onto the sidewalk and a police officer sidled up to his window. Benji's head was back and eyes were closed; the alcohol transported him backwards in time.

"Sir…do you know why I stopped you?"

After a while, Benji opened his bloodshot eyes and gazed blankly at the officer. After what seemed like an eternity of staring, his response was heavily slurred and barely understandable:

"Because that's the way it's got to be."

And then I knew he would never listen to that song quite the same way ever again.

CHAPTER 7

DON'T LET THE GREEN GRASS FOOL YA

"OK, so let's role play. You're going to be you...I'm going to be your best friend. And I want you to respond to me exactly as you would respond to your best friend."

It was one of Benji's many coaching tools—and a devastatingly effective one. At times when clients needed to balance their thinking to maximize their personal wellness or were struggling to meet a goal or didn't know how to proceed or in almost in any situation where clients felt indecisive, Benji would assume the role of the client's best friend in the world. After framing the friendship, within a few minutes Benji could get into character where the client would really get into the role play of talking to his or her best friend— then, Benji would pose the exact issue to the client that the client was struggling with. In providing advice to their "best friend" on the troublesome issue, oftentimes the clients' advice served as self-talk to themselves...and the self-awareness generally put the clients on the path to problem resolution.

That was the plan, anyway. Even on the infrequent occasions it didn't achieve the desired result, Benji employed an assortment of other tools and activities to successfully resolve his clients' issues.

In addition to an expert ability to apply the tools of his profession, Benji had an authenticity that appealed to clients and prospective business partners alike. Benji scorned the industry practices which forced many of his peers to repeat the same phrases and jokes for every workshop— he knew people would not be fooled by an insincere approach. So he listened and reacted with sincerity. He knew when to lead and when to follow; he knew when to talk and when to listen; and he was an expert at using open-ended questions to bring about client self- awareness. It was these qualities that made him among the best in the region. Benji turned on charisma and charm combined humor, inspiration, patience, and empathy. He was expert at facilitating in groups and avoided giving his opinion to individual clients, preferring to wait until his clients caught on so they could take responsibility for their own solutions. In his profession, he literally had no weaknesses.

Benji was a life coach—and a highly regarded, well- paid one. His job was to solve client problems, or stated more clearly, his job was to increase client self-awareness so they could identify and solve their own problems. It sounded simple; Benji was amazed clients would pay up to $400 per hour to discuss their personal and professional challenges with him. His groups paid $100 per person for up to twenty people for an hour of his time—that's $2,000 total an hour for his group work. He commanded up to $5,000 for a single speech, and his all-day leadership development, personality awareness, team-building, strength, and resilience seminars went for up to $14,000 a day. Benji was extremely well paid for his talents, and for good reason.

He was good. And he had an impressive inventory of material possessions to show for it.

He'd purchased for himself a stunningly beautiful luxury home, a modern palace complete with glass walls, a gourmet kitchen, formal and casual dining areas, and a state of the art entertainment system all set against the full beauty of nature. The furnishings were plush and reflected professional decoration, while a black Mazda Miata and a white Lexus competed for Benji's attention in his spacious garage. Awards for his professional expertise and commitment to the community were spread on walls throughout the home. An in-home movie theater never ceased displaying Benji's most inspirational movies or even videos of Benji himself being interviewed discussing his philosophies on personal development, personality theories, or diversity and inclusion.

He'd definitely come a long way from the days of making family Christmas presents from household materials and wrapping them in newspaper.

And yet, despite all he'd accomplished and accumulated, I knew Benji was not a totally happy man. His possessions...his accolades...his hard-earned professional standing in his industry— he thought all those things, individually or collectively, would fill the void in his life. None of his affluence could make him feel like he belonged. Like he'd really made it.

Like he'd finally found his way home.

Oh, but he could talk the talk, though. Benji's clients were almost mesmerized by his combination of instinct, intellect, and training. He could read people like he was inside their minds— it was a talent that stemmed from the days where he refused to wear his glasses so he was ultimately forced to pick up on clues, however subtle, in other people's tones, their inflections, their body language or even their auras…he even imagined he could almost smell what people were like and what they were about. It was as if he had developed a sixth sense. Accordingly, Benji could protect those who needed protection, listen to those who needed to be heard, tell a joke to those who needed a smile, or give straight talk to those who needed absolute honesty. He could see a room collectively and never gave the same workshop twice, even when the topic was the same, because no two groups were the same. It was a practiced skill that made Benji almost irresistible to his groups…and to his individual clients alike. He was in command of the group the minute he walked into any room.

And he could walk the walk too. To his coworkers, it seemed as though he were always in total control of the situation. Confident and mildly arrogant only to a level inspiring admiration as opposed to revulsion, he walked among his peers like their self declared emperor. And yet he carried a humility and a sense of dignity— he was never the loudest person in the room, never the obnoxious salesman, always the quiet hustler taking in the scene with just a hint of a smile, noting tendencies, moving from person to person, knowing just how much to say to show interest but moving on before he got tiresome. He was adored by his assistants and the firm's secretarial staff. He even spent huge amounts of time with the building's custodial team every chance he could— a few of the janitors were natives of Tanzania, and since Benji was teaching himself Swahili, he'd often spent an hour he could have spent making money by instead learning Swahili at the feet of the men whom he considered African *mkuu zangu*...the chiefs...the elders...although to everyone else, they were the building janitors.

But I knew Benji...so I knew what was wrong. I tried to have that conversation continually over the years, and I was still having it with him. I needed to make him understand.

I knew he felt the need to hold a part of himself back. There was a certain unspoken expectation from his professional community...and whispers followed those who did not conform to those expectations, as well as those who were deemed successful. Jealousies, both personal and professional, existed in this world. And for Benji— perhaps for anyone—it was extremely difficult if not impossible to feel like you were at home in this sometimes secretly cutthroat environment. Everything he said, every interaction he had—it all seemed like an audition...every time. He thought back to being tested as a teen; by the one who slapped him out of his seat in school, by Mexican gang bangers outside of Ricky's house, by the guy who confronted him with the golf club. Those were tests he'd had to pass every time too. These were different kinds of tests but he imagined his life experiences had prepared him well for these professional "auditions" that seemed to occur randomly. He'd never begged for his life back then, not once; he couldn't imagine himself begging for something as simple as anyone's approval now.

For example, Benji was aware that some in his firm considered his time spent with the Tanzanian janitors done for the benefit of his image…for reputation. Some asserted he only spent time with the custodial staff when it could be noticed by or reported to the firm's partners. Some derisively claimed he did it to look "cute." When informed by an ally, Benji dismissively claimed, "Love me or hate me…it's all good. Love me, and I'm always in your heart. Hate me, and I'm always on your mind. Either way…I win."

He thought it was a Shakespearean quote. Or based on one. Whatever it was, Benji learned it as an undergraduate and thought it had a street edge to it, so he loved it and filed it away mentally. But when it was reported back to him as evidence of his arrogance by another supposed ally, Benji realized he'd been betrayed by the initial person he thought was a friend. That incident taught him a valuable lesson.

There were no permanent friends in this business. A friend today would be competing for your spot tomorrow.

So not knowing who was friend and who was enemy, he held back aspects of his personality. In some situations, he was comfortable giving eighty percent of who he really was…in some cases he gave fifty percent of this true self. Sometimes he could only give ten percent of what was real, and oftentimes, the person he displayed at work to his professional teammates was nothing like the real Benji at all. Though it was necessary, it was during these times Benji felt like a carefully crafted corporate clown…like a puppet dancing for other people's enjoyment and comfort.

And it was a nauseating feeling.

But here, it was important to "fit," and there were times when Benji didn't want to fit…he just wanted to be Benji. He didn't want to hear about and feign interest in the same topics over and over. He didn't want to wear expensive suits…he wanted to wear casual attire, even jeans…and sometimes did so at the cost of being subject to the firm's gossipmongers. And he was weary of being asked to consciously or unconsciously represent every black person in world. It was as if the partners didn't realize not everyone who looks the same thinks the same way or has the same dreams, goals, aspirations, or outlooks. When his bosses asked him, "What do you think, Ben?" the question behind their gaze was "Tell us what minorities think," or "How might our minority clients respond to this?" And though Benji answered, he often thought, "If you want to know what minorities think, you need to talk to them. You can't just read one article…or talk to one black person…or two…or ten…and think you know black people."

It was simply exhausting at times.

Though it may sound strange…Benji also resented being asked to smile.

It was often an innocent request, one given as a compliment and accompanied by a sincere "C'mon, you have a great smile!" But somewhere inside him…he couldn't quite figure it out or where he'd gotten the idea or heard it from, but full-on smiles just to put people at ease seemed almost cartoonish to Benji. Maybe he'd learned that in college, or maybe it was something Marcus told him when they were kids. Maybe it stemmed from incidents like when he was in Tokyo and the Japanese lady on the subway brazenly requested to see his teeth to determine if they were real.

Smiling was ok for women; Benji loved seeing women smile, but when he saw men smile too wide, there was just something about it that repulsed him. Maybe it stemmed from where he'd grown up, where he did not see men walking around smiling at each other. Laughing? Yes, sometimes. But smiling? Seemed like a weakness. But he was asked to smile often. He imagined women who were unconsciously judged by their looks might feel the same way about being constantly complimented on how they were dressed—he imagined they sometimes wanted to come to work in the most basic attire possible just so they wouldn't have to hear "you look nice today"…again. Benji DID smile…but his smiles during workshops and individual sessions came naturally. During other times though, Benji would grin a little and nod when asked to smile. But in his mind, he would often think with some hostility, "What am I? A puppet?" Though annoyed, he was disciplined enough to not let it show. But through it all, his thinking was, "I don't fake smile…and I don't dance on demand."

But I knew that sometimes he did. Not as often as some others, but often enough that he was disgusted with himself after he did it.

He totally despised social media. All the firm's practitioners were strongly encouraged to become active and expert at utilizing the various forms of social media to attract clients, build networks, and expand the firm's reach. Some of his peers even conducted group workshops and individual sessions using the medium and strutted like peacocks at the earnings resulted; it was an efficient way to conduct business. But Benji was inwardly contemptuous of the practice…for him, it was the equivalent of being good at a boxing video game versus truly being able to fight. They all put their best selves, their best pictures, their best quotes on social media. They could labor over responses until they found the perfect response, and virtual workshops didn't require the focus and skill required to keep an audience engaged—it was more like a one- way lecture; it was nothing like the energizing in-person sessions Benji favored. Those online types earned more, but Benji was better. He knew it. And they knew it too. Benji's assistant maintained a minimal social media presence for him, but he considered it beneath him. It was ok for lesser practitioners, but wasn't worthy of a man of his skill.

What he really loved was going to his parents' house or to see family every chance he got. He didn't drive one of his luxury vehicles when he went…he had a used Nissan for when he went home because he didn't want to talk about or emphasize the world he was running away from—he wanted to enjoy the world he was running to…and his luxury cars were a distraction. He loved listening to Pops and laughing at his stories as they shared a glass of VO in the Frazier family's modest back yard. He loved playing spades and dominoes with his brothers and the playful shit-talking that accompanied each and every game. He loved taking turns claiming the family Monopoly championship, and he was almost ecstatic one time when he came home and found his parents purchased a karaoke machine that provided a score to each musical performance. It was something else for him and his brothers to have fun competing at, but Benji probably had even more fun singing duets with Nikki. Often, Benji and his sister would continue singing "*Beauty and the Beast*," "*Up Where We Belong*," "*A Whole New World*," or a favorite from his childhood, "*Don't Go Breaking My Heart*," long after his other siblings went home, Nikki's husband and children had fallen asleep waiting for them to finish, and his parents had likewise gone to bed. Benji thought maybe they were being too loud, but his parents never came out to ask them to keep it down. In fact…more than once, Benji would note Pops reappearing to quietly listen to his children sing. And smile at the sound.

He checked in on his childhood friends during those visits home too. Brian led a local band now, and though they didn't make much money, in true artist's fashion, Brian didn't care. Benji would attend his friend's sessions at beach parties, small bars, and wine-tasting sessions where they played for a plate of food and tips, and he was always excited when Brian would invite him to join as a guest vocalist on "Stand by Me" or "Super Bad ." But even better than that was Brian's backyard. Ricky would join them sometimes, and the three childhood friends would all sing along and drink liquor from plastic red cups as Brian strummed the chords to "*Betcha by Golly Wow*," the song Brian first sang in junior high school concerts and Ricky sang in Spanish on the way to school when they were all fifteen.

With Ricky, he noted how his friend bounced from job to job and from woman to woman. Ricky was not the same happy-go-lucky teenager he'd grown up with, and as Benji picked up on some things, he thought he could help his childhood friend. But offering help was a tricky thing: in this neighborhood, admitting a weakness was still a taboo, whether as the teen they once were or the men they were now. He had to help smoothly...easily...almost slyly...and in such a way, Ricky would not realize he was being coached. So Benji noted once, "Yeah, I can see myself in five years... I'm going to be doing this and that." He said reported on what he was doing immediately to reach his goals, and then on what he was going to do next week...next month...next year—and he went to Ricky for advice on how to do it all. Ricky fell right into it...in giving Benji advice, he was giving himself advice. And Benji was pleased as he saw Ricky begin to settle down, express happiness with his career, and plan to save enough to buy an automotive franchise. And he knew Ricky was able to maintain his pride because no one said anything was wrong with him or offered to help him... he'd come up with it on his own. It was very important to let a man keep his pride. Just like Ricky did for Benji in shop class when they were in junior high.

Yes, he loved going to his old neighborhood. Every time. The only negative was eventually he had to leave— he had to go back.

Back to his supposedly perfect life.

His attention was drawn back to his dark-haired client, who was excitedly speaking to him now as if she were speaking to her best friend. His technique was working...as it usually did. Since this technique required him to ask her to repeat back and restate what she was saying, he allowed himself a minor lapse in concentration.

He knew her…kind of. She was from the neighborhood, and Nikki asked him to see her. Benji agreed, and he was now trying to place her. She looked really familiar…where did he know her from? From her comments she'd made when the session began, it seemed like…maybe he knew her from…junior high school maybe?

Which took Benji back to that fateful year…the year his journey to the place where he currently found himself began.

Dr. Deen's science class.

He'd left the science class bound and determined to not complete his project. It was spring vacation, right after that party, and his girlfriend reminded him he needed to do it.

He'd been surprised when she said that, but he still hadn't intended to do the project. Until Angela stepped in.

His sister's idea was to develop a BASIC computer program that could serve as a computer dating service for teenagers.

The Beginners' All-purpose Symbolic Instruction Code, or BASIC, was confusing to Benji, but with Angela's tutoring, he began to pick it up quickly…

10 Input "What is your name: ?", N$
20 Print "Hello"; N$
30 Input "Are you a boy or a girl?", S$
40 Input "What is your birthday?", A

And from those initial inputs, Benji and his sister worked on a BASIC computer program that once it computed the users' zodiac signs and genders, would tell the users who in the school was a good match for them. Benji had to figure out what zodiac signs were the perfect matches for the other signs—Nikki helped him with that; she knew all about that kind of stuff. And once Nikki knew what he was doing, she became really interested in her younger brother's project too, so…and maybe for the first time, Nikki and Benji worked together to finish the project, working night and day together. And it was from that time, the two middle siblings got much closer. They'd always loved each other but they'd also love fighting each other. Well, not "fighting"—fighting was what Benji did with his brothers. It was more like…"sniping" at each other. But from this time, the emphasis between them became less on the sniping and more on the bond.

But Benji had more work to do…he needed to find out people's birthdays and figure out how to store them in the program's internal data base. Then he had to figure out how to tell the computer to select the best match. Then he had to figure how to tell the computer to select the right gender. It was confusing…difficult…and fun. It was a series of "if the person says this, then do that" statements within the program, and the further he got along into the program, the more he had to learn.

And for the first time in his life, Benji felt…smart.

When spring vacation ended and Benji turned in his project, he could tell Dr. Deen was surprised. And for some reason, Benji thoroughly enjoyed the look of shock on her face when he turned in and explained his now- treasured program— it was the greatest school thing he'd ever done.

Deen gave him a B-plus.

"It is an interesting take on combining computer science with the science of psychology, Benjamin. I applaud your effort, and you have obviously learned a lot. I note horoscopes have no scientific benefit, but if you are utilizing the concept, I would have liked to see the program use questions to ascertain the users' personalities and horoscopes instead of simply asking them their birthdays. But this is an impressive effort, Benjamin…extremely impressive. You should be lauded for your work on this."

"Not lauded with an A, though," I thought to myself sarcastically. I was annoyed with Dr. Deen myself. I made plans to keep Benji's spirits lifted.

But it was unnecessary.

Benji didn't care what his teacher said. He didn't care what his teacher thought. He didn't even care what his grade was. He knew how much effort he put into his project, he knew what he'd learned in a short period of time, and he knew his project was good. In fact, he knew it was better than some of the other projects, so he didn't care what anyone else did either. He simply enjoyed the brand new sensation of experiencing the feeling of being smart for the first time in his life.

Benji did not become a high performing academic, though. But what he had was the confidence to know that anytime he wanted to do it, he could do it if he wanted to work hard enough. He knew he was smart now.

He just didn't always want to show it if the subject was uninteresting.

His high school years saw him on an academic seesaw, sometimes displaying brilliance and sometimes displaying a lackadaisical attention to his required studies. But what started with Dr. Deen continued in his high school years…

when he thought his work was good, or when he knew his work was good, he didn't care about his grade or what anyone else thought about it. It seemed like teachers were always finding fault with him anyway; even when he worked hard, it was as if they didn't want him on the same level as the geniuses.

So as time passed on, he cared about impressing people less and less. But he found himself with an increasing fascination with people, personality, and relationships— and his poor vision caused him to focus on subtleties others may have missed but gave him clues about why they thought the way they thought and why they did the things they did.

His education extended beyond the classroom. He could spend hours watching and listening to Marcus opine about his philosophies regarding life and people; he watched Nikki and listened to her motivations and observed Sid's easy way of dealing with people and influencing them. There was no one he wouldn't watch…everyone was his teacher in the art of why people were who they were and how people interacted with each other.

He wasn't interested in going to college. Too many teachers trying to judge him. But when he was surprisingly accepted to a few, Angela helped him fill out the paperwork for grants and loans to help him start on his post–high school journey. Though he was becoming an above-average student, he was less impressed with the ramblings of his professors and peers, who loved to use big words and say long sentences in an effort to show how smart they were. He much preferred riding with his father on his route to watch his father interact with people along the way; he loved studying his mother and her interactions with each of her children, as well as friends and neighbors. He often felt like he learned more from watching his parents, siblings, and the people in his neighborhood than all his years in college put together.

Angela finished college, got a really good job, and left though. Benji missed her…but something was different. He never heard his parents talk about it; he never heard anybody talk about it. But something was definitely different.

Angela had gotten a job in public relations or communications or something. She was dealing with a lot of big shots now, and apparently they depended on her for whatever it was she did. Benji knew his parents were very proud of her, but the thing was…Angela just didn't come around much anymore. Maybe she was tired of being the big sister everyone always depended on, but she just came around less and less and less. And when she did come, she talked differently. She used a bunch of big words, like it seemed like she was intentionally trying to embarrass them all if they didn't know what they meant. Or…she seemed to assume they didn't know what the words meant. She talked a lot about the high-level people she was dealing with…it wasn't so much what she said but how she said it. Like…she was better than they were now. And being a student of people and motivations himself, Benji caught every deep breath… every small sigh…every eye roll. It was like she was laboring to be in the presence of her own family.

And his parents knew it too. They never said anything. They just shared little smiles with each other. Knowing glances. Then you could tell they knew what Angela was doing and feeling. But they let it go without comment. They were just proud parents.

As Benji watched these scenes unravel, he knew his sister was inside this stranger's body some place, and he didn't love her any less. Nevertheless, he made a vow…what happened to Angela would never happen to him. These were his people. This was his neighborhood. And he would never ever forget it…ever.

He didn't feel like the academic world appreciated him anyway. Ever since the project in science class with Deen, it was like they kinda liked what he did but they didn't want to let him all the way in. Probably because he refused to talk like them or think he was better…like they all seemed to think.

Including his own sister.

I interrupted Benji's constant mental rampage to say, "Benji— could it be that you don't get full credit because you don't fully follow the instructions? There is such a thing as a rubric, but you refuse to follow it—you won't even look at it. They appreciate your genius! But could it be they have to judge all students by the same standard?"

But Benji resisted this logic. He was determined to be accepted on his own terms. And since his work continued to fall just short of the compliance with academic standards exhibited by his peers, Benji increasingly began to judge himself not by grades but by his own internal standards and individual sense of accomplishment.

It created in Benji a situation where he almost felt like he was acting as a kind of double agent. He was fully capable of reading a rubric, complying with it, and participating in a discussion with his most studied counterparts and even his distinguished professors—he became fluent in their language, so to speak. But at the same time, he decried those who leaned heavily on research and academic study while ignoring how real people talked, thought, and interacted. For Benji's part, he maintained his balance by utilizing his accumulated knowledge through application to his personal circumstances. He developed an expertise in breaking down studies and academia into what he called "the language of real people." And as he advanced through his undergraduate and graduate studies, his knowledge was of great benefit to the disadvantaged people in his own community. Benji developed the ability to perfectly straddle what seemed to be two different worlds, seemingly comfortable in either world...but one was a facade and the other was real.

Benji easily found work upon graduation. First, it was basic entry-level counseling jobs—important work, but nothing that truly used his full capability...yet. At various times, he found himself employed as a crisis counselor working as an advocate for domestic violence prevention, a career placement officer, a group counseling leader, an alcohol and drug counselor, and the like. And at the same time, he continued to volunteer services in the community which augmented his paying jobs and rounded out his experience further. He also took advantage of every training opportunity...equal opportunity training, diversity, and various methods of personality assessment.

Benji had taken a midlevel coaching job with a large firm—they'd been extremely impressed with his ability to connect with audiences during different types of workshops and the array of situations he was comfortable in. Large and small companies hired them to indoctrinate new employees, develop existing employees, and provide coaching services to its senior executives. When one of the partners approached Benji with an opportunity to become certified in an advanced leadership development technique, Benji readily accepted.

The course intrigued Benji from the first day. His mind literally spun with all the possibilities of using the tools he was being certified to employ. As was his custom, he mostly stayed silent and observed. He was silently contemptuous of those who continually asked questions not in search of knowledge but to seem knowledgeable. It was a common practice in academia that Benji despised.

But then, toward the end of the course...Benji advanced a question.

"So...can this tool be modified for group coaching sessions?"

They been trained to administer the leadership development assessment to individuals and then provide follow-up individual coaching.

The instructor smiled knowingly and dismissed Benji's question out of hand.

"No, no, no, no, no..." he began.

"Five nos without even asking about what I have in mind?" Benji thought sarcastically.

"No, no...this tool is meant to be used one on one. It's not appropriate for a group session."

Benji's face was impassive. He even nodded slightly to indicate he accepted the instructor's explanation.

But inside— the statement was already embedded in his mind.

"We'll see about that."

Almost immediately upon graduation, Benji went to work turning what was intended to be a one-on-one developmental session into a group session that allowed him to develop thirty leaders for the cost of a single coach.

When he presented it to his bosses, they were thrilled with his proposal...but for different reasons.

They intended to utilize Benji's creation to charge the thirty leaders individually for each session...increasing revenue by thirty since a single coach could conduct the workshop.

And when the firm patented Benji's process...it increased revenues even further.

And Benji's financial fortunes and notoriety in his industry took an immediate upturn. Though as an employee, he received no direct benefit, he was known as the process's author. It made him valuable to similar firms, both in the United States and internationally. It made him more valuable to his firm— and the firm drastically increased his salary to keep him in place.

Or maybe they didn't want him to contest ownership of the leadership development process he'd created. Benji was unsure. But for what he was getting paid, they could have the process. He'd built that one; he'd build another whenever he wanted to.

And with his new wealth came the accumulation of material goods...the increased attention of new, similarly high-powered peers…and an increased agitation for Benji as he felt an increased pull away from his comfort zone.

He was almost embarrassed to have family at his home. He didn't want to seem like his sister. His parents didn't care about his wealth— they cared that he came home to spend time with his father, though. Pops had retired, but determined to stay busy, he bought candy and set up a neighborhood candy store in their garage. Benji treasured time riding with his father to buy candy in bulk and then bringing it home to help his father count his inventory, move the older candy to the front, and eat the oldest candy while his father told stories and reveled in the attention from his son.

His siblings didn't care about his cars. His brothers cared about their tradition of watching the fights together. He, Marcus, and Sid always watched the major sporting events together…the NBA playoffs, March Madness, the World Series, college football, the NFL playoffs…whatever was on depending on the season. But the brothers especially loved watching boxing together and arguing about current boxers and past fights. Each considered himself an expert. Benji had almost considered becoming a fighter once. He often fantasized about it.

And Nikki treasured their marathon karaoke sessions, of course.

And Mama? She just wanted to feed him. And she would call to make sure he was coming; she'd keep Benji on the phone for almost an hour telling him about the goings- on in their neighborhood, Pops's doctors' appointments, talking about her grandchildren, talking about good girls Benji needed to meet, when Benji was going to get married, why he needed to get married, and when he was going to give her more grandchildren.

Benji swerved Mama on that topic. Though he preferred to go home than have family over, he did not feel the same about the numerous women he often brought into his home.

Benji's insight into personality and human motivation made him quite an effective seducer of women. Interestingly enough—he rarely tried to seduce the numerous visitors to his home. He was a relaxed conversationalist: funny when humor was called for, an expert listener, and practiced at getting people…in this case, women…to reveal their inner vulnerabilities and thoughts. Plus…somewhere over the years, the dark skin that made him subject to taunts as a teenager was now considered exotic and enticing to women. All kinds of women.

Or maybe that was a result of his confidence and maturity.

Or maybe that was a result of his ever- expanding bank account.

But no matter the reason, Benji made frequent use of what he called his "Real Quiet Storm" playlist. First, Tony Tone Toni would gently ask his guests to *"Lay Your Head on My Pillow"*, before Silk requested the women to let Benji help them to *"Lose Control"*, then in the aftermath, L.T.D would remind them *"We Both Deserve Each Other's Love"* as they basked in the aftermath. And after a while it wasn't the singers singing anymore and creating an atmosphere where seduction was ripe.

It was Benji talking. With his eyes.

He didn't know why he seemed to be so good at talking with his eyes.

Benji enjoyed these women but never met any like his mama often suggested he should marry. Those kinds of women never looked Benji's way. But now…here…was the dark- haired girl from his old neighborhood. He did know her. Or at least…he remembered her.

Benji was fascinated. For some reason this girl had always fascinated him. She was different from any girl he knew back then and any of the women he had recently been with. She was smart, but also there was a realness to her demeanor. She was funny without trying to be. She was confident yet vulnerable. She shared, but yet…there was still a mystery about her. And her dark-haired beauty was unlike that of anyone he'd ever met.

And from the way she was sharing…the way she was looking at him…was she was developing a type of emotional connection with her life coach?

With Benji? After all these years?

Benji was a practiced and patient seducer of women… but he wanted to ask this dark-haired girl from his past for a real date. But not to his home. Seduction not on his mind, but he would also fight against any urges to seduce or have expectations of her being with him. Because he had zero expectations. No matter what.

And at that moment, Benji experienced a powerful sense of déjà vu . It was as if he'd had these feelings and internal conversations before.

I smiled.

And then…Benji told her she needed to go, that he was late for his next appointment, rushing her out of the room. As she departed, he told her he was very busy but he would definitely have someone from his firm help her and to make sure his assistant got her insurance information.

And just like that…she was gone.

I was puzzled.

In Benji's subconscious, I planted a question: "Why did you do that? Why did you let her go?"

I thought he would say it was because she was a client—that would have been an acceptable answer, though it had never stopped him before.

But that was not Benji's response.

He opined, "We're from different sides of the tracks now. It wouldn't be a good mix. Not anymore."

And I was flabbergasted.

"Not a good mix? Says who? Why not? Or do you mean…not a good mix for you? What is going on here, Benjamin? You spent all these years being real and staying connected, and now…a woman from your neighborhood with an obvious connection is not a good mix?"

I paused before I decided I needed to continue.

"What is the real reason you hesitate to bring your family into your home? Is it truly because you are embarrassed to display your belongings to your family? Or…is it because you are embarrassed to have your father, your mother, Nikki, and your brothers drive their cars in your neighborhood? Because you don't want your neighbors to hear you debating sports loudly with your brothers? Because you don't want the sounds of karaoke coming from your expensive house in your gorgeous quiet neighborhood?"

"Have you become Angela?"

There were times when Benji stared right at me. Though I knew I was invisible to him, it was almost as if he could see me clearly. This was one of those times.

And he was enraged.

And then he began to consider what I said.

In truth— with all of his wealth and possessions, there was definitely something missing from his life. He was great at his job — he was not being arrogant to consider himself the best in his industry; he was charismatic, sincere, knowledgeable, and versatile. He didn't do what he did for money…he believed in what he did. And it made him lots of money.

But the results of his talents didn't seem real. It was like he was trapped in another dimension. His coworkers were nice to him, but he just often felt like he didn't fit in, and the effort to pretend like he did was exhausting. His bosses, the firm's partners, were interested in making money. They used Benji and others out to make money— they were unconcerned with quality. The firm's reputation was such that their clients believed they were getting superior service when in fact they were getting average service. The partners stole Benji's creation and used it to extract even more money from their clients—and Benji allowed it in exchange for a higher salary.

He was tired of forcing himself to smile all the time. He was tired of living a separate life from the people who really mattered. He was tired of the endless series of relationships, if you could call them that, dalliances that all started the same, went the same way, and ultimately…ended the same.

I saw his quandary; to me, the solution was a simple one. Quit.

"Why don't you resign? You have plenty of money… you have a reputation in this industry. Why not go home? Remember how you helped Ricky? You can do that full time, Benji. They can't pay as much, and you may lose some things. But you can go home…freelance for a few smaller companies since you won't have your firm's resources. But you'll be OK with less. I know you'll be happier, and…you can pursue the dark-haired girl. Go after her—you wanted a date. Call her and ask her to go to a movie."

"Just quit this life, Benjamin. If you can surrender the material things you say you hate, you will definitely be OK."

A look of calm and pure peace entered Benji's spirit as he considered what I'd planted in his subconscious.

Home.

He would trade the comfort of home for his modern palace, complete with glass walls set against the beauty of nature. He would trade the comfort of home for his gourmet kitchen and formal and casual dining areas. He would trade the comfort of home for his state of the art entertainment system. There would be no more plush furnishings, and he would no longer be able to even afford the insurance on his Mazda Miata or his Lexus. He would surrender his in-home movie theater too.

He would give it all up in exchange for the comfort of being home and working in his own community. And to date the dark-haired girl who'd just left.

And then…slowly…almost as if it were happening in slow motion, the look of calm and peace on Benji's face was transformed into a look of worry, concern…and distress.

Benji took another mental inventory of all he would voluntarily surrender, including the considerable fortune he'd already invested in purchasing these items.

He remembered now…he expected to be offered a partnership in this firm. In fact, he was certain of it. When that happened, his already considerable income would triple, if not quadruple.

And like the current partners, he would get paid off other coaches' labor.

He checked his messages— there was an email from a beautiful female social worker he'd met telling him how much she enjoyed their meeting and that his talent was exciting.

He heard a voice message from a voluptuous woman he'd met at a professional conference saying she was in town on business for a week and asking what his schedule looked like.

I watched…and waited.

As Benji sat transfixed in thought, his ultraefficient assistant appeared in the doorway.

"Your stress management group is ready and waiting, sir."

Benji looked at his assistant and thought of how necessary she was to his success; she knew him, anticipated what his needs were in advance, and was talented and versatile enough to get him to appointments on time, plan his trips, manage conferences, or even fill in for him conducting workshops. She learned from her boss, accepted his mentorship, combined it with her own talents, and created a facilitation style all her own. She was very, very good.

And Benji knew she was another thing he would no longer be able to afford if he left his current life and went home.

Benji took a deep breath and closed his eyes for a moment…and when he opened his eyes, it was as if a huge weight had been lifted from his spirit.

"I'll visit the old neighborhood this weekend," he thought to himself.

"Or the week after…"

Then, with a huge, dazzling smile illuminating a charisma intended to charm paint off the wall, he exclaimed to his assistant with a sly wink, "Well, all right…let's go get 'em, teammate."

But I watched after Benji with some sadness as he departed. Clearly— in life, whether you "win" or "lose"…there always seems to be a price to pay.

Because…I don't think I'd ever seen him smile quite that way ever before. His now over the top smile had never been quite THAT big.

For me, it didn't seem quite…real. For good reason.

It wasn't.

CHAPTER 8

SOMEBODY'S GOTTA WIN, SOMEBODY'S GOTTA LOSE

Benji stuck out his hand, and Johnny slapped it in a display of misbegotten solidarity. Benji narrowed his eyes in dramatic fashion and addressing the current situation, said as hip as possible, "Ain't nothin' to it, J. D.—let's do this. In and out."

Benji's words did not betray his true feelings…he was terrified.

And for good reason. I saw clearly where the aftermath of this crossroads would lead. Maybe not specifically but it was clear to me no good would come from the path Benji was about to choose. I literally screamed at Benji, "No! You don't even need me to know THAT this is a huge mistake!"

I saw in Benji's eyes that he knew what I knew—I'd gotten through to him.

And yet…he was going to do it anyway.

Johnny slapped Benji's hand, gave a quick nod, and disappeared around the cornet at the speed of light.

Benji took a deep breath and glanced up and down the street— there was no one to be seen. Even the birds seemed to have stopped chirping, and to Benji, it seemed as if their eyes followed his every move. It was as if the entire neighborhood was frozen for this moment in time…completely motionless in fascination and anticipation as to what Benji would do next.

Benji glanced at his house to get a sense of whether or not his mama was passing by the window and possibly noticed her stationary middle son NOT on his way to school. Benji delayed a second; his feet seemed stuck to the ground. I knew in Benji's mind, it seemed like he delayed for an hour…and I knew why. Benji was unconsciously hoping his mother would come by the window, notice him, and scream for him to get to school, or maybe Nikki would come out on her way to school, a car would turn down his street and drive by, or anything would happen…anything that would halt the freeze, resume the flow of time, and disrupt the flow of events Benji and his delinquent neighbor were about to set in motion.

But fate was determined not to rescue Benji on this day. Benji looked after Johnny Davis and quickly followed him to his now inevitable destiny. He forced his feet into motion and willed himself to move faster…the sooner the deed was started, the sooner it would be done.

As soon as he was out of sight from the main street, he put his books down and turned his attention to the wannabe hoodlum who initiated this mess. Johnny was at the window but was standing there lingering until his accomplice came into view. Once the boys locked eyes, they both appeared to be silently telling each other the next step they took meant there was no turning back.

The boys looked up at the window, and Johnny silently looked at Benji, then imperceptibly at the ground, psychically indicating to Benji what he needed him to do. Benji wordlessly dropped on to all fours, and Johnny stepped on to his back and went to work on the window. Johnny teetered to balance on Benji's back as he began to work on the window's screen, which, though it was invisible to Benji on all fours, was bent nearly to the point of being severed. To get to the window, which was slightly ajar, Johnny expertly slid his fingers into the screen to gently dislodge it from the window frame; this was an extremely important detail, since if the screen was forcibly removed, it might not fit again when the boys tried to reinsert it into the frame.

Johnny maneuvered the screen with the skill of a professional and popped the screen out so easily, Benji instantly knew he'd done this before— probably numerous times. Johnny dislodged the screen and wordlessly handed the screen to Benji, who balanced on his knees and one arm to take the screen from his cohort and place it gently on the ground beneath him. I noted with frustration the boys seemed to be in sync.

It did not take much for Johnny to open the window wide enough for him to slither in and disappear from view. As he vanished, Benji stood up; he heard the sounds of steps and voices coming closer and closer. Not directly to where he was…he could tell there was a group of people walking down the sidewalk outside the house. He distinctly heard girls' laughter…girls his age…probably on the way to school.

He remained frozen in place as he waited for the voices to pass by or indicate they knew he was there and up to no good. He secretly wished it was Angela…or even Nikki. He wished his sisters' eyes were drawn directly to him and they started screaming, "Benji! What are you doing! I'm gonna tell!" But they were nowhere to be found.

As the group of girls who were not his sisters wandered aimlessly by, Benji noted he had seen them in school, but he couldn't remember their names. He thought he'd seen one of them— the most beautiful girl in the group with the dark hair. Maybe at a dance or something, but he couldn't focus— his mind was solely dominated by his fear and the irrational belief that if he remained immobile, he would somehow become invisible. But too engrossed in their own conversation and each other, the teenage girls did not see Benji as they passed by the residence on their way to school.

Just like Benji should have been doing.

In the aftermath of nearly being discovered, Benji remained nearly motionless as he seriously contemplated a thought: Why didn't he just leave? He didn't want to go in; he had assisted his neighbor, but— it wasn't like Johnny would snitch on him because doing so would involve admitting his own involvement. Neither boy was able to snitch on the other, no matter what, not for any reason. Of course, Johnny might want to fight him if he did as he was considering— but after humiliating Tootie Mo, Benji was unconcerned with fighting Johnny Davis. So Johnny Davis might have gotten angry, but Benji's reputation after that fight might have tempered any aggressive feelings on Johnny's part. That…plus his newfound friendship (kind of) with Nick Thomas. So Benji deliberated his new idea: Why didn't he simply go? He stared at the open window for what seemed like an eternity, and for a moment, I thought he might just leave Johnny Davis with his criminal ideals alone in AP's house.

I wanted Benji to leave, but truthfully...I didn't know if leaving would have altered the chain of events that had been already set in motion. I know every decision results in an altered future state, but for some reason, I was not permitted to see or even sense what the result would be or even could be if Benji simply decided he would leave. But even without my guardian insight— leaving had to be preferable to entering a dangerous man's home...right?

In an instant, Benji resolved any conflicting ideas he had on the matter. I don't know why he made the decision he made, but with a deep breath and a little leap, he and after a minor struggle to get his footing and pull himself up, Benjamin Frazier crawled through AP's window, and slipping in headfirst as Johnny did, he stealthily entered the home of the notorious Arthur Parker.

Benji crawled through the window on his stomach, and since his eyes were not yet adjusted to the darkness, he stuck out his hands to find the floor and support his weight. Once his vision cleared, he could see his hands were a few inches from the floor, so he realized he would have to fall in and swing his feet away from anything he might disturb or break upon landing. Once he was comfortable he devised a landing strategy, he let his body drop to the floor, using his arms to cushion the landing and guide his feet and body to a safe space. The entry was perfect. Nothing was broken, and he landed a pile of clothes laying haphazardly on the floor.

He was in.

Benji stood and surveyed his surroundings.

It was obvious he landed in the bedroom, darkened and smelling faintly of cigarettes, incense, and some other weird, thick smell. The bed sat low to the floor…in fact, it was on the floor and ruffled. Benji saw pictures of beautiful semi-naked women hanging on the wall, a dynamite "Velvet Smooth" poster was on the wall too, an ashtray by the bed that hadn't been emptied in about a year, it seemed, some kind of mirror with what looked like baby powder on it, and as his vision cleared, Benji saw a girl's wrinkled yellow panties on the bed.

There was a low music sound playing from an eight-track somewhere in the room. It was the People's Choice, over and over with a mesmerizing, thumping bass line Benji was familiar with. He almost forgot where he was as he listened to the almost- hypnotic beat in the semi-darkness. Hearing Johnny Davis's movement in the next room awakened him from his stupor.

He was keenly aware he wanted to get out of there.

Benji walked through the beads that hung from the door frame into the sparsely furnished living room. There was an explosion of color in the living room, but even Benji realized the furniture was old and faded. The furnishings consisted of a bright blue couch that used books to prop it up instead at least one of the legs and a green beanbag chair that was ripped and fixed with some kind of tape. The television looked kind of like the one Benji watched at home, but older—a big brown bulky box with the knobs missing and aluminum foil on the antennae. Benji literally tip toed through the living room as if he was afraid he would break something if he moved too fast. Johnny Davis came out of another room and glanced at Benji as he darted past and made his way into the bedroom to look for AP's gangster treasure. Benji thought, "We're here checking how AP is living, but the truth was, there was not much to check." It was like a normal house…kind of. It smelled different, for sure, and Benji was fairly certain there were some kind of drugs in the bedroom, and there were the panties, of course. Benji almost wanted another look at those, but he had seen panties before, normally when he was sneaking to put peanut butter on his sisters' panties because he thought it was funny. But Benji imagined he was going to see piles of guns and drugs and tons of alcohol and fur coats like in *The Mack* or maybe the last vestiges of a crazy, wild party…something like in *Super Fly*. But for the most part, it was just…a simple house like a bunch of houses he'd seen before.

The knowledge had Benji in a daze as he wandered from the living room into the kitchen, where sunshine was streaming through the window and was well lit— pretty much like any other kitchen he'd been in. There was a small table with two raggedy chairs off to the side by the kitchen door, and Benji sat, though he jumped up immediately as he heard the chair scrape against the kitchen tile. Curious, he opened the refrigerator and examined its humble contents— a half gallon of milk, ketchup, a pan with some kind of leftover food in it, a block of cheese, and a carton of eggs. As Benji slowly closed the refrigerator door, a thought crept into his consciousness: he was not going to take anything from this house. He didn't want to look for anything to take. He just wanted to leave.

Johnny Davis entered the kitchen, and he looked a little frustrated, probably because he had come to the same realization Benji had come to— there was nothing there to steal.

"Man, this mother fucker ain't got nothing in here."

Johnny sounded almost disappointed as the two boys stood in the kitchen waiting to make their next move. Benji felt relieved the ordeal appeared to be coming to an end and that they would soon be leaving.

"What'd you get?"

"Now Johnny is the one asking questions?" Benji thought ironically. But Benji was not in the mood to answer any of Johnny's questions. He was tired of being in this place. And even more than that— he was tired of being around Johnny Davis. Rather than answer, Benji elected to stare at Johnny with dead eyes…dead eyes didn't answer the question or even acknowledge a question had been asked. Dead eyes make a questioner feel stupid for asking a question or even speaking. They were dead eyes— dead eyes can't be faked. It was what Benji truly felt.

Johnny shrugged, and after looking around the kitchen for a minute, the self-described leader proclaimed, "Well, we gotta do something…we can't just come up in this mother fucker and leave."

Without a word, Johnny began opening cabinets until he found two bowls, and he placed both on the table, one in front of Benji. Next, he went and presented a box of Waffelos and filled each bowl nearly to the top with sweet, maple-flavored cereal. As he moved to the refrigerator, presumably for milk, he spitefully muttered, "This mother fucker ain't got shit, so we gonna eat his food."

What did he mean...we?

Benji's disbelief was now threatening to turn into full-blown rage. "I was on my way to school," he silently fumed. "We break into AP's house... I almost get spotted...we walk around...there's nothing here...and now we're eating cereal I could eat at home...so...we broke in here for nothing!"

Johnny Davis was busy slurping sweet Waffelos out of his bowl, and Benji literally had to hold himself back from smacking the spoon out of his hand and choking him with his bare hands . He stared at Johnny Davis and thought, "Why am I here? I got my own friends...I even been to parties at Nick's place where I ain't gotta sneak in. He can't beat me up...and he's always talking about what girls I talk to, and I never even seen him with a girl!! What am I doing?"

But just then...Benji has a thought that pushed away his escalating rage. A terrifying notion. A moment of chilling reality.

There was milk in the refrigerator.

Milk.

In the refrigerator.

Milk spoils.

If AP was going to be gone for a week, why did he leave milk in his refrigerator?

And as a matter of fact...why was the People's Choice tune *"Nursery Rhymes"* now humming from the eight-track in the bedroom? Why hadn't AP turned it off if he was going to be gone for a week?

AP wasn't gone. He was coming back. He could be back any moment.

Benji knew he had to go. And right now.

Johnny was leisurely finishing his cereal and looked like he was prepared to go for a second bowl when Benji, with absolute steel in his voice, commanded the room saying, "Check this out - you one stupid mutha fucka - for real. How AP gonna be gone for a week leaving milk in the mother fuckin refrigerator and music playing and shit?? He ain't doin no 7…he probably at work. You do whatever you want. I'm 'bout ta book, catch you on the flip side."

As Benji spoke, the look on Johnny's face slowly changed from one of complete scorn to a mask of pure horror as he realized his next- door neighbor was right. He jumped up almost whispering to himself, "Yeah…shit! We gotta go! C'mon, Doo—help me wash these dishes real quick!"

All the cool had been drained from Johnny's voice, attitude, and mannerisms. The pleading look in his eyes told the entire story. The boys stared at each other, but Benji didn't care…Benji again contemplated simply leaving. He wanted to. Being in Johnny's presence only threatened to further enrage him, but even through his anger, Benji felt a just a small hint of sympathy for the petrified young boy Johnny had turned into in front of his very eyes.

"C'mon, hurry up then."

"And stop calling me Doo."

Benji was in command now.

The boys hurriedly dumped the cereal, washed out the bowls, and returned the bowls and utensils to where they got them. After a quick inspection and confirming the kitchen looked as it was, the boys reversed their steps through the living room and back into the bedroom to depart. With the work done, Benji considered just leaping through the window first and leaving Johnny to get out the best way he knew how, but remembering the panic-stricken look on his face, he looked back assertively and quickly motioned to for him to get through the window. Johnny leaped up and through the window, seemingly in one motion, and just like that, he was out of the house.

Benji followed suit, and he noted it was much easier getting out of the house than it was to get in. As Benji climbed through the window, he realized Johnny had left him— he made it enough of the way through the window to see Johnny disappear around the corner, running as fast as he could in the opposite direction of their school.

"I don't need that sucka anyway," Benji thought sullenly to himself. He marveled he wasn't nervous even a little bit as he shimmied through the window and on to the ground below. As he dropped to the ground, he felt strong. Powerful. He didn't feel like running. He had a clear mind— if he ran, someone would notice him running. Or worse…he wouldn't notice someone who was noticing him. He had to be smart now…stay focused and aware. He took three or four steps toward the street when his newfound awareness served him well.

He hadn't put the screen back.

And without Johnny to stand on—there was no way to get it back inside the window frame.

Benji walked back to the window and looked up at the screen and quickly realized there was no way to put it back the way it had been before. So Benji held up the screen as close as he could to the window and let it drop. Then he did it again…then he did it again. He wanted to see where the screen might land if it just happened to fall from the window…maybe AP would believe the wind blew it off. Or a bird landed on it…or some other random occurrence caused the screen to inexplicably fall out of the window frame that normally held it in place.

Maybe, I thought. It's possible.

"But what would he think about the open window behind the screen?" I called out to Benji as he smugly sauntered away in the direction of the school.

But Benji didn't hear me. He never could. It would be so much easier, but…unfortunately…it just didn't work that way.

Benji went to school as if nothing of consequence had happened that day, but as the day wore on, the confidence and strength he initially felt slowly evaporated as the weight of the morning's events became increasingly burdensome. As the day progressed, he almost felt as though he were walking through a dream sequence and everyone was talking and moving in fuzzy, super slow motion.

When he finally returned home after what had become the longest day ever, he went straight to his room and lay down to contemplate what had transpired. Shante called but he told his sister he was sick. He didn't want to talk; he wanted to disappear…stay home from school, never go out anywhere, and never be heard from again. He wondered aloud why it was unreasonable for the entire family to move away as fast as they could…he internally debated ideas he could present to Pops later to justify why the family should move.

The door opened— and there was Marcus standing in the doorway. He stood there for a minute, and though Benji did not make eye contact, he knew Marcus was looking at him…staring at him…studying him as if trying to figure put a complex puzzle.

"We got McDonald's."

Benji smelled the food; he wasnt hungry so he didn't answer and chose to continue to lay on his bed with his back to his older brother.

And Marcus knew then that something wasn't right.

"What it is, young blood?"

It was not just the words; this was how Marcus spoke to his friends or to other guys on the football team. But it was more than the words…it was the tone. It was more of an adult tone; it was an inviting tone, and it was sincere. Benji turned and opened his eyes just wide enough to see his older brother gazing at him with actual interest…and waiting tolerantly for how Benji would respond. As the brothers exchanged glances for a time than seemed much longer than it actually was. And looking at Marcus, Benji knew…

He knew…that Marcus knew.

He probably didn't know the specifics…no, he definitely didn't know the specifics…but he knew something was up.

Benji looked at his brother and genuinely wished he could tell him what was going on; if he could tell him, he knew that Marcus would know what to do. He wanted to tell his brother how he had done something stupid; he wanted to tell his brother how he had been weak and listened to their stupid neighbor even though they both knew how much of a loser he was. He wanted to tell his brother how he had done something he truly did not want to do, how scared he had been when he did it, how they had done it for no reason at all, and how panicked he was now because it seemed like everyone he saw knew exactly what he had done. He wanted his brother's advice…he wanted his brother's comfort…he wanted his brother to say something to make him laugh… he wanted his brother to walk with him for the rest of his life now and to protect him. Because that's what his brother would do.

But he just couldn't say the words. He wanted to…he almost did. But when he opened his mouth to speak, what came out with a forced but practiced smile did not demonstrate his true feelings:

"It's all due to the extract."

It was a phrase both boys had heard from their father when he was talking with his friends…or sometimes with Mama. It was an expression normally uttered when the men were drinking, and it meant…well…everything, but at the same time, absolutely nothing. It was just a funny thing to say to lighten a debate, provide comic relief to a more serious topic, or make a point without making a point. None of the Frazier brothers ever heard anyone else use the term. Benji thought it was something his father brought with him from Memphis, Pops's hometown. But it was definitely a Pop-ism and a Frazier family trademark.

Marcus looked quizzical for a moment, then grinned at the explanation; his response was also a Pop-ism and the only acceptable response:

"What you know 'bout that doo bob quiver, black?"

The men never failed to bellow in absolute joy at this. It never occurred to Benji that perhaps the men were usually drunk and would probably laugh at anything during these lighthearted moments. But what did occur to Benji was the interaction had done with Marcus exactly what it did with Pops and his friends.

It disarmed the conversation and changed the topic.

The brothers shared laughter, and after sitting with him for a little while longer, Marcus slapped him five, and after looking back and peering at his little brother one last time, he left and closed the door behind him.

And once again…Benji was alone with his thoughts. He couldn't go to the party; that'd be dangerous now. He didn't sleep well that night.

But by morning's light, Benji felt much better. He was determined to feel better…because after all, nothing was missing, right? Nothing was broken, right? And nobody saw him anyway, right? He'd been extra careful…nothing was going to happen! He had dodged a bullet though, because what if AP had caught them in his house? Or if he or one of his friends had been coming down the street when they left? That would have been bad, but since none of that happened, it was a lesson learned— a lesson Benji silently vowed to always remember, and a lesson he promised to himself he would never repeat. Kind of like never waving to girls he didn't know.

That kind of stuff can blow up in a young blood's face. That's why he promised himself to never do it again. And he kept that promise.

Over the next few days, things began to return more and more to normal for Benji. He saw Johnny Davis playing street football while on his way to Brian's house and to show his contempt, he watched with sincere disinterest until Johnny dropped a sure touchdown pass (past the old raggedy red car with the taped up windows) and got savaged without mercy by the quarterback in front of everyone for the fumble.

"Doo Doo, you wanna get down? Take this soft ass nigga's place. Mother fucker scared to catch the rock even when ain't nobody hittin' his ass!"

Everybody on both teams laughed. Benji looked right at Johnny Davis and laughed too. "That pitiful look ain't gonna save you this time, sucka," Benji thought derisively. Benji continued to chuckle to himself at Johnny's misfortune before declining the invitation with a wave and heading over to Brian's house.

Talking without saying a word—another one of Marcus's "Frazier Man" rules. But the fact Benji remembered and did it so naturally meant that he was starting to feel better again.

It was a good time at Brian's house. Spring vacation was almost over, and when school started again, Benji would have to be inside before the street lights came on—which Benji thought was kind of silly since he was already fifteen. But since everyone was still out of school, Mama was relaxing a little bit and letting Benji spend the night at Brian's so they could go to the skating rink later. Benji loved hanging out with his funny, artistic friend. Brian would normally practice his guitar, which was cool because Brian also had this new handheld electronic football game for Benji to play while Brian practiced…and Brian's mom always kept the snacks coming. Brian loved to play the guitar and he was already writing songs that he always wanted to try out with his friends first. Benji thought Brian's songs were OK—he even wrote one real funky song with no words yet, but Brian called it *"French Toast Movie"*…french toast…it figured Brian would name a song after the thing he liked next best after music. Benji liked to hear his friend play, but he really liked hearing Brian play songs he recognized and sometimes sang along with; Brian could play the bass line to *"Brick House,"* and Brian was getting really good at playing the funky parts on *"Slide."*

But tonight? No time for cool new handheld football games and definitely no time for guitar practice. Tonight… it was all about the skating rink.

Benji loved the skating rink. He couldn't really skate too well like some of those cats he saw skating backward and doing circles, but he could skate around and around in a circle, holding a girl's hand, without falling; he loved the colored lights and the music, and everyone always seemed to be there, laughing and cutting up. But tonight he loved it for a different reason—that dark-haired girl wasn't going to the skating rink. She was staying home; Benji didn't think she went out very much. Shante was going, but he planned to ditch her to go over to that dark-haired girl's house. So Benji hatched a plan: once Brian's mom dropped them off, he was going to sneak over there. He'd finally talked to her a few times since seeing her in front of AP's house; he'd needed to check to see what she saw. Or maybe he just thought he saw her…she'd never said anything about it.

Anyways —she laughed a lot when Benji was around, and their interactions seemed easy. So that dark-haired girl said something about watching television. *Wonder Woman* and *The Incredible Hulk* were on since it was Friday night. That would normally be copacetic, but watching television would take too long; he had to be back at the skating rink. Beside, she had sisters and brothers. Too crowded. Benji wasn't interested in TV. He wanted to hang out on her porch with her then head back…maybe see if he could find Shante and skate around a little bit. If he felt like it.

Because he was going see if he could kiss that dark-haired girl…even on the cheek. Even on her hand. "Tonight's the night," he thought elatedly with a huge smile. He wasn't exactly sure how he was going to get her to want to kiss him though. Maybe he'd quote some song lyrics at her, real super smooth-like; that would definitely be player-style, especially if he quoted song lyrics that had her name in it. That was one of the benefits of occasionally listening to pop tunes and folk music; when he quoted the lyrics to sound like a player, nobody ever recognized the words.

Once they were dropped off, Benji waited until he was sure Brian's mother was gone. Brian knew where he was going, but he didn't care…he was going to meet Ricky to hang out anyway. Benji just knew he had to get there and get back. Brian's mom always came back early, even before she told the boys when they had to be ready to get picked up; she would come back early and wait in the parking lot. Sometimes she would get out of the car, go looking for the boys, want to hug them once she found one, then make the boy she found stay there until she found every child she was giving a ride to. Brian didn't mind—and honestly, Benji didn't mind either. He might have considered it annoying coming from someone else, but hey…this was Brian's mom, and that's just the way she was. Kind of like…a black Carol Brady. That lady on the funny show with all the kids.

But it meant Benji had to get going. He momentarily considered asking his friends to go with him. Brian would probably go after some prodding; Ricky would agree immediately just to see if he could kiss one of the dark- haired girl's sisters. But if they went, his kissing plan was sunk—so dismissing the idea almost instantly, he decided to head over alone. He figured he'd have about an hour to try to make her laugh some more and sneak a kiss in before he had to get back to the skating rink.

So the journey began.

The area outside the skating rink was an even tougher part inside a tough part of San Diego. Even so, Benji proceeded unconcerned…he'd walked these streets numerous times, going to parties, playing ball, and just hanging out. He'd sneak over here when he was younger…kind of like now. When he was younger, sometimes he and his friends used to just start running for no reason when they saw cops. The game was to see if they could make the cops chase them…just because they thought it was funny. Another time, just last year, he was shocked to see his friend "Little Charles" driving a car. Little Charles was not much older than Benji, but though I told him he shouldn't get in the car…as usual Benji did it anyway. The too-young-to-drive teens sped around the neighborhood at extremely high speeds until they caught the attention of a policeman who did give chase…

Little Charles was doing eighty miles per hour or more in the residential neighborhood; Benji had been scared that night…but scared like he was scared on the roller coaster. The boys were laughing and yelling and bouncing around in the car…until they crashed into a ditch. Benji thought for sure the gig was up, but the car was covered by shrubs and small trees. The boys sat still and hunched down on the floor but amazingly, two policemen drove up real slow, got out and seemed to shine the light right on them…and they didn't see them. Apparently unconcerned with wreckage, the policemen didn't investigate further and just backed up, then drove away. The boys got out laughing and giving each other dap…and they weren't even hurt.

I may have had something to do with that. I'm not an angel, but…sometimes I get lucky with my guardian powers.

So for those reasons and many others, Benji was unconcerned as he made his way through the streets outside the skating rink. He was more focused on practicing and repracticing his strategy on kissing and getting kissed. Mental rehearsals took a lot of his focus, and as he walked, he thought himself practiced enough to pull off his plan and make it seem natural.

Which explains why he did not notice the dark-colored Chevy Impala until it passed by him slowly for the third time.

When he saw it, Benji immediately sensed the danger. They called the area down the street from the skating rink "the zoo": there were bars, domino clubs, prostitutes, drug deals going down, people just hanging out; music seemed to come from every direction at once…but nothing normally happened this early. Any car slowing down while going in the direction Benji was walking and then speeding up again, then repeating the action, was more than a little bit odd.

Benji was tempted to peer inside the car in hopes of seeing Little Charles or some other acquaintance—even though he may not know them very well, he hoped whoever was in the car would not represent danger. But Benji knew that if he did not know the occupants, they would likely consider staring inside the car an act of aggression; additionally, since he was not wearing his glasses, he wouldn't be able to see who was inside anyway. So Benji almost instantaneously decided to just maintain a calm exterior and continue walking. "I need to just chill out," Benji quietly mused.

And then the car stopped. Right in the middle of the street.

Four men got out of the car, and now their intentions were crystal clear. After exiting the still- running vehicle, the four men headed straight for where Benji was standing.

Benji had never been through this before…not even when he'd been jumped by the Mexicans or chased home by the Filipino gang. He always escaped before, but those were boys, and though it was dangerous, Benji never had this sense of foreboding. Because these were not boys…they were not teens…these were men who were coming toward him now with obvious malice. And though Benji did not have his glasses on, there was one thing he could clearly see.

One of the men was Arthur Parker.

Benji slowly retreated when he recognized the feared gangster while keeping his eye on the rapidly advancing men. He turned halfway around to see what was behind him—it was his instinct to immediately assess the situation for an escape route so he could run but he saw that he was cornered in a closed lot with no alley for him to escape.

He was trapped.

"You been in my house, motherfucker."

Oddly enough— it was the first time Benji had ever heard the man speak. Arthur Parker was an almost mythical figure in Southeast Dago, and to hear him speak in that low-pitched, ominous rumble of a voice was almost enthralling in its own right…if Benji had not been paralyzed by intense fear. Benji immediately understood AP's declaration was not a question. It was a statement of fact and given in the malicious tone that served as an advance explanation as to what was getting ready to happen.

And through the lights of the street lamps, Benji saw the gleam of a knife in Arthur Parker's hand.

His instinct was still to run, but he knew he was trapped and was aware that three of the men moved to cut off any possible escape. Then they closed in on Benji, and forming a human wall between Benji and the street, they turned to face the street while shielding a still advancing Arthur Parker.

As he continued to retreat, thoughts flooded Benji's mind. He wondered if what was coming would hurt very much. In that moment, he saw his father looking stoic, lost and trying hard not to cry. He saw his mother screaming inconsolably and his sisters both holding her, each of the Frazier women sobbing uncontrollable tears. He saw his brothers standing off to one side in matching suits, stiff, sad, and unsure what to do, and he saw Marcus wipe at his eyes and grab Sid's hand to hold it…and Sid let him. He saw himself lying in the dirty cold lot with only empty liquor bottles, trash, used needles, spoiled food, and broken glass for company.

Arthur was close now, and Benji looked him in the eye. He was so close, Benji could see the redness in his tired, wild eyes; he could almost taste the smell of alcohol coming from his breath, and his nose was assaulted by the thick smell of cigarette smoke, weed, and incense trapped in his clothes.

It didn't occur to Benji to beg for his life or cry out. Strangely, he felt a sense of pride for not doing so…it was as if he was almost happy to know what he was inside. He thought back to the fight with Tootie and the confrontation with Topaz; he stood a little taller knowing even under stress or threat of physical danger, he would not break. He just stared at all four men with the cold eyes of the fearless. But Benji knew— even if he started crying like a baby or begged for his life on his knees, he knew it would make no difference at all.

Or would it?

But then without a word, holding Benji tight with one hand, he pulled Benji in close, seemed to snarl, and held him there while he punched him hard in his stomach— not only once…not twice…not three times…but four times, and upon the impact of the final punch, Benji slumped to the ground. But it didn't hurt, and Benji marveled at that. Even though he'd been punched four times by Arthur Parker and was on the ground, he was shocked that he was in no pain and felt a sense of gratitude realizing Arthur had only punched him.

But then it came.

Hot, searing, pain...

Benji grasped at it in his belly and found it was accompanied by a warm, red slickness that washed over Benji's teenage hands as Benji felt compelled to play with the warm slickness flowing between his fingers. The pain washed over Benji like a slow wave...and I knew if he could catch a breath, he would have had no choice but to cry out, but the pain was so intense it literally took his breath away. All his energy and focus were on breathing...but each breath increased Benji's agony until he started to lose consciousness from the intensity of the pain.

I moved in closer to comfort Benji. I knew he needed me more than ever now.

When Benji regained consciousness a short time later, he could hear cars driving by and music playing in the distance...but his vision began to fail him. Thankfully, the pain started to subside...but his stomach still felt very hot.

So very hot. But not painful anymore. Just blazing hot. Like his stomach was on fire.

Benji could smell the blood which started to pool around him in larger and larger quantities. Though barely hanging on to consciousness, he thought his blood smelled almost... like metal? He tried to open his eyes to look at his wounds, to see if it was really his own blood he was smelling, but...his vision was rapidly deteriorating...he couldn't see anything now. He could still hear— but his world had gone dark.

Even though the pain subsided a little, Benji found himself panicking as the sounds of the world around seemed to begin to drift away as well. He was aware that he was panting harder and harder...breathing faster and faster. He tried catch a single breath to control it, but he couldn't. He thought to himself that he needed to get up…but as he tried to will his body to rise, he could only manage to wiggle a single toe…and there was no one there to hear him whisper "I need to go home now…"

No one…except me.

Benji felt a sense of comfort as his panting finally slowed…and he was thrilled when he saw his mother approaching him. His eyes opened wide as he looked at her and thought, "Mama has come to rescue me…she's come to take me home." But his mother did not rescue him. She sat by his side, just as she sat by him in the car in those younger days…and they sang together. Benji's voice was no more than a whisper as he sang along with Mama and waited for his favorite part…Mama's favorite part…the part his mama always thought was so cute…

Benji did not have the strength to lift his finger to his lips, but he looked at his mama and whispered, "Shhhhh."

Mama smiled…like she always did at that part.

Benji was getting cold…he began to shiver uncontrollably…he was really, really tired now…he wanted badly to sleep…and he almost did. But his mother continued singing, and Benji's eyes jerked open as she got to the point of the song Benji wanted to finish… the part that asked for forgiveness. He tried in vain to mouth the words to their song.

Mama tilted her head, nodded and smiled at her beloved Benji again. He smiled back…comforted in knowing he was forgiven.

Benji saw the face of the beautiful, dark-haired girl who'd passed by AP's house that fateful morning; the girl he'd been going to visit…and she sat by his mother. What was she doing here? She was smiling too.

Benji looked directly at me and whispered to me, "I know her."

He could see me now.

For Benji, his world of darkness changed into a world of blinding white light now, the brightest light he'd ever seen. Benji didn't even realize lights could be that bright— whereas at first he could not see because of the darkness… now he could not see because of the light. As the light got increasingly brighter, it was accompanied by a roar— a sound as if every loud noise that had ever been made from the beginning of time all decided to play at maximum volume simultaneously. Then the entire area began to vibrate uncontrollably like the whole world was gripped by the same violent earthquake. The scene become brighter…louder… with ever more furious vibrations…until the whole scene seemed to meld into a single all-out combination of brilliance, clamor, and movement—and in the uproar, I lost Benji…I couldn't see him anymore. And then…

It all stopped.

Now, people in white were hurriedly rushing toward us as Benji, in a state of total calm, smiled at me. Even his eyes smiled. I knew he was tired, but he wouldn't close his eyes. He wouldn't because he could still see me, his mama, the dark-haired girl…and also a sweet, comforting presence that had just emerged from what seemed like chaos just a few moments previous.

Benji was determined to see us, to keep looking at us all…so he refused to close his eyes. He fought the urge. He kept looking at all of us with a hint of a smile in his eyes.

The people in white came close enough to touch Benji. They were talking to him now, trying to make sure he stayed awake…they were treating his wounds, doing everything possible to stop the flow of blood. They began giving him oxygen to help his breathing. Everyone was working on Benji… furiously…almost frantically…determinedly…and hurriedly…but ultimately…and finally…

Benjamin Frazier Jr., just fifteen years old…with eyes wide open…slept.

CHAPTER 9

EVERYTHING'S COMING UP LOVE

B enji slowly surveyed the scene and took it all in.
Everybody was here...how many years had it been? Though the family remained close, overcoming every daunting hill and rising from every inevitable valley, as adults tend to do, they'd all met their own crossroads, made their own decisions, chosen their own paths, and gone their own ways over time. This was the reality of life.

But the family came back together like this for weddings...and also for funerals.

Today it was a wedding. Nikki's daughter was getting married and the event had brought them all together.

Benji truly loved and appreciated days like today. It would be a day full of big, sincere smiles —the kind that warm hearts and create lasting memories. There'd be tight hugs, constant laughter, and affection born of history, decades of commitment, struggle, and shared triumph; a reaffirmation of loyalties never forgotten and not dimmed by the passage of time or length of absence.

And there'd be food— a veritable feast. He was happy his niece ignored those who said fried chicken was not a wedding food...the menu included country fried chicken with white gravy on the side, pot roast, macaroni and cheese, sweet potato casserole, mashed potatoes, southern green beans, greens, cornbread, rolls, deviled eggs...Benji had no intention of going anywhere near any salad that didn't have potatoes or macaroni in it and the colorful fruit was likewise safe. But they were there too if anyone was so inclined. The color was pretty and made for a beautiful spread even if no one touched the healthier wedding alternatives.

Benji was normally not a huge fan of wedding cakes; he didn't think they were sweet enough. But this cake had promise...Nikki had ordered a cake where each piece of the cake was going to be a different flavor: lemon, strawberry, chocolate, vanilla, caramel...Benji was a sugar addict and ready to take up the challenge of getting through each one of the flavorful treasures contained within the sugary temptation.

Then the music and the dancing would come. They would all take turns dancing with the beautiful bride and with each other. It was a family with a wide diversity of musical tastes, which the bride and groom respected—they would all jostle to dance with Mama to Frank Sinatra's "*The Way You Look Tonight*"; Benji would grab whichever female relative was nearest when they played his requested, "*How Sweet It Is to Be Loved By You*"; Beyonce's "*Single Ladies*" would be a hit with the family's women, and everybody would dance with everybody when the ultra-popular *"Cupid Shuffle"* inevitably got remixed into a fifteen-minute song.

Benji didn't know how to do that dance yet, but he vowed to learn it today.

All families have stories stretching back to when its elders were adults, when its adults were children, and when its children were infants, stories told over and over, the punchlines and endings known but still told with relish as if it were the first time telling it or hearing it. And they would use the time not just to rehash the old stories and memories. Since everyone was here, there was time to catch up…to fill in the blanks created by the necessity of separate roads dictated by life, fate, and destiny that had been taken by the individual members of the Frazier family.

Almost everyone was there.

Pops had passed away two years ago, and though merriment was in the air, his loss stung and was felt by all. His father was the hardest-working man Benji had ever known. He did whatever was necessary to ensure there was harmony…and food… in the home. Benji marveled at his father's humor when he overheard his dad and the other men cutting up, but with his family, there was a simple all-encompassing goal—ensure their well-being. Pops was just not a simple garbage man…he'd served during World War II, earning three Bronze Stars and a Meritorious Service Medal. He was a hero, at war and at home. None of them would have been anything without the most influential man any of them had ever known. Nikki wanted to do a tribute to their dad during the wedding, but Mama gently nixed the idea, saying he wouldn't have wanted it— always humble, he would have wanted to keep the focus on the wedding. But no one could nix the feeling of absence they all felt in their hearts at seeing the empty place at the table Nikki had ensured would be set for her daddy.

Mama was in her seventies now, still alert, strong, and even more beautiful and mentally feisty today than she had been thirty years ago. Her vibrancy was undeniable, and even her gradually diminishing eyesight could not lessen the sparkle in her eye. Watching her play with her grandchildren reminded Benji of the woman who, when asked by her children how the record player worked, had responded, "a red light comes on in the studio whenever we play the record… they have to get up and play when they see the light." She was also the woman who told her children she was the first woman to play for the Harlem Globetrotters—and they believed her. Benji's mama had the skill to cook with her girls one minute, then play football with her boys the next. She could still make each of her five children and numerous grandchildren all feel as special as an only child but feel simultaneously like a committed, loyal Frazier family member. Family was everything.

Angela was a professor of sociology now. She'd married in her thirties, and had two sons, ages nine and seven . Benji thought his oldest sister was too driven to ever have a family, plus she shouldered such numerous responsibilities as the oldest, Benji would not have been surprised if she had permanently run away from the responsibility of raising kids. But there she was, doting over her sons just like she had cared for her siblings. Her boys were a little "proper," but a little time with their uncles would definitely loosen them up. Her husband was plenty boisterous, and it occurred to Benji that his sister married someone who was like her brothers. Benji imagined despite being a professor and all… she missed her siblings.

Marcus was a supervisor with an aerospace manufacturing company, in charge of integrating his company's component designs with other aircraft. His beautiful ex-wife gave him three equally beautiful daughters aged twenty-two, twenty-one, and eighteen. He was never one to be without a gorgeous lady on his arm, and his second wife added a son to his brood. Though his athletic build had not totally left him, the beginning of a paunch initiated his entry into middle age. Still as bombastic and charismatic as ever, he remained the loudest of the Frazier men, could still be found relentlessly teasing his younger brothers on occasion— but Benji knew he was proud and freely bragged about them every chance he got.

Nikki was living a storybook romance with the man of her dreams in a house a couple of blocks away from where the Fraziers grew up. Benji recalled when they used to play the Game of Life, Nikki was the one who had to give her spouse peg a name; the same peg everyone got when they passed the marriage square, Nikki had to name hers and have conversations with the peg. She named all the children too, always with different names. She never even cared if she won…she was just famous in the family for holding up the game by having conversations with little blue and pink pegs that represented her husband and children while her brothers would yell at her to "Just spin the wheel! Come on, Nik!" But she was such a great mother to her twenty-one-year-old daughter who could have been her twin and to her twelve-year-old son as well. It was amazing how much she was like Mama in that regard.

Sid was a stock broker and a good one...even great. Ever since he'd been a child, he'd been drawn to unpredictable endeavors that offered fun and adventure, and not only did he love his work, but he was also described as having brilliant instincts, even though he could not convince his financially conservative family to invest. He'd married a woman who could almost match his infectious energy—a kindred spirit who shared his love of fun and laughter. They had plans to start their own investment firm together so they could rotate between making money and raising their two sons.

Benji was thrilled his childhood friend Brian was at the wedding. Benji was somewhat surprised that his long time friend had finally curbed his insatiable appetite—he was slimmed down now and in great shape, but he still laughed like a jolly fat man. But to no one's surprise, he had never curbed his appetite for music. He was going to play today.

Brian's presence only highlighted Ricky's absence, though. Benji was devastated a few years ago upon learning Ricky had been shot in the face and killed while defending his sister Lety from an abusive boyfriend. Benji kept imagining his fearless friend charging in to defend his sister. It was like the Ricky he remembered, but Benji's world was permanently lessened by Ricky's senseless slaughter. He wished Ricky were here today.

Shante was also absent; she'd ended up joining the military, which surprised Benji when he heard. Nikki said she was still in the navy, with the top rank of master chief officer commander or something like that; he couldn't keep up with that military stuff. She had a high rank though; was the first woman to do something or other - Benji was unsure what. Tina had been a lifelong friend, ever since that day she'd walked up behind him and started speaking Swahili. She went by her given name of Tatiana now, had moved to another state after college and married, so they only talked sporadically lately, but when they did, it was like they were locker mates all over again.

Thinking about the old days made Benji wonder what had ever happened to his old neighbor Johnny Davis. He'd barely seen him since that day long ago he refused to rob the house across the street with Johnny. He'd seen him around for a couple weeks or so, then he'd just disappeared and Benji lost contact. He finally eased people into not calling him "Ice"; it sent a message he didn't want sent. He'd heard a rumor about Johnny back then; he hoped it wasn't true though. It all seemed like a million years ago now.

He gazed with pride at his four beautiful but altogether different children: the supremely talented vocalist, twenty-one - year-old Tabitha, her father's physical twin, a musical marvel who had already made a popular gospel record as lead singer with her group; the fiercely independent and inventive nineteen-year-old Samara, smarter than her father had ever been with her 3.6 college grade point average and possibly following in her father's professional footsteps; the tall, physically imposing, and athletic Solomon, six feet six inches tall, already getting notice from several college basketball recruiters at sixteen; and his youngest, Abraham, handsome, intelligent, nearsighted, insightful and intense at age fourteen, and mildly spoiled by his sisters…just like his father had been all those years ago.

And as much as Nikki channeled their mother's familial spirit, Benji was determined to model his father's commitment, love, sacrifice, and dedication to his children.

Benji had known his dark-haired wife since they were teens; it all stemmed from that fateful youth conference.

They'd finally met and gotten a chance to talk during the conference, and Benji always swore his future wife was flirting with him— a charge she vehemently denied even until this day. All she would admit later was it was the first time she realized he wasn't a thug. She'd actually heard him say something funny at the conference and thought he was cute. When Benji said, "See? You had already noticed me!" she calmly pointed out, "Yes, but you noticed me first…I just got tired of waiting for you to talk!"

And she was right. He was totally mesmerized by her from first sight. He found it amusing she knew it and was willing to say it out loud. She found it amusing when Benji tried to use pop song lyrics that he thought she didn't know to try to sound smooth.

"With a little luck, you think we can work it out, huh?" she had thought with a laugh. He had tried so hard—they were at the Harbor Drive-In when he said it and she had laughed all the way through the first movie. Not because the movie was so funny—it was just so cute how he said it. Even today, he didn't know that she knew about his penchant for using obscure song lyrics back in the old days… when they first began.

But once initiated, their relationship advanced slowly; Benji found an increasing comfort in her presence. As they went from being acquaintances to being friends, Benji found it easy to make her laugh without trying to and found she had a way of interpreting his actions and emotions that made him feel more comfortable expressing his himself. In return, Benji became her sounding board and her champion and helped her frame her idealism against Southeast San Diego reality.

Their paths diverged after high school. Each chose a different path, but Benji constantly recalled the haunting silhouette of her excitedly waving goodbye on their last day together.

He missed her more than he would admit.

He wrote her a letter one day. There was nothing deep or intimate in his writing; he just explained what happened that day, just as he would have done if she was still there. Then he wrote another…and a postcard arrived from her… then another…then a letter. Secure in the knowledge he was reading the situation accurately, he wrote back, and before he knew it, he was writing every day…every single day. Sometimes twice a day. And though Benji was not what anyone would call romantic, even then…it was Benji who first wrote to her, "No matter how far away you are, remember when you look up in the sky at night, we're really not that far apart—we're always looking at the same moon. Don't forget."

It wasn't romantic to Benji. It was simply a fact he was pointing out.

Almost as soon as he dropped the letter in the mailbox, though, he wondered how he might recall it…he thought it was way too sensitive sounding. He immediately regretted sending it, but when the return letter came back from her, it closed with the phrase "Same moon."

Without realizing it, he'd completely melted her. Each of their letters closed that way from then on. And Benji had accurately defined the couple's philosophy for life.

Same moon.

Marriage for the two was entirely predictable. And with that, Benji was free to grow into the man he was destined to become with his dark-haired beauty of a wife as his full partner.

As the new Frazier family began to grow and develop, Benji realized that outside of his wife, he was for the most part unwilling to consider the emotions of others—and sometimes he didn't even consider hers. He found it difficult to even interpret emotions, and I knew why. So did his wife. Like many things in his life, it stemmed from teenage bullying—emotions never helped his situation. Without being able to gauge expressions, he was forced to go by his intuition and the result was a man who sometimes took offense when none was intended. Moreover, Benji was a man who grew to be unconcerned with emotions he could not interpret. His wife earned his trust…but with others, he struggled to respond to their emotional cues and needs even though, thanks to the advent of soft contact lenses, he could now see.

Many perceived Benji as arrogant, and though he was unconcerned, his wife was fully aware of this shortcoming and disarmed a trait that could have ultimately threatened her husband and their family. Using humor, insight, and a growing trust, she gently pointed out things Benji refused to or was unable to see. She helped him to make light of other things, to see the humor in other situations, and bolstered his own self-image in a way that made him more willing to give others the benefit of the doubt. Their intimacies bound them. I thought the way she would randomly pick up a box of dark chocolate, hug it, then suggestively look at her husband with a "What's my favorite flavor?" comment was genius. She also came to realize her husband was sometimes clueless on romance. Sometimes he got it right, but other times, his idea of romance was eating from her plate or drinking from her cup. She could see it from his view though; she knew Benji would not eat or drink after any other person, not even their children…only her— so that made it an intimacy between them. The sum of what she truly did was to provide an influence that completed Benji, settled him, and resulted in clearer, better, more informed choices in his life.

In short— she made him a better man.

Now she obviously didn't know quite as much as I did… but her influence definitely made my job easier.

Benji's natural tendency was toward introversion; I was often concerned for him during those early teenage days— for many young people, the continual attack on self-image often resulted in serious self-esteem issues through puberty, young adulthood, and adulthood. The opposite appeared to be true for Benji—as opposed to insecurity, he'd grown to be unconcerned with anyone's opinion of him. Though shy is not how anyone would describe him, he would abruptly leave a conversation or gathering with no notice and without comment if he'd decided it had consumed enough of his time. His wife softened that stance too, though—her humor and ability to carry on a conversation with whoever happened to be present allowed Benji the freedom to either observe the situation or get used to unfamiliar participants at his own speed, increasing his comfort during gatherings that did not involve family or close friends.

In truth, Benji often looked on in amazement at his wife's ability to liven up any atmosphere and to connect with various kinds of people. They shared their private jokes—Benji truly believed himself a great dancer, but his wife, a truly great dancer herself, would humorously point out to whoever was present that as sweet as Benji was, he couldn't dance to save his life. And Benji would always assert his dancing prowess by showing off the pop-lock moves of his youth, while his wife wryly asserted, "Those are the three moves he knows," before joining him in a short, spontaneous, musicless dance with her hand resting lightly on his stomach, fingers tapping imperceptibly to help Benji stay on the beat.

Benji still required solitude at times, but because they understood each other so well, each knew when the perfect time came for her to fulfill her own need to be around positive people, and Benji felt no resentment when those times came. And whenever Benji surprised his wife by saying "Same moon" with a kiss and a smile before she left at such times, she often hurried back, cutting the event short, to celebrate the bond she felt with her husband during those special times.

I know you know what I mean. Celebrate…yes…THAT kind of celebration.

But no relationship is a perfect one, of course, and despite their strong chemistry, the two had their inevitable bumps. Benji's wife was always concerned with harmony and tried to avoid conflict as much as possible, but she took criticism personally. When Benji offhandedly commented he wished she would calm down because he found her enthusiasm draining some times, it was a comment it took her years to forget. Though it was unintentional, there were other times her feelings were stung in similar fashion. Also, they were both extremely independent, a trait that can prove toxic to a relationship if both are not moving in a similar direction.

Benji's lack of emotional intelligence was also a source of occasional strife; his wife was not only keenly aware of her own emotions and emotional needs, but she also had an instinctive insight into the same for others as well. But it was not a talent that came to her husband naturally. He usually knew what he was thinking…but he either didn't know what he or others were feeling or didn't normally consider it significant. Yet these instances served as times to shake things up, which ultimately was to their advantage as each despised the routines that were common in marriage. They were both strong enough to stand their ground when necessary, smart enough to know when to give ground, and focused enough to remember their chemistry and connection when excessive moodiness threatened their bond.

I saw clearly what neither of them consciously realized—Benji relished the familial role his father had modeled for him his entire life: taking care of the family, being its strong protector and defender, sometimes silent, but enabling the connections that kept a family strong. His wife served as the family's inspiration, giving it excitement and color; she was its heart and soul, making sure love and passion were never far from the forefront. They started with no money, having spent all they had a used blue Mazda 323 and a 19-inch TV; those were their only possessions to start. But they grew together to expertly fit their family roles; and the same thing they did for their family as a unit they did for each other in all areas of their lives. It was a partnership marked by laughter, dreams, loyalty, support, and an almost ferocious defense of each other. And whenever they reminisced about where they first began, Benji wondered where he would have been if he had followed his plan of convincing his mother that he was too sick to participate in the youth conference. He told himself he would have "reeled her in eventually" no matter what path he'd chosen.

I knew differently.

I also knew that he might not have begun a different type of relationship with an extremely unlikely ally—Nick Thomas. The same Nick Thomas who as a youth, terrified Skyline, including parents, teachers, fellow students, and many of his fellow gangsters.

It was a condition of Nick's probation, his participation strongly recommended by his probation officer. Nick wasn't required to take part in the religious aspects of the conference, but anxious to have his four-year probationary period cut in half, he agreed to take part in a panel hoping to help the community to understand why its youth were attracted to the gang lifestyle. It was supposed to be a panel of three current gangbangers, but Nick was the only one to show. Surprisingly, he relished the opportunity to have the entire stage to himself, to tell his own story, and to represent gangbanging to the squares. What he didn't anticipate was the sincere questions and concern demonstrated to him that day; he didn't anticipate experiencing the strength and positivity that emanated from the event; he didn't anticipate the standing ovation he received in the aftermath of his session...and he didn't anticipate the offer to return. He didn't intend to go back...he shot pool, got drunk, then got high later that evening, in fact.

But something brought him back the next day.

Fate, perhaps.

He was surprised to see Benji there. He knew Benji was a square...a civilian...but he'd never forgotten this little kid blasting Tootie in his nuts. It was funny then—it was funny now— so when he nodded in recognition at Benji, he unknowingly started a conversation and partnership that would extend far beyond the end of the youth conference and would greatly impact both of their lives.

Benji and Nick became extremely involved in the community over time, and they were often introduced as having served the community since they were fifteen years old, a reference to their involvement with the youth conference in '78. That conference triggered a series of events which ultimately led to a partnership to fearlessly combat Southeast San Diego issues regarding street gangs, drug dealing, prostitution, depressed economics, and the apathetic schools that existed in the community. Both prescribed the best antidote to the issues was to prevent them from becoming issues in the first place. Each recognized the issues were vast and there was no one reason the community's men and women joined gangs. They realistically assessed they would not solve every issue but every thing they did, big or small, was better than doing nothing at all.

So the issue they focused on was youths who longed for a sense of community, who wanted to feel as if they belonged and were needed— who wanted to feel like they were "home." Neither Benji nor Nick was a great student, but they enlisted the assistance of those who were to create a tutoring program in Southeast, using boys' clubs, recreation centers, the Any Boy Can Boxing Club, and any other place that wanted to participate. The tutors were volunteer students, teachers that cared, recent high school graduates, college graduates from their neighborhood and others. Some provided mentorship; others gave free apprenticeships in areas like automotive repair or tattooing. Benji and Nick took turns negotiating with the gangsters who congregated in those areas to ensure safe passage for all participants… Nick spoke the language and was immediately recognized as someone of respect whom the gangsters should listen to. Benji was amazed by the power of his own reputation— he'd had one altercation with a gangbanger, during which he'd been terrified, but over time, that single instance morphed into his reputation as a savage street fighter, which gave him the credibility he needed to talk to gangs or physically break up fights…which he often did without being sanctioned by the gangs involved.

Southeast San Diego had a murder rate comparable to its more well-known neighbor to the north, South Central

Los Angeles, but its make up was substantially more diverse. Skyline, the neighborhood, was primarily black, but Barrio Logan was primarily Latino, and the Paradise Hills area was dominated by Asian immigrants. Benji and Nick differed over the perceived importance of attempting to link the various racial factions that existed among the Southeast's communities; Nick thought it would damage their efforts to curb gangsterism by being seen as weak by the gangs, but in this area, Benji's focus was not so much the gangs but on the entire community. He recruited and led an army of volunteers to help celebrate significant events in its culture and increase appreciation of the other cultures that existed in Southeast San Diego. Though he and Nick parted ways over his change in focus, Benji created a campaign he coined "I've Been There," where he convinced a sizeable number of Southeast San Diego residents who had been victim of a certain issue to wear a certain non-gang-related color as a measure of community solidarity. He chose different issues: not treated fairly in school, harassed unfairly by police, being laid off and others. The wave of color displayed in the community was Southeast San Diegans telling each other "I see you…I've been there too…we will get through this together"…it started slow but became wildly successful.

That and other initiatives gave Benji a voice, so that when a local councilman proposed the city stop using the term "Southeast San Diego" because the name carried a negative connotation, Benji countered with, "No! How can where we live be considered a negative thing? It's our reality! We…Are…Southeast. That's not going to change. Instead of trying to erase what's real, let's define for ourselves what our name means." And with that, Benji organized a soon-to-be annual "We Are Southeast" event, complete with T-shirts emblazoned with the term, all the community's schools represented on the T-shirt, and commitments from store owners and professional athletes to provide shirts for those who could not purchase their own. The community was drowned in the sea of yellow —the selected non-gang-related color for the shirts and the biblical color of joy. Benji considered the councilman's request for the city to stop using the term "Southeast San Diego" silly and a nonsensical political ploy...but the councilman was successful in convincing the city to adopt a resolution banning the use of the term. Benji was also successful... the inhabitants continued to refer to themselves as being from "Southeast" and celebrated it. Benji found it interesting that as a result of his efforts, he'd been approached to potentially run for a councilman seat representing District Four—the district of his beloved Southeast. Benji didn't have the professional pedigree of his potential opponents, but he was fearless...and uncaring if he lost. He realized he would get the chance to give voice to some issues whether he won or lost, so...he was giving serious consideration to running for the office.

When that happened, I'd gotten close to Benji's ear again and whispered:

"*Crossroad...*"

Then I watched for his reaction.

But that's a story for another day.

However, taking the youth conference road served as a spiritual springboard for Benji...although it didn't start out that way. Even though Benji decided not to try to fool his mother, he still didn't give his all for his presentation. He'd basically read it from a paper without any emotion, and he could barely be heard. In truth, the only reason he went back every day was the girl he met—the teenage girl who would later become his wife. But it turns out he got much more from the youth conference than just the chance meeting with his future spouse.

There was little to no spiritual impact in the aftermath of the conference. In fact, he still went to Sunday School as directed by Mama and remained a below-average student who occasionally got in trouble. His father got him a job at the gas station— he knew the Arab guy who owned it, and Benji was hired to pump gas and check oil for $1.50 an hour after school, but he got fired after a week. The owner claimed Benji stole $140 or the register was short. Benji denied stealing the money. His parents believed him. Well…Mama believed him, anyway. I knew he'd stolen it though…I was with him when he stole it.

You don't want to know what he did with the money.

Then there was Alonzo Allen, a high school gangster on parole who out of nowhere asked him to come over one afternoon. Once Benji got there, he asked Benji to hide a gun for him…to hold it because his probation officer was on the way. Benji foolishly took the loaded gun, walked home with it, and hid it in his closet, knowing his mother was fed up with cleaning his room and would never look in his closet. Except for that day, of course…Mama was in an extra good mood, so when Benji stashed the weapon and left to play ball, he was paralyzed to find Mama cleaning his closet when he returned. He was amazed she finished cleaning the closet but never found the gun.

I wasn't. Like I said…sometimes I get lucky with my guardian powers.

It got better…but even as he got older and his behavior changed and he matured somewhat, there was something missing— the something that defines and highlights a person's core values…not the values instilled by a person's parents or from watching TV. He knew what his parents expected of him. But what he was lacking were the values defined by a deep, over arching purpose, that unseen thing that powers a person to act in accordance with an enduring purpose even when no one is around to make sure that you do.

It all came together for Benji on a Saturday morning in his twenties.

Benji drank alcohol. He liked drinking it. Like all his friends did. He was trying to do positive things with his days; he had a girlfriend; he was no criminal, but…he liked to drink. He didn't smoke marijuana, though—he'd occasionally take a puff or two if someone passed him a joint, but he didn't purchase it on his own…primarily because he didn't know how to roll it. And he didn't want anyone to know he didn't know how to roll it. So when a friend unexpectedly offered him a small bag of marijuana instead of gas money for picking him up way out in Poway one Friday, Benji had no choice but to take it or forgo payment for the ride he provided. Once alone, Benji was perplexed about what to do with the bag. So he bought a burrito from the closest taco shop, poked a hole in the long end of the burrito, filled the burrito with the marijuana, closed the burrito, drowned it in hot sauce…and ate it. And nothing happened.

Until later.

A noise woke him that Saturday morning…a loud one. Benji thought it might be a dream, but…his eyes were open. And the voice spoke to him was so clear he thought that he had left his television on; but the voice was clear with an equally clear message:

"You believe there is one God. You do well. Even the demons believe— and tremble!"

Benji got up and went in to check his television…but it was off. And even if it had been on, church stuff comes on Sundays, not Saturday mornings.

The words stayed with him all day. That night, he couldn't get to sleep from hearing the words resonate in his mind. He thought maybe it was the aftereffects of the weed, but he'd smoked weed before, and nothing like this had ever happened. Besides—that was YESTERDAY. Of course he'd never eaten it…he just didn't know. But what he did know… was that he'd heard those words before. Those exact words.

Then it came to him. The youth conference. He'd heard those words at the youth conference while he was wandering around. In the same voice. And in an instant, it all come back to him:

"You believe there is one God. You do well. Even the demons believe— and tremble! Believing in God does not save you…believing in God may be our motivation to study Christian doctrine, go to church, pray, have Bible study, preach sermons about Jesus, give to the poor, memorize scripture, and even come to this conference, but it's still not enough to ensure our salvation. We can't think believing in God will ensure we end up in heaven, because James says the devil and his demons believe too! And when the demons think about God and the judgment awaiting them because of their sin, it makes them shudder from fear. If men could but see what awaits them because of their sin and rejection of Christ, no doubt we would shudder, too…but we don't. Humanity may claim to believe in God, but we have never trembled at the thought of standing before God to give account for our sin.

"It takes more than just belief."

It may have been several years since hearing that sermon when he was just fifteen. As a child, Benji joked that when he died, he would just be sure to ask for forgiveness right before he died so that he would be ok to go to heaven no matter what he'd done. And as the sun went down that Saturday evening, Benji realized he didn't remember hearing the sermon those many years ago…or maybe it had taken all those years for the sermon to make it from his subconscious to his conscious thoughts. And with it came a moment of clarity— he was living a pretty good life by human standards. Decent…as in trying to help the community, not committing crimes, still kind of a square, but a pretty good person…and he did believe in God.

But it takes more than just belief.

Benji joined his church the next day.

He didn't join as a fiery speaker, eager to tell his story and make a difference in anyone else's spiritual journey. No…as was his nature, he watched, read, learned, asked questions, read more, learned more, and shared, and slowly, over the years, he began to assume greater and greater responsibilities inside the church. He began to put things together in his own mind first, and the result was an inner peace, enhanced focus and well-defined purpose. He had to answer questions in his own mind as he advanced, but he didn't demand all the answers immediately to questions such as "How could God allow so much suffering?" But as his spirituality grew, his capacity for knowledge and understanding grew.

As he married and began his family, this newly refined clarity, focus, and purpose came to the couple's great benefit as they struggled through the pangs of growth experienced by all newlyweds with young children. Fights happen in the strongest of relationships, and frustration invariably follows. Rare is the relationship where one or both of the parties does not question the wisdom of their decision to marry and question if they would be better off single once more. Despite his love for his wife and children, Benji found himself at such a point in his marriage and had no doubts his wife was wondering at times whom she'd married as well. But the focus and purpose of his burgeoning spirituality manifested itself in a discipline to wait…and a faith that if he trusted the process and refrained from saying or doing anything he would later regret, his relationship would blossom as it had before.

And once again…an unconscious message from the youth conference that he hadn't realized was planted in his soul sprouted at exactly the right time. He'd overheard adults discussing something during a session with young spouses—the premise was, "If you can do one thing a day…just one thing…small or big…something that is totally for the other person…and you get no benefit from it or even let the other person know you're doing it…you will build a relationship to stand the test of time, no matter how young or old you are as long as you do it while not seeking or accepting credit for it." And when Benji was reminded of the memory, he believed the reasoning to be sound and considered, "Why wouldn't that work for me?" So that's what he did: a glass of water…a kiss for no reason…listening when he was busy… these small things and more, Benji did one thing daily. And when a day was ending when he hadn't done his one small thing, he scrambled to find something to do for his spouse so that he would fulfill his internal vow. And it worked. His relationship strengthened as the small, unselfish acts became second nature to both husband and wife.

And now, Benji was an influential leader not only in his family and community but within his church as well. Normally he wouldn't speak at his own family's marriage ceremony, but he'd been granted the privilege and scanned the congregation—smiling warmly, developing a spiritual connection, mentally inviting them all in. His gaze settled on his niece and her fiancé. She was exquisite…and a mirror image of her mother. Benji nearly laughed out loud at the thought of describing his older sister in those terms after all these years— but it was true. Her intended was a good man— he laughed a lot, was of strong spiritual character, and demonstrated wisdom beyond his years. There were never any guarantees, but Benji felt extremely positive the family was about to get even stronger with this young man's addition.

Comfortable that he'd made the required connection with the audience, he began to speak as he was moved to say:

"Aladdin…had a magic lamp…didn't he?"

Benji had mastered a vocal delivery designed to keep the crowd enthralled with the words. He literally thundered the first word and stopped…then delivered the rest of the introduction in a soft, gentle tone accompanied by a wry smile, a wink, and an embracing openhanded gesture.

Then he paused— the congregation collectively chuckled and tittered with anticipation. They knew him, both from his speeches in Southeast and from inside the church— they knew he often went off on unexpected reflections, and though some did not truly appreciate Benji's willingness to freestyle from the norm and wanted him to get to the point, the majority knew there was a method to wherever it was he was going.

"Yes, Aladdin had himself a magic lamp," he continued.

Then he lowered his voice into a more conspiratorial tone in a manner such that every person in the building felt like he was speaking only to them.

"You know Aladdin, right? He rubbed the lamp or something…then a genie came out of the bottle…all smoky and what not, right? Then he started folding his arms and granting wishes!"

Benji paused to bring the crowd further in to his story before he continued.

"Wait, wait! No, he didn't fold his arms! He blinked, right? Then he…hold on, y'all…"

The crowd was with him now; some chuckled, some laughed out loud, and all were focused on the charismatic speaker who was addressing them now.

"OK, that's not no genie, is it? That was the one girl who came out the bottle for the soldier man…right, right…no no, he was in the Air Force…well…I don't really remember but I know she wrinkled her nose up and made wishes happen, y'all! Wait, wait…no, that wasn't Aladdin…that was the good witch who…hmmm…clicked her heels three times… aww man…naw, that ain't it either…"

The laughter of the crowd became more constant as Benji pretended to fumble with the story; the entire assembly literally exploded with laughter when Benji, with fake indignation, loudly exclaimed: "It's Aladdin! I mean the genie! Y'all know how I'm talking about!"

Benji kept a stern, offended look on his face as the laughter continued and then, with perfect timing, allowed his mouth to form a sheepish grin as he continued.

"Yes…Aladdin…and Aladdin's genie? He granted wishes…and you could wish for anything you wanted. The genie would blink or wrinkle or do whatever genies do and grant your wish. 'Genie, make me beautiful! Genie, make me rich! Genie, make that girl love me!' But…brothers and sisters… let me tell you something.

"Our God ain't no genie in no bottle."

Benji paused for effect.

"We don't need no magic genie wishes to experience the strength and the love of Almighty God…

"We don't need no magic genie wishes to experience the joy in His only begotten son Jesus Christ…

"We don't need no magic genie wishes to give us confidence and a spirit of lightness, gentleness, and truth that comes from the Holy Spirit!…

"We don't need no magic genie wishes to follow the path prepared for us and to use our abundance or our lack of abundance to advance His will and give glory to God!

"So my brothers and sisters— we are not going to make wishes of the Lord our God today…we do not need to wish for marital bliss for this happy couple; we are not going to wish for days of happiness; we're not going to wish for these two beautiful souls to keep the strength to withstand the inevitable storms…we are going to celebrate what God has already given them and remind them to always share these things with each other.

"Love based on a promise, not on feelings.

"Comfort in each other's arms and presence.

"Peace in the knowledge that in his eyes there is no better woman in this world, forever his queen…and in her eyes, there is no better man in this world, forever her king.

"Confidence that the words they both hear today will ring forever in eternity and that this day they become each other's forever legacy!

"The smiling souls who will become one today don't need wishes. They have God's promises and they have each other. And as long as they remember God's promises and let us all remember it in our lives as well…as long as they remember this and that even the memory of looking into each other's eyes today will remind them of this: with you by my side and you in my heart, home is not what we do; home is not even where we are or where we live. Home is living your core values and following your purpose. Home will never leave you…and you can't ever leave it.

"So if you can remember these things— wherever you are, whatever results from whatever crossroad you take—that road…will always…lead back to one place:

Home."

And Benji sat down.

He knew he wasn't just talking to the congregation.

He was talking to himself.

And in the moment he realized that he too had finally made it. He embraced the thought… it actually gave him goosebumps. He felt it in his spirit and knowledge welled up inside him and seemed to have captured the full essence of his entire being.

In his heart, in his mind, in his very soul he felt contentment in an emotional and spiritual place that worldly success could never substitute for, a place you can't charm your way into, a place that can't duplicated, a place money could never buy.

His crossroads had brought him where it seemed he was always destined to be.

I smiled. I knew it too.

We'd made it. Because Benjamin Frazier, Jr's crossroad had finally brought him to place he'd been looking for and never wanted to leave…Benji's crossroad had led him home.

AFTERWORD

Benji's mama was still gazing at him with an adoring look. Benji smiled back, but not for the reason his mama thought he was smiling. His mama thought she had gotten through to him. But Benji was smiling…because he knew.

He knew he was going to deceive his mother.

And he knew it was going to work.

I wish that he could see me and that we could just have a conversation. It would be much easier, but unfortunately… that's not the way it works.

But I suspected Benji was right. He was going to deceive his mother. And it was going to work.

His mother's smile followed behind him as her fifteen-year- old middle child departed the house on his way to school. Her smile was genuine. She was full of joy over all her children— she felt like a blessed woman. It was not easy to bring children up the right way in this neighborhood, but she had faith in her husband, she had faith in her children as well, and accordingly…she had an unwavering faith that Benji would make the right decision.

Although in this case— she didn't need faith.

"He thinks he's slick," Mama thought with a smile. "He probably thinks he's going to do that 'pretend to be cold' thing the boys like to try to get out of school.

"But he's speaking at youth conference whether he wants to do it or not.

Because I say so."

Lina Frazier paused for just a moment; she had a busy day ahead and she needed to call Rose back first…but instead of starting her day, she went outside to take in the beauty of the morning and was surprised to see Benji standing on the sidewalk talking to that little Davis boy from next door. They looked like they were going across the street but when her middle child saw her, they waved to each other, then her son quickly ran off in the direction of the school.

Benji's mother came back inside…and looked directly at me.

"Mama got one of them guardian people too," she said with a knowing smile, a wink in her eye and a twinkle in her soul.

If I didn't know better…I would have sworn she could really see me.

It's My Turn: A Message from the Author

A wise person does not look where they fell…
a wise person looks where they slipped.
—African Proverb

This is a story about choices.

My story's main character is good-hearted but augmented some of his choices by abusing alcohol, ignoring important people in his life and being unfaithful to his spouse, to name a few bad choices. Even the positive choice regarding higher education was polluted by his future arrogance.

My hope is my audience will make choices that align with your personal core values and purpose in life. The true message of this fictional account is not to make perfect choices. We are human, so living a mistake-free life is beyond our capability. Rather, my message is when making your choices, plan for destinations that reflect who you truly are or want to be and recover whenever you feel you are off your chosen path.

Remember---resilience involves preparing for life's inevitable storms, withstanding the storm, then learning lessons from the experience so you can prepare all over again.

I thank you for joining me on this literary journey. I hope you enjoyed this account and look forward to seeing you again.

> *If you don't know where you're going, ANY road will take you there.*
> —African Proverb

www.ingramcontent.com/pod-product-compliance
Lightning Source LLC
LaVergne TN
LVHW041755060526
838201LV00046B/1005